HARVEST HOUSE

HARVEST HOUSE

CYNTHIA LEITICH SMITH

CANDLEWICK PRESS

Copyright © 2023 by Cynthia Leitich Smith

First edition 2023

Library of Congress Catalog Card Number 2022915235
ISBN 978-1-5362-1860-2

23 24 25 26 27 28 LBM 10 9 8 7 6 5 4 3 2 1

Printed in Melrose Park, IL, USA

This book was typeset in Sabon.

Candlewick Press
99 Dover Street
Somerville, Massachusetts 02144

www.candlewick.com

For Stacy, in memory of a spooky-fun night,
for everyone who feels haunted,
and for those searching for someone they love

CELESTE

The Bad Man has many faces, and I remember them all. So how is it that I share my own name with the heavens, my clan's name with this winter breeze, but I can't always recall what they are? Tonight, I know I am Celeste, though I am not yet celestial.

Wisps of memory taunt me. I can't be sure, might never be sure, if The Bad Man seeks to kill or if he simply relishes frightening young women—frightening *girls* really—or if he intends something awful in between.

So far, I've managed to hold him at bay. But *so far* doesn't equal forever.

Moon is my trusted lookout. She nudges me awake.

His latest prey, yet another girl with dark hair that ripples like ribbons, exits through the front door of the . . . pub, yes, that's it . . . and walks toward the two-lane country road.

This latest girl, she knows to look both ways. Someone who loves her taught her that. Someone who loves her will miss her, mourn her, if I fail.

The thought of love uncoils a memory.

I left home—*home*—after high school graduation for a love of books, a love of poetry, for the promise of education, with every intention of returning.

Is she seventeen, nineteen? Younger or older than I was then?

The girl waits, shifting her weight from one foot to the other, stalled by a passing motorcycle, a passing sedan, a passing pickup truck. She's stalled long enough that the lurching, desperate shadow of The Bad Man will catch up with her soon.

In the gutter atop the empty building on my side of the road, the mourning doves sense my dread and shudder in their cozy nests. Their kin have flown to warmer, brighter skies, but they remain my steadfast companions.

I'm grateful, though I long to fly, too. But as long as The Bad Man lurks, another girl may need me. As long as The Bad Man lurks, I will stay.

Red dye streaks the girl's flowing hair. It's bold. Formidable. She doesn't know I recognize her, *almost* recognize her, that I almost recognize *myself* in her. She doesn't know I'm her sentry, soldier, sister, salvation. I protect girls like Mother Mourning Dove protects her chicks.

Skittish, this girl hesitates at more oncoming headlights. Can she hear him scraping forward? Can she sense the danger that she's in? I silently urge her, *hurry, hurry, hurry, hurry, please*. I wish it was autumn, when I can see better, hear better, sometimes speak.

Local folks used to tell stories about me. Maybe they still do.

Yes, I'm the reason the now-abandoned restaurant closed so abruptly. All that's left is this boarded-up building, this shell of a structure where birds huddle.

Finally, here she comes! Brisk, focused. White shirt, black jeans, black shoes—the employee uniform remains unchanged after all these years. But only a handful of girls fit the description—dark brown hair, deep brown eyes, lovely brown skin—brown and beautiful.

I know The Bad Man's type.

She's shivering. She should cover her head with that red winter scarf, zip up that red winter coat against the dangers of the cold. Ice glistens. *Hurry, but watch your step!*

The streetlight points away from me, toward the road and the pub, for the benefit of passing vehicles and cautious pedestrians.

Clouds pass over Moon. Night wraps the girl in its dark blanket.

No doubt she helped close the pub. Swept the floors, refilled the salt and pepper shakers, married the barbecue and ketchup and mayo and mustard bottles, wiped down the worn wooden tables and sprawling leather booths. Maybe she got caught up in conversation with the last few customers, made sure no one was driving home drunk. She looks like someone who cares.

What did we call the diners—the lovebirds and lost

souls and heavy drinkers—who lingered past closing time? Stragglers, campers, lonely hearts?

I recall loud laughter and louder music . . . greasy smiles and grabby hands. The revving roar of motorcycles. Faint metallic thuds as car and truck doors shut.

No witnesses left tonight except me and the mourning doves. *No reason to fret,* I thought, she thinks. At this sleepy crossroads between the old town and the new suburb I didn't live to see, it appears as if nothing much happens—the display of a handmade quilt at the antiques store, a friendly game of pool, the occasional illicit meetup—highlighted by NCAA basketball on mounted TVs. It's a tidy intersection of rural commerce and camaraderie on the vanishing prairie.

"Less . . . less," The Bad Man whispers. He's on my side of the road now. The last thing I said to him was "Hvtvm cehecares." I warned him—him wearing a rounder face and thinner form, but still and always him—that he wasn't rid of me, that I would remain vigilant.

The girl with red streaks in her hair glances over her shoulder. Does she hear him approaching? She reaches to open the driver's door of a compact yellow car, rusty around the fenders. A fresh bumper sticker reads CUSTER DIED FOR YOUR SINS.

Mother Mourning Dove welcomes my presence, trusts that I won't stay too long.

She doesn't want to lose her life like I did.

"Less . . . less," The Bad Man hisses. "Less . . ." The

voice comes from behind a minivan parked next to the girl. His faded bumper sticker reads SUPER BOWL CHAMPS. I remember place names better than people names. Maybe because people come and go but land endures. This is currently called Kansas, named for the Kaw or the Kanza. The Bad Man is a fan of the Kansas City football team. *"Less . . ."*

The girl's spine goes stiff, her chin lifts. One hand is on her boxy, beaded leather purse. The fingers of her other hand are threaded with keys like claws. "Who's there?"

He's gaining on her, his eyes full of blood and stars. "Less . . ."

My wings—*our* wings—rise, dive, our talons strain for his face. Our flock follows, and the girl gasps at the sudden presence of whistling feathers. A word rushes back to me, the memory of my great-grandmother's voice. Wind recognizes my language, fuels my scream. "Letkv!"

The girl's car door slams shut, its engine fires. Wheels spin, slide across black ice, rush her to safety. She is safe. We have won.

The Bad Man will try again.

52 DAYS UNTIL HALLOWEEN

It struck Hughie as odd that the first after-school theater meeting was scheduled in the faculty director's English classroom instead of the auditorium as it had been in the past. The classroom didn't offer enough space for a flashy reveal or a line reading or a group exercise like he'd normally expect. But he didn't care. The important thing was that theater was beginning, and soon Hughie's sophomore year would start to take shape. For him, it wasn't only a school activity; it was a calling that came with a social scene, jam-packed schedule, and chance to shine.

As he approached the door, a petite girl in a MAMMA MIA! T-shirt paused in the hallway to double-check a room number. "You lost?" he asked.

"You're Hughie Wolfe!" she exclaimed, starry-eyed. "I'm Joy! I saw you in *Little Shop of Horrors* last spring. You were so funny!"

"Glad you enjoyed the show." He was flattered that his performance had stuck with her.

"You were a freshman last year, and you landed a major role! Two roles actually, but . . ."

"The Tin Man turned out not to be a good fit for me," Hughie said in the understatement of the day. Anyone who followed student theater at East Hannesburg High knew that Hughie had backed out of the Tin Man role the previous fall after finding out L. Frank Baum—the author of *The Wonderful Wizard of Oz*—had written and published newspaper articles advocating for the genocide of Indigenous people. Baum's words were forever connected to the killing of three hundred Lakotas at Wounded Knee in 1890.

Hughie went on, "I had fun playing Scrivello in *Little Shop*. My dad's a real-life dentist, so he got a huge kick out of it. What's your dream role?"

Joy pointed to her MAMMA MIA! T-shirt. "Big surprise, I know. I used to say Sophie, but now I'd go with Donna, her mother."

"The more complex character!" Hughie exclaimed. "A mature choice for a freshman."

Joy beamed at him.

As they hurried in behind a half dozen fellow thespians, he saw A.J. Rodríguez waving him over. Calling "Break a leg!" to Joy, Hughie headed to where A.J. was saving him a seat.

In this crowded room, overflowing with big personalities, Hughie was surrounded by kindred souls who shared his love of the stage, and he slowed for hugs and high fives on his way over. "Hey, bro," he greeted A.J., slipping into the desk beside him. "Good to see you."

"May I have your attention please?" the faculty director called. *"Attention, please!"*

The anticipation in the air was palpable. Everyone was eager to hear Mrs. Qualey announce the name of the fall production.

"You psyched?" A.J. asked, leaning over. "You know it'll be between us for the lead."

Hughie grinned. "Unless the girls get their way, and we do *The Wolves*." There had been pushback after both of the prior year's productions had been musicals—which were popular with theatergoers but worked to the advantage of the handful of actors with strong singing voices—so Hughie expected they'd be putting on a straight play this fall. Still, even without singing in the mix, he and A.J. were clear favorites for any male lead roles.

Chatter quelled to a low murmur as Mrs. Qualey began, "I'm going to keep this brief. Or at least brief by the standards of someone who teaches both English and theater." She squared her shoulders. "Students, please be advised that in his 1651 book *Leviathan*, Thomas Hobbes described the life of man as 'solitary, poor, nasty, brutish, and short.' I'd be remiss in not warning you that life on the stage is often the same way."

Ominous.

Mrs. Qualey stood, strolled around her desk, leaned

against the front of it, and sighed. "There's no easy way to say this. Our vice principal has informed me that while our spring production is still a go, the fall show has been cut from the budget. As an alternative, we—"

The room erupted in protest. Mrs. Qualey raised her hands, palms facing the crowd. "Quiet, please. *Quiet!* I'm still in charge here. Allow me to explain." She took a breath. "It's not only theater. They cut the school newspaper budget, too. The *Hive* will have to raise the money if they want to attend the state press association competition this year. TV, radio, and orchestra are on life support. It's a miracle that the library emerged largely unscathed—this time. Supposedly, the only alternative was to raise student activity fees, and there's already a lot of talk in the PTO about the financial burden that places on larger families."

"We can find sponsors," Hughie suggested. "We can crowdsource or sell ads—"

"Don't you think I already thought of all that?" Mrs. Qualey exclaimed. In a more subdued voice, she added, "I'm sorry. The matter is settled. I'm coaching JV volleyball this semester instead. Coach Rummel is retired now, and I played volleyball in college. The varsity coach is covering for me at today's practice. I should be in the gym right—"

"This makes no sense," argued Madison Cohen, who was seated on the other side of A.J. "The school just spent a kajillion dollars on a freaking jumbotron."

"Wake up, Madison!" Kelly Oh exclaimed. "Football is a second religion, and we're—"

"Be that as it may," Mrs. Qualey interrupted, "we will still have a production coming up this spring, and I have an intriguing development to announce. A few of you have been asking for a more *now*, more *wow* production. So, *write one*. As of right now, I'm officially in the market for a brand-new script. Take this unexpected windfall of time as an invitation."

Hughie was barely listening. Early planning for the spring production wouldn't kick off in earnest for another *five months*. What was he supposed to do with himself in the meantime?

"All of you are storytellers," Mrs. Q insisted. "Visual, performing, and yes, literary. Well, congratulations on this unprecedented opportunity! Write your dream roles, the stories of your hearts! The deadline is November fifth. I'll choose three finalists, and then *you'll* vote on our spring play." Her gaze fell on Hughie and A.J. "All of you have the potential to win this thing. Show me, show *everybody*, what you can come up with!"

51 DAYS UNTIL HALLOWEEN

The next morning, Hughie kept mostly to himself, stared out the windows during his morning classes, and tried not to think about the looming, empty fall semester or his dashed theatrical expectations. He was already in a lousy mood when he turned down the sophomore hall, carrying a newly checked-out library book, and noticed that the Vogel brothers were at it again. This time, their target was new girl Sophie Miller.

Hughie doubted that it was personal, them choosing Sophie to harass. Granted, she was a self-described shit-kicker—more rez than burbs—but nobody except Hughie knew Sophie well enough yet to have figured that out. And sure, she was a brown girl in a mostly white school, but really, the Vogels were insufferable to everybody.

It's not that Jonas and Elias Vogel *looked* all that menacing—they were skinny white guys who projected *average*. But on a whim, they'd pick on anybody without the social currency to stop them. They even had a rep for taking potshots at squirrels, birds, and neighborhood cats with their BB guns.

While Hughie liked to think that he would have stood up for any of the Vogels' victims, he had a soft spot for Sophie. Now that his big sister, Louise, had graduated, he and Sophie's stepsister, Buffy Mitchell, could've ended up the only Native students at his high school, so he was glad to have Sophie there, too. While Hughie was Muscogee and Sophie and Buffy were Prairie Band Potawatomi—different tribal Nations, different cultures—they still had an Indigenous solidarity vibe going on.

"Chill, new girl," Jonas Vogel said, leaning over Sophie, whose back was pressed against the orange cinderblock wall. "We just want to talk to you. You don't want to be rude, do you?"

"So talk," Sophie replied.

It seemed like the brothers didn't have anything specific to say.

Hughie scanned the hallway, looking for a teacher, janitor, administrator—any potentially useful grown-up—and came up empty. He headed toward the situation without a plan.

"Check it out," Elias said to his brother. "The letters on her beads spell out, uh . . ." He reached forward to turn a hoop earring so he could read it better. "De, deco . . ."

Hughie's mom was a beader. His sister wore square beads just like those. Hers spelled out *dress* in bold, red capital letters.

"Decorate?" Elias ventured with a chuckle.

Decolonize, Hughie thought, picking up his pace.

"Decolonize," Sophie announced, smacking away Elias's hand—*whack*—and stomping her bootheel into Jonas's open-toe leather sandals.

Elias's "Ow!" was drowned out by Jonas's "Shit!" and Sophie took advantage of the moment to break free, running full-out, sparing a glance over her shoulder. Hughie, on his way to her rescue, found himself caught between a sauntering wall of girls from cheer and a cluster of hotly debating gamers. As he slipped between the groups, Sophie barreled into him, accidentally knocking Hughie flat. Meanwhile, Jonas hopped on one foot, yelling at Elias, "Get her!"

"You okay?" Sophie asked Hughie, offering him a hand.

"Fine," he replied, fumbling to push up. "Keep going. I'll hold them off."

"Yeah . . . I don't think so," she replied, grabbing Hughie's wrist and dragging him to his feet and pulling him along behind her. The clock was ticking, and the hallway was clearing out as students hurried off to their next class or to the cafeteria. "Come on!"

Hughie wasn't inclined to argue. The previous spring, the Vogels had been suspended for fighting in the parking lot. Elias had waved around a pocketknife. Jonas had broken a guy's eye socket. Rounding a hallway corner, Hughie slipped in his new kicks on the freshly waxed tile floor, and Sophie lost her hold on him. Regaining his balance, Hughie caught a glimpse of someone accidentally-on-purpose dropping—more like *tossing*—a backpack in Elias's path.

"Oof," Elias exclaimed, flailing as he tripped and crashed—face-plant.

"Mr. Vogel and Mr. Vogel," boomed a masculine teacher's voice from behind the brothers. "What fresh form of malfeasance are you inflicting on these hallowed halls?"

"Hold up," Hughie called to Sophie, who paused in front of the trophy cases outside the administrative offices. "We're clear." He studied their hero, the kid trying to look casual, retrieving his backpack like he was just minding his own business. It was a big school. Even after a year and a half in Kansas, Hughie didn't know a lot of people. "Who is that?" It was a rhetorical question. He wasn't really expecting Sophie to know, since she was newer than he was, but she surprised him.

"Sam Rodríguez," Sophie answered. "Junior year. Lives down the street from me." She turned to Sam as he jogged up. "Thank you for the rescue, Sam—and for trying to help me out, Hughie. I've got to run to meet some girls from my homeroom, but I owe you both." She took off toward the cafeteria.

"I owe you, too," Hughie said to Sam. "I'm—"

"Hughie Wolfe. I saw you in *Little Shop*. A.J.'s my cousin." The boys began strolling across the enclosed bridge attaching one side of the school to the other. "How do you know Sophie?"

"I went to her Tribe's powwow last spring," Hughie said. "An auntie of hers knew an auntie of mine and that she'd be going to school here this year, so they introduced us." Hughie had learned to make a low-key, early effort with potential friends to work a reference to Indigenous heritage into a conversation. That way, if they were going to say something bigoted, it happened before he got emotionally attached.

Hughie was reassured when Sam simply said, "Nice. Glad we happened to be there when the Vogels started hassling her. They've got anger issues."

"You don't say," Hughie agreed.

In the quickly filling cafeteria, Hughie grabbed a hummus cup with cheese and a flatbread while Sam went for chicken strips with honey mustard.

"How was your summer?" asked Hughie. "I went to Oklahoma with my family. Did a theater camp and a science-and-tech camp."

Sam chose a table. "I worked at the plant nursery just west of the crossroads. It was sweaty work—grimy, but I dug it. Get it? *Dug* it? That's plant-nursery humor for you. The old couple that owns the place said I was a natural salesman. Too bad they had to let me go."

The nursery was located between the suburb and old town. Hughie and his family sometimes stopped there to shop on their way home from church. "What happened?"

"It's sad," Sam said, dipping a chicken strip into mustard. "Since that garden superstore opened, they've had to lay off the part-timers. They're planning to boost sales with a pumpkin patch, Christmas trees, you know, quick-turnaround seasonal stuff where a country atmosphere brings in customers. If that doesn't work, well, they're already talking about early retirement."

Hughie asked, "Are you looking for a new job?"

Sam brightened. "Nah, I've got this new gig. It's a fundraiser. One of my mom's good friends from yoga class—Ms. Fischer—her appendix nearly burst over last Fourth of July weekend. She's fine now, health-wise, but she got blasted with these huge hospital bills. She needs cash and a lot of it—stat."

Hughie put down his flatbread. "What kind of fundraiser?"

"That's the best part," Sam said. "You know that empty building across the street from the pub at the crossroads? Used to be a chicken restaurant? Ms. Fischer is putting on a haunted house there for Halloween weekend. It's going to be so fun. People are volunteering and donating supplies to help her out. Ticket and merch sales will go to paying off her medical debt."

Putting on a haunted house did sound fun. Building sets, staging lighting, costuming, and acting . . . like theater. Hughie sighed and pushed his lunch away.

After choosing a dark green vinyl seat at the very back of the stuffy school bus, Hughie was glad when Sam slid in next to him, as it suggested that their lunch might not be a one-off. That was an especially welcome thought since Hughie would obviously be spending a lot less time with the theater crowd this semester than he'd originally envisioned.

Suddenly, the passenger seated alone in front of them pivoted, phone in hand. "Hughie Wolfe?" She was a striking white girl with a huge mop of auburn curls and light blue eyes set off by cobalt-blue cat's-eye glasses that looked fanciful and no-nonsense at the same time. "Mind if I ask you a few questions about the theater program for the *Hive*? I'm the new arts and entertainment reporter."

Hughie winced at the thought of answering questions about the now-nonexistent fall play. "I'd rather not talk about—"

"What do you mean, questions?" Sam asked as the doors swung shut and the driver put the vehicle in gear. "Who're you? What's with the third degree? Can't you tell that my friend here needs a break from the tempests of adolescence and banalities of suburban life?"

"I'm Cricket Stewart. You're Sam Rodríguez. I've seen you with your family at Holy Trinity. And that doesn't make any sense. Think about it: either there's conflict and emotion from the tempests *or* nothing blah-ness from the banalities. You can't have it both ways."

Sam didn't miss a beat. "Says who? Banalities aren't nothing. The weight of infinite banality can crush the human spirit. Exhibit A: my man Hughie. He currently has nothing in life to look forward to. It's tragic. It tears at the soul."

"Conceded," Cricket replied in a pleasantly surprised tone. "Are you in theater, too?"

"Nah," Sam said. "I'm more of an offstage, rogue improv kind of guy. I heard about the fall theater drama from my cousin. For the duration of this conversation, you can think of me as Hughie Wolfe's personal public relations representative." When that failed to rouse a thumbs-up or protest from Hughie himself, Sam added, "Or life coach. I'm not sure. Our fledgling friendship is a work in progress."

Hughie appreciated Sam's attempt to cheer him up, but he didn't even try to engage with the quick wit of the more socially gifted. Staring out the bus window as they rode past football practice, he found it hard not to begrudge the players their pricey jumbotron.

"Be that as it may," Cricket replied, persistent, "Hughie, do you have anything to say about the cancellation of the fall play?"

Plenty of words sprang to mind, but none that his parents would be happy to see attributed to him in the school newspaper. "Sorry, no comment."

Thumbs flying, Cricket keyed that in. "When I talked to Mrs. Qualey, she said that there was a script-writing competition for the spring production. Are you entering?"

"Absolutely!" Sam said, quick to pounce on the affirmative. "Hughie intends to—"

"No, no comment. Don't listen to Sam. He's just joking around."

"He comments!" Cricket and Sam exclaimed before bursting into laughter.

"About you, not the fall play," Cricket added.

"At least it was full sentences," Sam replied.

Hughie was glad *someone* was having a good afternoon. "If I give you a quote, will the interview be over? I'm trying to wallow, and you two are interrupting me."

"Sure," Cricket said. "I've already got something teachery from Qualey and pretty colorful from Madison. Tomorrow morning, I'll corner Vice Principal Delaney and start typing."

Hughie sighed. A couple of guys toward the front of the bus were tossing a hacky sack back and forth. A jacked-up gray truck in the next lane was playing music so loud he could feel the vibration. Cricket fiddled with her phone and pointed the camera lens at him. "Today, we're talking to Hughie Wolfe, a well-known sophomore actor who starred in the EHHS production of *Little Shop of Horrors* last spring and, before that, stepped down from the role of—"

Hughie surprised all of them, himself included, by covering the lens with his palm. He'd been a huge part of the news coverage around theater last year. He didn't regret his choice, but he didn't want to rehash it, either. "I changed my mind. No comment."

"What was that?" Sam asked, following Hughie down the stairs off the bus at the landscaped entrance to the

19

Emerald Hills subdivision. "I get that you're bummed," Sam said. "But a cute, smart, funny girl was talking to you, and you shut her down—boom! Shut her down, shut yourself down. How does that help?"

As they hiked up the sidewalk, Hughie said, "Cricket wasn't talking to me. She was flirting with you. I was just a convenient source with a clickable backstory."

"Come again?" Sam asked.

"The only reason she wanted a quote from me is—"

"No, no, not that. You thought she was flirting with *me*?"

"Wait a minute," Hughie said as they strode in the general direction of the subdivision pool. "This isn't your bus stop. You could've stayed on and talked to her longer."

"You looked like you could use a friend," Sam said. "Listen, I saw you onstage last year, and that was something. I also watched you take off down the hall like you were going to physically defend Sophie from the Vogels, and no offense, but you don't exactly project badass."

It was true. Hughie Wolfe was many things, but a badass he was not.

"You've got heart, man. Look, I watched that *Hive* video about how you bailed on the *Oz* show because the guy who wrote it was a racist . . ." He trailed off, noticing a preschooler on a tricycle, followed by her mom, peddling down the sidewalk. "Tool," he finished.

Sam lowered his voice. "Solidarity to you, my friend. I've got my Mayan ancestors, you know? The way I see it, you stick up for people. You're loyal. I could use a friend like that." Before Hughie could reply, Sam added, "But enough about you. How could you *tell* Cricket was flirting with me? When was the moment I bowled her over with my charm?"

Hughie couldn't suppress a smile. Maybe the fall wouldn't be a total write-off after all.

CELESTE

My voice of now is not my voice of then. It's braided with the stories of my Elders, the songs of my sisters, even the poetry of invaders from schoolbooks. I have matured—turned fear into power and frustration into strength.

I have not been a teenage girl in a very long time.

I will be a teenage girl forever.

Last call. Last chance to make a buck, last chance to pour poison into your body. I sold it, I served it, I never drank it. I knew better. No, that's not right. Once, *once* at a 49 after powwow, a Sac and Fox fancy dancer, a longtime crush, cracked my beating heart, looking for a quick snag. I spiraled. My girls—my cousins, my sisters, my auntie who was my age—they carried me home. I was crying, making a mess of myself—I'd known him since I was a tot.

He played guitar. His big sister was married to my best friend's brother. His hair was prettier than mine. How could I have forgotten his name?

I've hung on for decades, trapped in the ebb and flow.

I can't remember my girls—not my cousins or sisters or aunties. But I'll protect the girls at the crossroads from something far worse than a full-of-himself tipi creeper. They deserve better than that.

I've known better. I've even known love.

The tipi creeper wasn't the boy there when I died.

50 DAYS UNTIL HALLOWEEN

It wasn't until Friday night that Hughie's phone vibrated, alerting him to a text from Louise. He was already in bed, his algebra 2 and sociology homework finished. The family dachshunds, Bilbo and Frodo, slept side by side at the foot of his puffy comforter, grunt-snoring in turn. He could faintly hear the twenty-four-hour TV news coming from his parents' bedroom down the hall.

Hoping he didn't wake up the dogs, Hughie video-called his sister. When she picked up, Louise looked tired. Her long brown hair was twisted on her head, and she was sitting on a stone bench outside Watson Library. "Sorry I didn't check in earlier. Mama took me to Billie's for dinner."

"You went to Billie's Down-Home Diner without me?" Hughie was teasing. Given that the women of the family were both enrolled at the University of Kansas in nearby Lawrence—Louise as a freshman studying journalism, and their mom as a law student—it was only natural that they'd take advantage of being on campus together for extra mother-daughter time.

"I didn't know you were in crisis! Mama told me about the play. She says you seem okay. You look okay. Are you okay?" Louise had moved into the dorm a few weeks earlier. Since then, she had returned home for her birthday dinner, and she and Hughie had exchanged messages on their all-family thread, but they hadn't talked just the two of them. That wasn't only unusual; it was unprecedented.

Then again, Louise had never been a college student before, either.

"I'm okay, I promise. I was not okay at first, but I'm fine now." Hughie smiled at Frodo flicking his paws in his sleep. Chasing rabbits. "My friend Sam thinks I should write a script to enter in the spring production contest."

"You're writing a script?" Louise exclaimed. Hughie was a solid-enough student, but unlike her, he wasn't an academic overachiever.

"You know how me and A.J. have been pushing Mrs. Q to put on a play written by somebody with melanin? This might be our chance to make it happen."

"Yes! That'll keep you busy." Louise waved at someone out of view of the phone's camera. Hughie could picture where she was on Jayhawk Boulevard, the most quintessential and the highest-traveled stretch of the campus. "I say, go for it. Write a script."

"Just like that?" he said. "It's not that easy. Can you help me?"

Louise wrinkled her nose. "I'm a news reporter, not a playwright."

It was late at night for her to be studying at the library. The area was well lit, but Hughie hoped she had someone to walk back with. He hoped she was making friends. He suspected that Louise was feeling more lost and overwhelmed than she might otherwise because her best friend was attending community college instead of KU and because Louise's previously attached-at-the-hip boyfriend had chosen to go to K-State, which was located about an hour and a half away.

"Rock Chalk, sister!" Hughie replied. "You're the writer of the family. Besides, it'll give you an excuse to come home and do your laundry."

She feigned an aghast expression. "I need an excuse now?"

Hughie laughed, and Louise grinned, clearly pleased with herself. "I might be able to help you," she said. "But you're going to have to figure out what story you want to tell."

42 DAYS UNTIL HALLOWEEN

Within a week or so, Hughie had embraced a new routine. Dad dropped him off at school in the mornings before continuing to his dentist office in Olathe. Hughie had lunch with Sam in the cafeteria and then rode the bus home with him and Cricket, who—despite the continued flirtation between her and Sam—seemed to click in and out of the boys' conversations without any of them feeling like a third wheel.

One sunny Saturday morning, Sam surprised Hughie by showing up in his driveaway in a boxy yellow station wagon with faded fake-wood side paneling. "Gorgeous, isn't it?"

Hughie made a show of circling the vehicle, which looked for all the world like it was being held together by duct tape and a dream. "A beauty all right."

In the driver's seat, Sam flashed a set of pearly whites that even Dr. Wolfe would approve of. "She's all mine," Sam said. "A hand-me-down from one of my great-uncles in St. Louis. He says it wouldn't be worth much on trade-in anyway." Sam patted the steering wheel. "I told him not to talk too loud so he wouldn't hurt her feelings."

"People can be so superficial," Hughie said.

"Man, she is our ticket to freedom."

The paint was chipped, and when Hughie tried to get in, the front passenger door handle felt loose. But the interior was clean, and the dashboard and seats were in good condition. A rosary dangled from the rearview mirror, and hip-hop was wafting from the speakers. "Freedom to do *what* exactly?"

"I thought we'd hit the outlet mall," Sam said. "I've got to buy an anniversary card for my parents to give to my aunt and uncle today. It's supposed to be"—Sam used air quotes and raised his voice in imitation of his mother— "'pretty and simple, not funny, whatever you think might be funny.' My mom forgot to pick one up at the grocery store, so she gave me some money."

Hughie grinned. "New wheels! Errand for Mom! Way to set the world on fire!"

"Come on, you can keep me company, come to the party. There's always too much food."

The outlet mall wasn't the worst idea Hughie had ever heard, and he liked the idea of spending celebratory time with a large extended family, even if it would make him homesick for his own relatives in Oklahoma. Hughie got in and texted his parents—his dad at work, his mom at the law library—that he was heading out for the day with Sam.

At Burnham Outlets, Hughie helped Sam pick out a simple, not-funny anniversary card with an illustration of white roses on the front. Meanwhile, a store clerk was filling slots in the display with Halloween cards and envelopes. Hughie grabbed a card and read the front of it. "When do ghosts come out to play?"

Sam replied, "I don't know. When do ghosts come out to play?"

Hughie opened the card and read, "On Fright-day! Happy Halloween!"

"Nice one!" Sam chuckled. "Hey, speaking of Halloween, you should join me in volunteering at Ms. Fischer's haunted house. It'll be spooky fun for a good cause. And now that I've got a car, I can drive us everywhere. From school to home to the crossroads to old town."

Hughie put the ghost-joke card back in its slot. "That's everywhere?"

"You know you want to," Sam cajoled as he went to pay at the counter.

"I do," Hughie admitted. "Okay, I'll ask my folks if I can volunteer."

"That's spooktacular!" Sam crowed.

Hughie appreciated the festive atmosphere of the outdoor mall, a manufactured neighborhood of commerce and local government buildings brought to life by discount shoppers, a guitar player in the gazebo, and the laughter of little kids riding a miniature carousel. As the boys wandered around, Sam scanned the yellow bricks that paved the walkways, each bearing the name of a donor to the public library located at the complex.

"What're you looking for?" Hughie asked, squinting in the bright sunlight.

"This!" Sam knelt, pointing his phone lens at one of the engraved bricks. "My family gave money to help build the library. Or my parents did anyway. See, right here, it says 'The Rodríguez Family.'" Hughie wasn't sure why that merited a photo shoot until Sam added, "You think I should post it or text it to Cricket? She loves books."

"Life's short. Be bold. Post and tag." Hughie's mind wistfully turned to a certain Ojibwe girl who he'd befriended through his cousin Rain and gotten to know better through a Native youth summer camp in old town. He was in a good mood. The sky was blue. Life was—

"Afternoon, boys," an outlet security guard called, strolling up. "How's it going?"

Hughie tensed up. He and Sam were the only brown kids in sight. The woman working at the kiosk of Kansas-themed gifts was South Asian, but other than her, it was a largely white space, including the mall cop. Sam said, "Everything's fine. We came to buy a greeting card."

"A greeting card?" the mall cop asked, as if he'd never heard of such a thing.

"For my mom," Sam added. "An errand for my mom."

The security guard was only about ten years older than

they were. He began walking away. "Nothing wrong with being a mama's boy. I love my mom."

"I love my mom, too," Sam replied, a little too enthusiastically.

"Seriously?" Hughie added, under his breath. Resentment mingled with relief. Running a hand through his short-cropped hair, he wondered if things might've gone differently if he wore it long like some of his cousins and uncles.

As the boys exited the mall between the waterfall-style fountains on either side of the entrance, Hughie noticed Elias and Jonas Vogel strolling in their direction. It was the first time Hughie had crossed paths with the brothers since the incident in the hall with Sophie Miller on the second day of school.

"Prick," Elias audibly muttered, and theoretically it could've been meant for either Hughie or Sam. But the tension between his friend and the brothers was as dense as the humidity. Fortunately, the Vogels kept walking, and so did Hughie and Sam.

With an exaggerated wave, Sam called to them, "Jesus loves you!"

Hughie was grateful for the heavy flow of shoppers, but where was the security guard when he might be a useful deterrent?

Elias paused, glaring back at them, but Jonas said, "Leave it," and Elias did.

Hughie had the sinking feeling that there was something important he was missing. "Sam, bro, what was that?" No answer. After a moment, Hughie realized out loud, "When you tripped Elias with your backpack in the hall, that wasn't only about helping out me and Sophie."

The silence emanating from Sam was louder than the crash of water falling into water, louder than the nearby toddler screaming for ice cream, louder than the country music blasting from the open windows of the convertible cruising through the parking lot. It wasn't until the boys were in the station wagon that Sam sighed. "You could say that."

"You want to talk about it?" Hughie nudged.

Minutes later, weaving through subdivisions, Sam finally replied, "You've got a sister, don't you? Louise Wolfe, graduated last year?"

"Louise M. Wolfe," Hughie said with a hint of pride. His sister favored her power initial.

"And she's pretty. Like, long wavy hair, curvy, popular, dates jackass jocks."

Hughie stopped fiddling with the useless air vent. "She's also brilliant and hilarious and a really good writer, and she dumped that jackass jock for a guy who's—sure, kind of full of himself, but a huge improvement—"

"Exactly. I get where you're coming from. I've got a big sister, too. Ximena. She's a hostess over at the Grub Pub. Ximena's the best—she's always looking out for me. She's supersmart, too—a techie and a runner. Came in third in girls' cross-country at state."

"Impressive," Hughie said. "Do you run?"

"Not unless somebody's chasing me. Anyway, lately, Ximena has been staying with our abuela at the trailer park in old town." Sam paused at an intersection. "Her boyfriend and our stepdad don't get along. Point is, last summer, she was still living at home—lying out in the sun on the back deck, reading on her phone—and one day, my parents were gone and the Vogels were over at our house—"

"You were hanging out with them?" Hughie exclaimed. "Socially? By choice?" With effort, he dialed down his shocked, judgmental tone. "Y'all used to be friends?"

"Yeah. I know, it's embarrassing. *Used to be* are the operative words, and anyway, they wouldn't shut up about my sister. About how 'hot' she was, what they wanted to do with her . . . or to her. It was . . . disgusting." Sam's phone buzzed, and he glanced down at it.

"Bike!" Hughie exclaimed, and Sam jerked the wheel to the left as the biker swerved out of the way and lost his balance.

"Thanks," he said, waving an apology out the window.

The rider picked himself up from the side of the road and gave them the finger.

"I can't win today," Sam added, glancing at the screen again. "That's Ximena now, probably checking up on me." He tossed the phone to Hughie. "What does she say?"

Hughie summarized. "Your sister is stuck at work, so she won't be able to make it to the party. Oh, and the air conditioner at the pub broke down." The temperature that afternoon was in the low nineties. The air felt thick and muggy. "Doesn't sound like she's having a great day."

Sam hit the brakes for a squirrel scampering across the street. "Uh, what was I—"

"The Vogels were saying stuff about her."

"Yeah, I got pissed, and they made out like they were kidding, like it was so funny getting a rise out of me, but they wouldn't drop it, either. The more they talked, the madder I got. Finally, I told them I'd had it. I didn't want to be friends anymore."

"How long have you known—"

"Forever. We used to play T-ball together. But they've changed. Every year, they've gotten worse. I'd tell myself that wasn't the real them. Except . . . it *was* the real them."

A lot of history, Hughie thought. As Sam's station wagon veered onto A.J.'s street, Hughie noticed that there were several parked cars and trucks. A couple of motorcycles, a couple of bicycles, a tent in the front yard—definitely a party. The phone buzzed in Hughie's hand, and he grinned. "Cricket hearted your pic of the library donation brick."

"Let me see that." Sam turned off the engine, then took his phone back. "I'll text Ximena really quick and"—the phone buzzed again—"that's weird."

Hughie unbuckled his seat belt. "What?"

"Ximena's still griping about her day. Now she's complaining that she's chilly and so are the waitresses and customers and they keep whining to her about it."

"With the air conditioner out?" As Sam's little cousins rushed out to greet them, the boys got out of the car, and Hughie wiped the sweat from his forehead. "That is weird."

41 DAYS UNTIL HALLOWEEN

The sign in front of the Grub Pub read HIDE YOUR STUFF. TAKE YOUR KEYS. LOCK YOUR TRUCK.

Hughie was no stranger to the intersection where the pub was located. The crossroads was out in the country, which meant that the police departments of towns to either side tended to leave it to the county sheriff. Despite the sign, it was a low-maintenance area, except for the occasional drunken scuffle or fender bender.

The north side of the business district, if you could call it that, was scarred by a boarded-up two-story building that was destined to become Ms. Fischer's haunted house. It was located next to Sunflower Tea Shop and Antiques and a storefront on the other side that frequently changed hands. Currently, it was a year-round Christmas shop. The south side was home to the Grub Pub and the plant nursery, which was located down the road a piece and over the hill. The east–west road connected old town to the relatively new suburb. The north–south road connected vanishing cattle pastures and fields of corn and wheat to more vanishing cattle pastures and fields of corn and wheat.

As they had many Sundays before, the Wolfe family chose the pub for their after-church brunch. "Hello, and welcome to the Grub Pub," a feminine voice piped up.

At the hostess stand, Hughie glanced at Ximena's name tag and said, "You're Sam's sister, right? I'm his friend—"

"The famous Hughie Wolfe!" she said. "He told me all about you, and of course I was in the audience for your standing ovation last spring." Ximena gathered up a handful of menus. "You're a better singer than my cousin A.J., but don't you dare tell him I said so."

Hughie ducked his head, flattered. "Your secret is safe with me."

As the family settled into their meal and conversation, Aunt Georgia asked Louise how her college classes were going.

Louise deflected by replying, "Hughie is thinking about writing an original playscript to enter in a high school theater competition. If he wins, it'll be produced this spring."

He playfully tossed a waffle fry at her. "That information was off the record."

From across the long table, his sister replied, "Hughie, if you tell people you're working on it, it'll help keep you accountable and motivated when you run into writer's block."

"Or it might freeze you up from too much pressure,"

his cousin Rain added with a hint of criticism. A high school junior who lived in old town, she fell between the Wolfe siblings in age, and unlike Louise, she preferred to scribble poetic reflections in private journals rather than use her writing to compete for headlines. But both girls were journalists—Louise, a news and information major, and Rain, a part-time photojournalism intern at the *Hannesburg Weekly Examiner*.

"What's this y'all are talking about?" asked Aunt Georgia. "An original script?" She was an Elder of their grandparents' generation, an auntie in the Indian way, originally from Oklahoma. Hughie had gotten to know her through his old-town cousins and by participating in her Native youth camp, focused on science and technology. "Hughie, I thought you were an actor, not a playwright! My goodness! You can just do it all, can't you?"

"I don't know about that," he replied, his cheeks warm.

While Hughie's mother explained what was happening with budget cuts at EHHS, he slowly shook his head at his sister, who didn't in the least seem to regret her words.

Hughie always felt relaxed at the Grub Pub. It wasn't only the greasy food that made the place popular. The local diners' conversational hum was punctuated by the sound of breaking pool balls, spinning foosballs, and cheers rising from friendly games of darts.

There was a TV on every wall showcasing sports coverage as well as two above the bar, though one of those had been dedicated to a twenty-four-hour news station.

"How's everybody doing?" asked their waitress, Shelby, a hardworking white girl who was also Louise's best friend. Hughie noticed that, since he'd last seen her, Shelby had gotten a small tattoo of a sunflower on her wrist. She refilled ice teas with a pitcher in one hand and coffee with a carafe in the other. The waitstaff routinely circulated with free drink refills between carrying out trays of food. It was a big selling point, especially during happy hour.

"Yeah, how is everybody doing?" echoed a booming voice that belonged to the pub owner, Doug Boucher. "How's the grub? Is Shelby earning her keep?"

Mr. Boucher was a broad man with a wide grin and a big belt buckle. Everyone murmured praise for Shelby and for the food, and as Mr. Boucher moved on to greet the next table, Grampa Berghoff started speculating as to how much the crossroads land might be worth now and commenting on how odd it was that Mr. Boucher, who owned it all, hadn't already cashed out and retired.

Technically, Grampa Berghoff was Rain's grandfather from the other side of her family, but he'd invited Hughie and Louise to call him that, too. He said, "Now, the pub, it's been in these parts longer than I have, and I'm born and raised." Pouring maple syrup over his pancakes, Grampa added, "Some of my fellow old-timers like to say the property is haunted."

That's when Hughie noticed the Vogel brothers following their mother through the front door of the pub. In a dour church dress with sensible shoes, Mrs. Vogel was all forced smiles, waving to friends across the dining room. She was plump and pretty, with a heavy layer of makeup that didn't disguise how pinched she was around the eyes. Hughie suspected the widow would've been stunned by how her sons had bullied Sophie, how crudely they'd talked about Sam's sister, Ximena. Then again, having been suspended for fighting wasn't the kind of thing Jonas and Elias could've slipped by Mrs. Vogel. Jonas and Elias's father had died recently, but maybe it wasn't only the grief wearing her down.

In any case, Hughie had to hand it to Jonas and Elias. Cleaned up, wearing church clothes, and absent their signature sneers, they looked downright wholesome. Tracking their gazes, Hughie confirmed that they hadn't noticed him yet.

"Is it just me or is it cold in here?" asked Dad.

"The air conditioner vent is right there," Mom commented, pointing at the wall above his chair. The conversation reminded Hughie of the previous days' text exchange between Sam and Ximena. *Must have gotten fixed,* he thought.

Still focused on local gossip, Grampa Berghoff leaned back in his wooden chair. "*I* say it's that old chicken restaurant across the road that's haunted."

As Mr. Boucher passed by again, he joked, "So far as I'm concerned, the whole damn crossroads is haunted. That is, if a good ghost story helps drum up business!" He let loose with a booming laugh.

The sound drew other diners' attention. Hughie watched Jonas turn his head in their direction, witnessed the moment of recognition. Jonas nudged Elias and leaned in to say something. Then Elias's gaze zeroed in on Hughie, too. Elias used two fingers to point to his own eyes and then at Hughie as if to say, *We're watching you.*

39 DAYS UNTIL HALLOWEEN

In Mrs. Qualey's English language arts class, the desks were arranged in a circle, and each day a different student took a turn leading a discussion of the reading homework.

Today was Sophie Miller's turn. "We're going to be talking about 'Young Goodman Brown,' a short story by Nathaniel Hawthorne." She tapped her purple pen on her desk. "According to the syllabus, the fact that the protagonist's name is 'Brown' is the closest we'll get to reading about a brown character all semester."

That was bold. Hughie's gaze flicked to Mrs. Q, and he was surprised to see her lips twitch as if tempted to smile. It made no sense to him that, after fighting as theater director to integrate brown and Black student actors into major roles, she wouldn't do the same for brown and Black voices in her classroom. Then again, his own mom used to be an English teacher in central Texas, and she had often complained about the politics of the prescribed curriculum. Sometimes teachers were held hostage by narrow-minded people.

Sophie read aloud a section to refresh the class's memory of the assignment:

> "Well; she's a blessed angel on earth; and after this one night, I'll cling to her skirts and follow her to Heaven." With this excellent resolve for the future, Goodman Brown felt himself justified in making more haste on his present evil purpose. He had taken a dreary road, darkened by all the gloomiest trees of the forest, which barely stood aside to let the narrow path creep through, and closed immediately behind. It was all as lonely as could be; and there is this peculiarity in such a solitude, that the traveller knows not who may be concealed by the innumerable trunks and the thick boughs overhead; so that, with lonely footsteps, he may yet be passing through an unseen multitude. "There may be a devilish Indian behind every tree," said Goodman Brown to himself; and he glanced fearfully behind him, as he added, "What if the devil himself should be at my very elbow!"

Sophie looked up from the textbook. "Anything jump out at you about this passage?"

Sophomore class president Amy Wagoner raised her hand. "He's putting a ton of pressure on his wife, Faith, to be . . . pure and angelic—'a blessed angel on earth.'"

"It's romantic," her boyfriend, Aiden Walker, replied. "When people are in love, they see the best in each other. It's called 'Through the Eyes of Love.'"

"That's the title of the theme song from *Ice Castles*," Mrs. Qualey muttered. In response to blank faces, she added, "Historical reference. Move it along."

"He thinks all of his people are pure. Pur-i-tans, pure," basketball star Logan Moran said. "He's shocked to find out they're partying in the woods."

"Anything else?" Sophie asked, with a not-so-subtle head tilt toward Hughie. "What about talking like Indians are evil, the devil. Did anyone notice that?"

Even though the question was directed at the entire group, Hughie felt obligated to say something. But before he could form a sentence, Carter Harris said, "Give it a rest, Sophie. Literally everybody back then used to think that way."

Hughie spoke up. "Not *literally* everybody. For sure not Indians themselves."

Carter's parents were among the loudest members of Parents Against Revisionist Theater, and he was among the contingent of PART-family students who seemed on board with their worldview. Carter replied, "You know what I mean. They didn't count."

"Of course they did," Mrs. Q declared, putting an end to that line of discussion. "Also, kudos to Mr. Wolfe for his refreshingly accurate understanding of the word *literally*.

Ms. Miller, perhaps you'd like the class to address Hawthorne's use of symbolism?"

After the bell, Hughie and Sophie fell into step as they headed toward the sophomore hall. The part of him that had called out L. Frank Baum for his pro-genocide newspaper editorials admired that she'd called out Nathaniel Hawthorne—or at least his protagonist, Goodman Brown. The part of Hughie that wanted to make it through English class without feeling like he had to play Cultural Spokesperson felt cranky and exhausted by the fact that people like Carter always seemed to default to bigot mode. But Hughie also knew how hard that assignment must've been for Sophie. If she had ignored the anti-Indigenous content, other students might've assumed she didn't think it was a big deal. "You were good in class today."

"Thanks," she replied. "I was so nervous."

"I couldn't tell." They briefly separated to make way for an incoming tall girl preoccupied with her phone. He added, "You know, you should try out for the spring play . . . or whatever it turns out to be."

"I don't think so." Sophie was wearing dangling beaded earrings in greens and blues. "In ninth, I tried to give this oral report in history on Shirley Chisholm. I choked out a few high-pitched noises . . . like a sheep being strangled . . . and then ran to the girls' restroom and threw up. I'd had burritos at lunch that day. It wasn't pretty."

Hughie chuckled and gave her a wave as they parted ways under the spirit banner for that weekend's football game and headed for their respective lockers.

Having always attended mostly white schools, Hughie had sometimes imagined that if there was at least one Native student in his grade, they'd become best pals, but . . . no. It wasn't that he didn't like Sophie. She was nice enough. He'd always have her back—like with the Vogels and in ELA class. It's just that he and Sophie didn't click that way.

Hughie opened his locker and spotted a book that he hadn't put there—*Apple: (Skin to the Core)* by Onondaga author Eric Gansworth. The price sticker on the back confirmed that it had been purchased at an independent bookstore in Lawrence. Hughie pulled out the handwritten note tucked inside the front cover.

> Hughie,
> Here's another one by your favorite author!
> Your Friend, The Librarian

He wasn't surprised that Ms. Zimmerman and her library aides had access to his new locker combination. They'd managed to get last year's, too. Hughie had consumed a steady supply of good books through their covert deliveries, which subversively served EHHS readers while foiling parental censors.

Glancing down the hallway, Hughie noticed Sophie smiling at a note as she held *Elatsoe* by Darcie Little Badger, which he recognized from his own bookshelf at home. He made a mental note to ask her sometime soon what she'd thought of the story.

By the time the video call came in that evening, Hughie had spent what felt like a productive half hour or so at the desk in his bedroom researching playscript formatting and adjusting his open document accordingly. "Howdy, cousin!" he said. "How's it going? What's new?"

Rain had her phone camera turned toward herself and her black Lab, Chewie, as she slowly rocked on her creaky porch swing. "Pretty good. I've been babysitting Yanni a lot and helping Grampa Berghoff remodel our darkroom in the attic—we're almost done." With her father stationed in Guam, Rain lived with her twenty-something big brother, sister-in-law, and their toddler in a house only a block away from Grampa Berghoff and her step-grandma.

As Hughie made a mental note to call his own grandparents in Oklahoma, he could faintly hear his parents' laughter as they climbed the foyer stairs to go to bed.

"Want to come with us to the football game?" Rain didn't need to clarify that "us" referred to herself and their mutual friends from Aunt Georgia's youth camp. Rain's boyfriend, Dmitri Headbird, was a placekicker on old-town varsity.

"Sure," Hughie replied. "Mind if I bring my friend Sam?"

"Bring him! Just so long as he knows that we're Harvesters fans!"

"Will Marie be there?" Hughie asked with intense casualness. He had been trying not to regret that he hadn't made his romantic interest in Marie Headbird, Dmitri's twin sister, known the previous summer. The Native youth campers' road trip to the Leech Lake Ojibwe rez in Minnesota was becoming an annual tradition. But it was also very much a group activity, and in case Marie didn't reciprocate his feelings, Hughie hadn't wanted any awkwardness between them to taint her trip or their shared connection to Rain, Dmitri, and the others.

"Yes, Marie will be there." Rain arched her left eyebrow and touched her seed-beaded, small pouch necklace. "She never misses her brother's games." Rain tactfully changed the subject. "How's the script?"

Standing to pace on the Berber carpeting in his bedroom, Hughie almost would've preferred that his cousin quiz him about his feelings for Marie. Almost. "I have created a word-processing document. It has a file name: 'Untitled.'"

"Well! That's a glass-half-full answer if I've ever heard one. Are you thinking about a play with singing or a play without singing?"

"Straight play, not a musical," Hughie replied. "Playlet actually. On the short side." Because that sounded less intimidating.

"Fiction or nonfiction?"

It was the first time he'd considered the latter option. "Nonfiction about what?"

"Up to you, but we can brainstorm, if you want. You could even fictionalize something that really happened. People call that *loosely inspired*. It's not cheating. All stories somehow spring from stories that came before them. It would give you something to work with."

Hughie wasn't surprised that, despite both his sister's and his cousin's flurry of encouragement at the recent after-church brunch, it was Rain (rather than Louise) who'd offered practical support. Rain had a tender but determined quality, which made her particularly good at looking out for people she cared about.

"Or you could write something fantastical and escapist like *Star Wars*," Rain said. Hughie's geekdoms skewed more to superheroes than sci-fi, but he did have a poster of real-life Chickasaw astronaut John Herrington tacked to his wall and a pair of binoculars resting on his nightstand. *Star Wars* was always a stellar idea. Rain added, "How about a mystery with an X factor? Something spooky and mysterious. You know, a real mind-bender."

"Let's keep thinking," Hughie replied. "I'm not a huge fan of scary stories."

CELESTE

Time is slippery, liquid. Seasons swirl—the freeze and the thaw, the heat and the harvest. With the corn ripening, memories merge again. I'm watching over yet another new girl. White T-shirt, black jeans. Brown hair, brown eyes, brown skin.

The last one drove away and never came back, hopefully never looked back—she was smart, so smart. This new girl, she's arguing with her boyfriend, their words spewing with passion and bitterness. She's spit and tears, her face scrunched and snot grody. He throws up his arms, furious. Then he slams the door of an old sports car and peels out, wheels screeching on the country road.

In a mix of Spanish and English, she's confiding in . . . her grandmother, I think . . . her abuelita, she says, on the phone—phones are so strange now, like walkie-talkies on outer-space TV shows.

It's unseasonably chilly, and I'm on the lookout for The Bad Man. Sometimes he waits years between his appearances. Sometimes it's a matter of seasons, weeks.

This time it's not only me and Moon and Mother Mourning Dove watching. Feral eyes shine from the brush along the barbed-wire fence—Coyote.

The birds rustle, ready. Awaiting my call.

Would the same trick rebuff him again? He's always different, always the same.

"*Less,*" The Bad Man calls, appearing from the shadows. "*Less . . .*" His voice has a sharper pitch. It's eerie how it changes, how his face and body shift. It reminds me of tales I'd rather not think about.

His voice unnerves the girls, makes them more likely to panic. The way the soles of his shoes or boots scratch against the gravel and pavement is even worse.

Headlights flash by. Dandelions strain through cracked asphalt. Coyote huffs, hidden. Where is Coyote's pack, her band? Why is she alone?

The girl ends the phone call. Wary, she circles around the far side of the building.

Maybe she senses Coyote.

"Less . . ." A familiar word, a stranger's voice.

The girl's head snaps up. No hesitation. She takes a step back, pivots, runs.

How far is it to town?

"Less," he gasps.

She's fast, focused. Our main advantage—he always walks—*staggers* like he's weighed down. No way can he catch her now. I'd be breathing easier if I could breathe at all.

Then she slips on loose gravel, trips like a slasher-movie victim. "Damn!" The girl pushes up, her palms and chin bloody. Her knees will bruise. She's scared of a too-common threat, a hateful man in the darkness. Nothing's happened that can't be explained away. Not yet.

The Bad Man lurches forward.

Not this girl, Bad Man. Not this night.

Coyote welcomes my spirit like a long-lost friend.

37 DAYS UNTIL HALLOWEEN

That Thursday afternoon, when Louise offered to pick up Hughie after school, he was impressed that she'd set aside time exclusively for her little brother. That was, until he noticed the three bags of laundry in the back seat. But Louise had more on her mind than tossing her stuff into the washer. "Let's swing by the Grub Pub for a snack," she suggested. "I got a text from Shelby this afternoon, and she sounded frazzled."

Hughie agreed, and as the Wolfe siblings approached the pub, he noticed a HELP WANTED sign in the front window. He looked around for Sam's sister, Ximena, but he didn't spot her. Louise led Hughie to her favorite leather booth, which had a view of Sunflower Tea Shop and Antiques and the year-round Christmas shop. Hughie glanced out the window at a middle-aged woman in a gray tailored suit carrying out a garden statue of an angel.

"In the weeds," Shelby declared, setting glasses of ice tea on the table. "The usual?"

"Dry-rub wings," Louise confirmed. "But we can wait. You need help? We can run food. We can bus tables. We can make distracting small talk with customers."

"Can you pour beer?" Shelby replied. Pointing at Hughie, she added, "Not you." By Kansas law, he was too young to serve. "Hughie, you clear tables."

With that, Shelby sprinted toward the restaurant kitchen to check on her orders, and Hughie began gathering up dirty dishes, discarded napkins, and emptied glassware while Louise grabbed a frothy pitcher from the bar.

It wasn't the first time Louise had helped out at the restaurant. Mr. Boucher didn't officially approve, but having to hire and pay more staff would've bothered him more.

"Fill up everyone with a beer mug on their table," Millie, the bartender, said to Louise. "It'll buy us some patience and goodwill." On the TV screen mounted above the bar, a blond, white woman holding a microphone in front of a McMansion announced that a different blond, white woman, this one from Pennsylvania, had been reported missing earlier that week.

Hughie texted his dad that he was out with his sister and not to hold dinner. "What happened?" he asked Millie. "How did everything get so backed up?"

"Another girl up and quit—no notice. Mr. Boucher still hasn't found a new waitress, and hostesses usually run backup for the waitstaff . . . clearing tables, fetching food from the kitchen, that sort of thing. So we're down by two."

Hughie found the service cart on the other side of the waitstaff station and made quick work of returning the dining room to a less messy state.

A couple of hours later, another waitress had clocked in, Shelby was spraying off dishes in the stuffy, greasy kitchen, and Louise was loading them into the machine while the Wolfe siblings waited on their own food. Karl, the pub cook, was deep-frying mozzarella sticks "on the house" (in addition to the wings they'd ordered) as a thank-you. Suddenly, as Hughie reached for a nearby dishrag to clean up some spilled sweet tea, he felt a sharp chill that made no sense, especially in the kitchen. "Did anyone else feel that? The cold?" The back of his hand prickled with rising gooseflesh and a shimmer of sweat.

"I did." His sister pushed a rack of dishes into the machine. "Shelby?"

"The regulars are saying our resident ghost has been acting up more lately," she said.

The moment Shelby mentioned *ghost*, the cold dissipated. At Louise's scowl, Shelby added, "Hey, it's not like I'm encouraging them. But Boucher is all over it. He even wrote up the legend and had it printed on the back of our October specials menu. Millie helped him with it." She reached into her apron for a folded-up copy on orange paper and handed it to Hughie. The front was decorated with a pumpkin border, which tied in with several of the dishes, notably the pumpkin pancakes. Shelby had scribbled lists of ingredients to memorize next to each. The back of the menu read:

THE LEGEND OF THE CROSSROADS GHOST

Over a hundred years ago, a beautiful, exotic Indian maiden was plagued by a heart full of suspicion and jealously. One windy wintry night, she tracked her lover—an upstanding old-town boy from a good family—and her own younger sister, who was even more lovely than she was—to a secret romantic rendezvous at the crossroads.

By the light of the full moon, the maiden witnessed their passionate embrace and threw herself, sobbing, into the dry prairie grass. As her tears fell, the night clouds began to sleet, but in her sorry state, she couldn't summon the strength to seek shelter.

Instead, she remained there, freezing to death, until the last beat of her broken heart. Yet her anger was too powerful to die, and it tied her soul to the crossroads. Here, she remains, seeking revenge on her sister by haunting innocent young women.

So beware, raven-haired beauties! This spurned maiden's spirit may come after you next!

Realizing his big sister was reading over his shoulder, Hughie braced himself. Louise could spend the rest of the evening ranting about the word *exotic* alone.

"Shelby," Louise began. "Do me a favor. Try to 'forget' to give out the specials menu next month."

"Roger that," her best friend replied. "Forgetting already."

"Order up!" Karl slid the platter of dry-rub wings and fried cheese onto the metal kitchen shelf separating him from the teens. "Get them while they're hot."

"Does anyone know what her name was, the girl who died?" Hughie refolded the menu and handed it back to Shelby. "Or where she's buried now?"

"I seriously doubt she ever existed," Shelby said, glancing briefly at the piece of paper in her hand before crumpling it up and tossing it into the trash can by the register. "God, if she was a real girl, that would've been tragic. Can you imagine?"

"There's probably at least one bullshit legend about Indians in every state in the country," Louise said. "The exotic, beautiful brown woman. The angry, dangerous brown woman. The white man she doesn't blame for cheating on her—no, it's her conniving sister who deserves to be punished. It's all so bigoted and cliché."

"It doesn't say he was white," Hughie pointed out.

"It's implied," Louise said. "*Upstanding* and *a good family*, they're code for *white*. At least in this part of Kansas."

Hughie was glad that college hadn't dulled his big sister's edge. "Does anyone know what Tribe she was supposed—"

"Enough nonsense!" Karl scolded, waving his spatula around. "You're good Christian kids, aren't you? You should know better than to be making light of the dead with that silly ghost talk." He raised his voice to be heard over the sizzling skillets and boiling oil, but it still sounded too loud in the cramped cinder-block room. "It's goddamned disrespectful!"

As Karl slammed a metal lid onto a metal pot, Hughie flinched. His family had changed churches enough times that he considered himself generically Protestant, leaning mainstream Methodist or Baptist. But he couldn't remember the Bible saying much about ghosts or the subject ever coming up in Sunday school.

With a loaded oval tray balanced on her shoulder, Shelby led the Wolfe siblings out of the kitchen. "Don't mind Karl. When he got sober, he got religious. He lost a brother some months back and took it hard."

Moving down the wood-paneled hallway, Hughie felt for the cook. He understood that grief didn't always look like sorrow. Sometimes it bared its teeth.

"Sorry to hear that," Louise said. "What happened?"

"Heart attack. Karl is in charge of elder care for his mom, and he's been helping out his sister-in-law with her sons—Jonas and Elias. They're a handful." It was news to Hughie that the bullies were closely related to the pub cook. Using her back and shoulders to hold open the swinging door to the dining room, Shelby added, "Poor Karl. There were three boys in his family. He was the oldest, and now he's the only one left."

That night, after finishing his European history homework, Hughie opened the document currently named *Spring Play*. He typed Karl's name and then deleted it. He typed the word *ghost* and then deleted that, too.

Hughie stared at the mocking, blinking cursor for about twenty minutes, then closed the computer and reached for his binoculars to drink in the stars.

He longed for a clearer night, for the clouds to disappear.

36 DAYS UNTIL HALLOWEEN

From the bleachers, Hughie caught sight of Rain's boy-friend, old-town placekicker Dmitri Headbird, sitting on the Harvesters' team bench with his forehead cradled in his hands. It was the fourth quarter, and the EHHS Honey-bees were leading 21–7, according to the overpriced, ego-maniacal jumbotron.

It wouldn't be fair to call Hughie a fan of the sport, but having grown up mostly in Texas, he'd learned a lot about football through osmosis. Hughie felt his loyalties cheer-fully divided between his home school and his friends' team—not that he cared much who won, but Sam, who'd gamely joined him on the Harvesters' side of the bleachers, and the girls had been having fun razzing each other over the old-town/new-burbs sports rivalry.

"Come on, Dmitri!" Rain shouted to her boyfriend. "It's not over yet!"

"*Yet?*" Hughie shook his head. "Was that you being supportive?"

His cousin shrugged. "It's me being honest." She tried again. "Let's go, Dmitri!"

On the other side of the stadium, Louise, her boyfriend, Joey, and Shelby were seated with their class of graduates in the Honeybees' cheering section. But it had become customary for Hughie to join Rain and their friends in the old-town fans' bleachers whenever their schools played each other. Tonight, it was a small group—aside from Hughie, Rain, and Sam, it was just Dmitri's twin, Marie, and Rain's forever friend, Queen. They'd hit it off with Sam, who'd excused himself a few minutes earlier to fetch drinks and snacks. Hughie noticed that Sam was making an extra effort to get along with Hughie's friends, which Hughie appreciated.

"Queen, did you tell Hughie about our school musical?" Rain prompted with an eager grin that suggested there was exciting news to be shared.

"I don't want to be insensitive!" Queen exclaimed, raising her voice to be heard over the band. "If a bunch of busybody parents got our theater program slashed in half, there would be smoke wafting out of my ears."

"Very considerate." Rain adjusted her long knitted scarf. "But did it ever occur to you that Hughie might be happy for you, especially given . . . ?"

"Oh, yeah," Queen said. "You might have a point."

"Just tell him already!" Marie exclaimed with a laugh as Hughie pleaded, "Tell me!"

Was it a good sign that they'd said almost the same thing at the same time?

Hughie hoped so.

What was it about Marie Headbird that dazzled him? She possessed a quiet, quirky appeal, the kind that shined from a generous heart. Marie collected PEZ dispensers— her one purely personal indulgence. She gravitated toward Elders, especially Aunt Georgia, and was a stalwart supporter of her friends and brother. Spending time on her rez the previous summer had been a privilege. Her humor had come out more, her strength and sensitivity.

Only problem? Hughie was a hopeful romantic with zero experience with real-life romance. The rom-coms he'd watched with his sister had taught him that love was about the meet-cute, the battle of wills, and the grand gesture. None of that was Hughie's style. He'd known Marie since shortly after he'd moved to Kansas, so they'd had time to get to know each other. Low-key and casual, like real human beings . . . always in the company of other friends.

The one downside to community? It wasn't conducive to sparks flying between shy beginners. Case in point: Rain and Queen were seated between him and Marie. With the noise of the crowd, Hughie couldn't always hear Marie talking. He'd asked twice for her to repeat herself only to have one of the other girls chime in on her behalf. Though he caught an occasional glimpse of her leaning in to say something, all Hughie could really see of Marie was her sneakers—they featured a floral design and green-and-white polka dot shoelaces. Hughie, who'd always been a serious fan of footwear, appreciated their whimsical appeal. Not that he could *tell* Marie that with his beloved cousin and their mutual friend in the way.

"I don't know," Queen said in a tone that let them know she'd already made up her mind to share and was now enjoying their bubbling anticipation.

Hughie rolled his eyes, but he really did want to know. "If you don't go ahead, I'm sure Rain will spill."

"Hughie's right," Rain warned. "If you don't tell him, I—"

"Okay, fine!" Queen said. She took a breath and straightened her posture on the bleacher bench. "I'm pleased to announce that I landed the role of none other than queen of the damned, the grand dame of darkness, the all-time hottest housewife of horror—Morticia Addams herself—in Hannesburg High's upcoming production of *The Addams Family* musical."

"That's amazing!" Hughie exclaimed, reaching over his cousin to give Queen a congratulatory hug. Being around a fellow thespian was like getting a booster dose of the theater vibe he was missing. She rocked in his arms, hugging him back.

"It probably didn't hurt that you, A.J., and Chelsea Weber killed it onstage at EHHS last year. To be honest, I was surprised to get a fair shot at the audition. We're talking Morticia, traditionally known as a tall drink of *pale* ale, but here we are . . ." Queen leaned into her character's voice. "Gomez!"

Everyone applauded. Hughie felt gratified to hear

that old town had joined EHHS in opening more roles to student actors of color. Queen's heritage was Black and Seminole, and she was the daughter and granddaughter of enrolled tribal members.

"I have no idea how you two can perform in front of a whole auditorium of people," Marie said. "I can't imagine doing that."

"You should try it sometime," Queen said. "You might surprise yourself."

"True. So true," Marie said. "There are many layers to the mystery that is me."

Everyone laughed, delighted by her confident declaration. Queen and Rain had been tight since they were little, and ever since Marie's family had moved to Hannesburg a few years earlier, the girls were a sisterhood of three.

Like Hughie, Rain was Muscogee-Cherokee-Ojibwe by heritage but Muscogee by tribal affiliation. Hughie, who'd been wholly raised around Oklahoma Indian people, hadn't known much firsthand about the Ojibwe before visiting Leech Lake with the youth camp the previous summer. He still couldn't believe that they'd gone on a road trip together all the way to Minnesota—almost twelve hours each way on US 71 North—and Hughie *still* hadn't let Marie know he liked her. But they were older now, with more access to transportation. The distance between old town and the suburbs wasn't nearly the obstacle it had been only months ago.

Sam climbed the bleachers, hugging five cups of cocoa

against his puffy vest. "A little help?" he asked. Hughie and Rain scrambled to meet him halfway and distributed the drinks.

"You could've come with me," Sam said under his breath.

"I figured you had it handled," Hughie said.

"Nah, your brain is somewhere else." Sam grinned. "And don't try to tell me you care about the game. Talk to me, Wolfe Man. What gives?"

"Keep it down," Hughie said, leaning closer. "I, um, I'm kind of . . . . I like—"

"Queen?" Sam guessed in a low voice. "I'm not trying to hurt your feelings, but she's seriously out of your league. By which I mean, I'm kind of interested in her myself."

"What about Cricket, your journalist bus crush?"

"I like her—I do—but I'm not sure yet if it's mutual, so I'm keeping my options open."

"It's mutual!" Hughie said. "Anyway, no, she's . . . it's Marie."

"Oh, that makes perfect sense." Sam took a sip of cocoa. "Left to your own devices, though, the two of you *might* finally have a one-on-one conversation . . . before senior prom. Let me help." He stood up. "Hughie and I are going to move down a row, so we can talk to everybody easier."

Hughie was half-annoyed, half-grateful. He followed Sam to the bench in front of the girls. Sam, who ended up closer to Marie, asked, "What were you saying?"

"I've been looking for a part-time job," she replied. "But there's nothing available in old town; you have to compete with the college students in Lawrence, and juggling who gets our family cars is an ordeal."

"The Grub Pub is hiring at the crossroads," Hughie said, pleased to have something to contribute to the conversation. "My sister's friend Shelby works there."

"So does my sister, Ximena," Sam said. "I'll text her and find out if the job's still open." He sent a brief message. "You know, me and Hughie are volunteering at that haunted house fundraiser at the crossroads, so if you get the job, you'll be seeing a lot of us there. Answer incoming." Sam held up his phone so everyone could see the dots indicating that his sister was writing him back. "We're supertight, me and Ximena." He leaned in toward Hughie. "Uh, you did ask your parents about volunteering?"

Hughie answered, "I did."

"And they said yes?" Sam pressed.

"They did—so long as I keep up with my homework."

"Outstanding!" Sam glanced down at his phone. The dots had disappeared, but Ximena hadn't answered him either. "Huh, that's not like Ximena. I hope she's okay."

35 DAYS UNTIL HALLOWEEN

Hughie was eager to meet Ms. Fischer and learn more about the haunted house. As Mom slowed the Honda Fit, turning in to the parking lot, he noticed that the wooden boards had been taken down from the building's windows, which hugely improved the look of the place. Hughie scanned the two-story beige facade. It beckoned like a blank canvas. This Saturday morning might only be the initial meet and greet, but he was already beginning to imagine the possibilities.

Hughie got out of the car, unhooked the dachshunds from the seat belt extensions, and attached their harnesses to a double-dog leash. Mom had asked him to help her take them to the mobile groomers, located out front.

Bilbo and Frodo had spent the car ride with their heads stuck out the window, sniffing the landscape, but once their paws hit asphalt, they began to whine and howl. They even tried to scramble back inside the car. "What's gotten into them?" Mom asked.

"Beats me." Hughie scooped up one pup in each hand

and handed off Bilbo to his mother. "Frodo, stop it! You're fine! Everything's fine!"

"They've always been happy at the groomer before," Mom said. "It's not like we're taking them to the V-E-T."

At the Pawsitively Gorgeous Airstream, angled alongside the property entrance, a pierced and tattooed groomer greeted them with exasperation. "This makes it unanimous! Either we've lost our dog-whisperer street cred or some unknown force is spooking the pooches."

"It's not only our rowdy little mongrels?" Mom asked with affection.

"Not even close. I've had it! As of next weekend, look for us in the empty lot next to the Unitarian Church off Main Street in old town."

Hughie felt for them. "I bet it's the barbecue smoke coming from the Grub Pub across the street," he said. "The dogs always get riled up when my dad fires up the grill."

Once the dachshunds had been whisked away, Hughie jogged to the Honda to grab the extensions from the back seat and hugged his mother goodbye.

Mom paused. "Do I need to meet this Ms. Fischer?"

"She's a friend of Sam's mom from yoga class."

"And you're sure Sam is a safe driver? He'll stay off the highways?"

"Sam is terrified of highways, awkward silences, and cute redheads."

Mom clapped. "That's what I like to hear. You boys

have fun. Text me a photo of the dogs when the groomers are done. Your father will be home for dinner."

A moment later, Sam bounced out of what used to be K.V.'s Chicken Restaurant and Lounge. "Where have you been? I was just talking to Ms. Fischer, and I told her all about you. We'll be helping to convert this mild-mannered, bland building into a spooktacle for the masses." Sam took off his Jayhawks ball cap. "I'm figuring we'll ask to paint. Once the lighting and effects go live, it's not like it has to be perfect."

"It'll be like building a huge stage set," Hughie said with growing enthusiasm.

"Yep, you'll be a natural! You— Hang on." Sam reached for his buzzing phone and frowned at the screen.

"What's wrong?" Hughie asked over the howling of a standard poodle emerging from the back of an SUV. The owner was trying to calm it to no avail.

"It's . . ." Sam ran his fingers through his windblown bangs. "My sister Ximena is messing with me. She finally texted me back from last night, and all she says is: *Stay away from the crossroads!*"

Hughie grinned. "I'm quaking in my kicks already."

"Me too." Brightening, Sam added, "Ready, Wolfe Man? It's time to come face-to-face with . . ." He swept his arm toward the building. "Harvest House!"

"Harvest what exactly?" Hughie asked as they strolled toward the front door.

"Uh, fall harvest. You know, harvest season." Sam

lurched forward—his arms bent and raised in a ghastly pose. In a deep, hollow voice, he intoned, *"Harvest your life, harvest your soul."*

Hughie chuckled. "Good luck with that. Zombies?"

"No, ghosts! It's an old-school haunted house theme. The guy who owns the lot told Ms. Fischer that he didn't want anything cheesy or churchy or too scary for families." Sam made a show of gazing at the rolling countryside, at the senior ladies sipping tea at a café table on the front porch of the antiques store, at the elderly gentlemen shooting the breeze on a beat-up wooden bench in front of the pub. "It's pretty wholesome out here."

As the boys approached what was to become Harvest House, Hughie could hear voices coming from inside, through the front door of the boxy building that had been propped open.

Out front, a few workers were unloading wooden planks from a pickup.

A petite blond girl was directing a couple of twenty-something guys staking a roadside sign in front that read HARVEST HOUSE: FEAR THE REAPER.

Between all that and the yipping, yapping, barking, howling dogs and their baffled owners at the mobile groomer, it was the most activity Hughie had ever seen on this side of the road.

As he climbed the cracked concrete front steps and entered the building, Hughie was surprised that the dusty interior looked historic in an early twentieth-century kind of way. Whoever had designed the place had integrated antique fireplaces, doors with transom windows, and heavy, tiered moldings to add gravitas to the country-style wallpaper and commercial carpet tiles. In Hughie's opinion, the place already looked the part of an old-timey haunted house. The air smelled musty and thick. Hughie sneezed from the dust.

With each step forward, the muffled voices sounded louder, clearer, and Hughie hazarded a guess that the kitchen toward the back of the building had been converted into a makeshift office.

In the tall foyer, Sam patted the finial on the wooden handrail of the staircase. "Every dining area will feature its own ghost or ghosts, and so will the attic and the grounds out back."

The boys proceeded down a broad central hallway, divided by wooden support beams. Sam paused briefly at one empty dining area after another, giving Hughie a moment to envision the faux horrors to come. The furniture had been sold off years before. Cracks split windowpanes. Light fixtures were gone, leaving dangling wires wrapped with electrical tape.

Hughie and Sam turned around at the kitchen door, which suggested to Hughie that the haunted maze would split the hallway along the beams, with ticket holders moving in both directions. For now, the sides mirrored each other, an otherwise barren landscape. Hughie felt his imagination tingle. The space had fourteen-foot ceilings, hefty square footage, and tons of potential.

Returning to the foyer, Sam added, "Then people will go up this staircase to the attic, and finally, they'll *whoosh* down superlong slides set up side by side over the staff staircase at the rear of the building, through total darkness, out to a haunted burial ground."

Hughie's mind filled with images of old-timey farmer ghosts rising from a make-believe historic family cemetery. Just then a middle-aged white woman in a faded plaid shirt and even more faded jeans called out, "Hello again, Sam! Is this your friend?"

"Meet the one and only Hughie Wolfe. Hughie, this is Ms. Fischer."

She offered her hand, and Hughie shook it. "Thank you for volunteering, Hughie. Let me show you around. You know, I'll be glad when the groomer packs up. I can hardly hear myself think. Sam, if you'll excuse us for a few minutes . . ."

As Sam took the opportunity to jog to the restroom at the pub, Ms. Fischer slung a companionable arm around Hughie and walked him through the long-abandoned restaurant kitchen, away from the canine chaos out front. Outside the open double doors, a handful of workstations had already been set up. Paint cans and lumber were stacked beneath the overhang. "Hughie, I grew up on this side of old town. I've always worked—don't think that I didn't. I even had a real good job with the county for a few years, but it got axed in the last budget cuts, and there went my government health insurance with it."

Nodding politely, Hughie was tempted to reassure Ms. Fischer that she didn't owe him any explanations. But as she continued to speak, he came to understand that what she had to say was more about reassuring herself.

"I'm a churchgoer, too," Ms. Fischer added. "Born and raised Catholic, just like your friend Sam. Not that I've . . . Well, you might say I'm lapsed."

Wind blew through the black oak trees along the barbed-wire fence, and birds rustled in the gutter around the top of the building—interrupted now and again by a muted but still explosive rant of a dog. As Hughie and Ms. Fischer sank to sit on the concrete steps leading from the building to the wraparound parking lot, he resigned himself to listening.

She went on, "I guess what I'm trying to say here . . . and you'd think I'd be better at it after repeating myself all morning . . . is that I'm sure as hell grateful. A kid your age, there's a million other things you could be doing with your time, but here you are, willing to lend me a hand because . . . you're a good boy. I can always tell, Hughie. And I never forget a kindness."

Ms. Fischer was tearing up. It was a lot of unexpected grown-up emotion for him to process. But Ms. Fischer seemed like a nice lady who'd been down on her luck for a while. She added, "Truth is, I'm not used to people showing up for me like this. I'm half-afraid that once the real work starts, volunteers will peel off, leaving me holding the bag."

"I'm not like that," Hughie assured her. "I'm in it—"

"For the duration?" Ms. Fischer asked.

Feeling grown-up and responsible, this time he was the one who extended his hand. "You've got my word." And they shook on it.

A few minutes later, fully committed to the haunted house project, Hughie accepted Bilbo and Frodo's double leash at the side door of the groomer's trailer. "How much do I owe you?"

"Your mother already paid," the groomer said. "Both of these sweet boys did pretty good. But Frodo tried to nip me when I shaved his haunches."

"Sorry about that," Hughie said, distracted by the sight of Marie Headbird emerging from the front door of the Grub Pub across the road. "Small dog, big world. You know how it goes."

"Sure do." The groomer grinned. "Occupational hazard."

Coming up beside him, Sam tracked Hughie's gaze to the Ojibwe girl. "Cue the orchestra," Sam said. "This is your big chance. Go say hi!"

"Huh?" Hughie replied as the dachshunds pulled on their shared leash and barked at the mysterious whatever that was setting off every canine on-site.

"Take the dogs!" Sam called, continuing back to the work site to bring Ms. Fischer a takeout cup of coffee, courtesy of Mr. Boucher. "Girls love cute dogs. Good luck, Wolfe Man."

What happened next was almost instantaneous. The dachshunds surged forward, and with Hughie's attention divided, the leash slipped through his fingers. Bilbo and Frodo dashed full barrel into the two-lane road. They barked frantically at the air as a motorcycle roared by, and then they paused in the center in apparent confusion as a gray hatchback sped toward them. While it was possible the hyped-up dogs would stay put and survive unscathed, it wasn't likely.

Dread coiled in Hughie's belly. There was no time to save the dogs—not unless Hughie wanted to end up as roadkill himself. He felt his blood rushing in his ears, and he could've sworn he heard a whisper of "Em vnicvkvs," as if on the wind. His subconscious, he figured, speaking to him in Mvskoke. His feet felt frozen to the ground.

Meanwhile, Marie—sprinting toward the potential tragedy—held out a fistful of hot chicken tenders from her carryout bag. "Hey, dogs! Over here!" She tossed the deep-fried meat toward the pups on the safe side of the road.

As the overexcited dachshunds pounced to gobble it up, the vehicle sped by, and Marie hurried to successfully intercept their leash and guide them securely onto the Grub Pub property.

"Marie!" Hughie dashed over. He would've swept

up both dogs in a hug, but it was a bad idea to touch Frodo when he was eating, so he settled for giving Bilbo a loving scratch on the top of his head and held out his arms to Marie. She welcomed the embrace, which lasted longer than the friendly, quick ones they'd previously exchanged—a mixture of adrenaline, relief, and maybe something more. Hughie could feel the seed beads of her drop earrings against his cheek. "You saved their lives," he said, misting up. "You're a hero!"

"I burned my fingers," Marie said, as if only just noticing it.

"Oh no." Hughie pulled back. "Are you okay?"

Marie grinned, waving her singed hand in the air and using the other one to pass the leash handle to Hughie. "I'll live!" She laughed, giddy. "We'll all live!"

"I sure hope so," Hughie said. The dachshunds had finished off the chicken and were now circling the teens, yipping and hopping against their shins.

"Let me help you get them loaded up in your car," said Marie.

"It's Sam's station wagon today," Hughie replied as they started off in that direction. "I just met with the woman in charge of the haunted house."

"And I scored the part-time hostess job. I'll been running food and busing tables, too." Her tone somehow failed to suggest that congratulations were in order.

"That's good news, isn't it?" Hughie asked. "You don't sound that excited about it."

Marie wrinkled her nose. "I'm not that excited about my new boss."

The closer they got to the old chicken restaurant, the more rambunctious the dogs became. "I swear they're not usually this wild." Glancing at Marie, he asked, "Mr. Boucher?"

"Your sister's friend Shelby is really nice. She took my application to him in the management office, and he came out to interview me in one of those big leather booths. He did most of the talking, which was fine. He said that the last hostess quit without notice and bragged about how much land he owns out here and how he'd worked hard for it his whole life." Hughie recalled hearing that the land had been inherited, but he kept that to himself. He liked the sound of Marie's voice, even if it was being interrupted by a nearby ballistic Pomeranian, which riled up Bilbo and Frodo even more. Marie added, "What's *with* these dogs today?"

Hughie couldn't explain it. The dachshunds had briefly calmed down in front of the Grub Pub, though, of course, Marie's chicken strips had served as a banner distraction.

"When Mr. Boucher finally asked me a question, he called me María, said he'd heard San Miguel was 'a safe place to visit in Mexico,' and wanted to know whether I'm an American citizen. Plus, there was this *tone*, you know?"

He knew. Hughie had been mistaken for Mexican American more than once himself—sometimes as a compliment, sometimes not—but it was never neutral. Plus, her name was Marie, not María, and she spoke with a vaguely rez and vaguely Minnesota accent.

Hughie opened the back door of the station wagon. "Hopefully, you won't have to deal with him much."

Marie hooked the dogs' harnesses to the seat belt extensions. "Hopefully, you'll visit me at work."

Even as a romance novice, Hughie recognized the invitation in her voice. This was his moment. He was going to ask Marie out. He searched his mind for something, anything charming to say. He considered and rejected mentioning that the pub was a regular hangout for his sister and a Sunday brunch destination for their family. He considered saying something about how much he liked the wings.

"Obviously, I owe you some chicken tenders." That wasn't bad. "I could buy you some chicken tenders." It wasn't about money. "Not now because I'm spending the day with Sam." Hughie gulped a breath. "Sam likes chicken, too. He'll eat practically anything." Spiraling. "Forget Sam. He's not important." Marie's eyes widened at that, and Hughie could feel himself flailing. "Uh, would you like to . . . could I . . . not at the place where you're working because that wouldn't be special or . . ."

Marie turned in the passenger car doorway to face him. "I know you like me, Hughie. I like you, too. If you want to join me for chicken tenders at the pub, or—even better—for pot stickers at Clifford's Chinese Kitchen—and not just because your adorable dogs ate my lunch—I'd be legit jazzed about that. I can even drive, so you don't have to ask Sam to chauffeur."

Marie was a hair older than him. Old enough to have an unrestricted license.

Hughie felt an enormous surge of joy and relief that she reciprocated his interest, and then it dawned on him to ask. "How did you know . . . ?" Of course, there was only one explanation . . . or two, to be precise. Hughie had thought he'd successfully hidden his crush from them, but apparently not. "Did my cousin or my sister talk to you?"

"Since the football game, both Rain and Lou have texted me, and both just happened to ask what I thought about you. Your cousin is subtle, but your sister is not."

That tracked. "Which one should we give the credit for helping us connect?"

"I'd say any credit goes to these good boys," Marie said, petting the dachshunds. "I hope to be seeing a lot more of them in the future." As if it was nothing, she added, "How's tonight?"

Hughie blinked. "Wait. What?"

Marie laughed. "I'm a new hire at a restaurant. It'll be a while before I get a Friday or Saturday night off." She sounded confident, but a hitch in her voice betrayed her nervousness. "Are you in or what?"

This was all moving fast for Hughie, but on the upside, it didn't give him much time to overthink the whole thing or get nervous. "Absolutely!"

CELESTE

The way the boy, Hughie Wolfe, carries himself catches my attention—the hint of clumsiness that hides untapped strength. He's still growing into his bones, into his potential. The echo of my mind asks, *Brother?* The memory of my heart beats, *Kin.*

That girl beside him, Marie—her hair falls beyond her shoulders like a powerful cape. Like so many of the girls before. Her lips point with intention, and her brown eyes shine. The echo of my mind wonders, *Cousin?* The memory of my heart thumps, *Community.*

He's awkward but gaining grace. She's shy but raising her voice. What they just did, admitting their affections, is among the most courageous things any of us can do. I only hope they find love and survive the experience. I only hope it turns out better for them.

35 DAYS UNTIL HALLOWEEN, DATE NIGHT

Hughie and Marie exchanged small smiles and tentative waves in the Wolfe family's foyer, their greeting hampered by the benevolent presence of Hughie's parents and their exhausting list of things to watch out for (bad drivers, drunk drivers, drivers on phones, potholes, road construction, weather, loud music). Standing on the porch with their arms around each other, they waved goodbye.

"Have fun!" Mom called.

Dad held up his cell phone. "Be safe!"

"Dad!" Hughie exclaimed. "You don't have to video us."

His father was undaunted. "Someday you'll be grateful that I did!"

When Hughie finally shut the front passenger door of Marie's family truck, he said, "I'm sorry my parents are enjoying this so much."

"Mine are just as bad," Marie replied, turning on the ignition. "Don't be surprised if we 'happen' to run into them tonight."

By the time they arrived, Hughie's nerves had calmed to the point that he noticed the effort Marie had put into her appearance. She had dressed up fancy in a long skirt and ruffly blouse, accessorized with a beaded Kermit the Frog purse. "You look pretty," Hughie ventured as he held open the door of Clifford's Chinese Kitchen in downtown old town. Had that been the right thing to say, to do? He was supposed to be respectful of Marie—his parents had reminded him of that a half dozen times.

"Miigwetch," Marie said, tucking a strand of her long dark hair behind one ear. "I've been looking forward to some just-us time."

Clifford's Chinese Kitchen was a family-owned institution, conveniently located in front of an old-school arcade in a red brick commercial alley. Hughie and Marie planned to drop in at the arcade after dinner.

The highlight of the restaurant decor was the ornamental fish tanks. Vases and tea sets were displayed on asymmetrical shelves above red leather booths and gleaming black tables. The dining room had also been festively decked out in paper and plastic Halloween decorations.

Hughie's phone pinged—Sam. Hughie adjusted the setting to vibrate. "Cool table!" he exclaimed, settling into the low swivel chair across from hers. He couldn't help noticing the game controls on the tabletop. "It *is* a table, right?"

Marie laughed. "Technically, it's a table-style arcade maze game. You ever played?"

"No, but I've heard of it. *Pac-Man*?"

"Ms. *Pac-Man*. The player"—Marie indicated a yellow dot with a huge mouth, one eye, and a hair bow—"tries to eat as many pellets as possible without getting eaten by one of the ghosts. Eating fruit racks up more points, and eating a big power pellet flips the game."

A waiter dropped off a teapot and two small cups.

"Flips it how?" Hughie asked.

"Between the player and the ghosts. The player becomes the predator—"

"And the ghosts become the prey. Got it."

As Marie poured herself a cup of hot tea, Hughie drummed his fingertips on the clear tabletop screen. "But ghosts are . . ." He searched his vocabulary. "Disembodied, ethereal—"

"Incorporeal." Marie set the pot in front of him.

"Good one," Hughie acknowledged. "Why would anyone want to *eat* a ghost? What's the point of . . . consuming the . . . incorporeal?"

She ventured a guess. "It's better than the incorporeal consuming you."

Not surprisingly, Marie was better at playing *Ms. Pac-Man*. "It's practice."

"Being a girl," Hughie joked, "maybe she's on your side."

As he jostled the joystick controller, she said, "*Ms. Pac-Man* is harder to play than *Pac-Man*. More random. Less predictable."

"You've logged a lot of time on this machine."

"Sometimes it's lonely here in old town. I've got my family and Aunt Georgia and Rain and Queen. But it's not the same as being with people who've known me since before I was born. Who've known my parents since before they were born."

Hughie understood how Marie felt. He'd noticed how relaxed she was at Leech Lake. She'd grown up there and in Minneapolis, which was home to an urban Ojibwe community. In contrast, Hughie had been raised in suburban communities with only a handful of Native people in the immediate vicinity, with no Muscogee people who weren't also family. And he'd noticed that the Hughie he was in East Hannesburg, Kansas—and that he'd been in Cedar Park, Texas—was different from the Hughie he was on visits to Muscogee Nation.

Still, on that early autumn evening, playing *Ms. Pac-Man* with Marie at the Chinese restaurant, Hughie felt completely comfortable, wholly himself. "The *Ms. Pac-Man* ghosts are weirdly morbid. Especially considering how colorful and friendly looking they are."

"Death always wins in the end," Marie intoned, in an exaggerated voice, gesturing at the skull-shaped holiday lights strung across the ceiling of the bar area. In a more sincere tone, she asked, "Do you believe in ghosts?"

"Honestly? I'm not sure." Hughie did believe in an afterlife. But he wasn't so sure about supernatural spirits, electronic or otherwise. "Why do you think these ghosts are so obsessed with Ms. Pac-Man? Why don't they go to ghost heaven?"

"As opposed to non-ghost heaven?" Marie picked up a pot sticker with her chopsticks. "Hm. What if they're not trying to kill Ms. Pac-Man? What if they just want the killing to end?"

"Deep." Hughie used his fork to spear a pot sticker and chewed thoughtfully.

Then came the generous platter of moo goo gai pan and a bowl of egg fried rice, which they split. Over dinner, Hughie and Marie talked about chopsticks, superheroes, stargazing, and her collection of PEZ. She asked him how his sister was doing at KU. He asked her about Dmitri and the rest of her family, including her grandmother back home.

"Nookomis isn't what you'd call high-tech," she replied. "But we mail each other postcards every week. I'm always on the lookout for funny ones."

Hughie remembered the postcards that had been posted all over Marie's grandmother's refrigerator the previous summer. "She misses you."

The conversation flowed. Hughie made Marie smile. Marie made Hughie laugh. It was shockingly not hard, maybe because they were already friends.

After they left a cash tip for the waiter—each offered to pay before they ultimately decided to split it—Hughie's phone vibrated again. "It's Sam. He's been trying to get ahold of me."

"What does he say?"

Hughie figured that if your date *asked* you what was on your phone, you were allowed to look. Skimming, he said, "He just heard from Ximena. He sent me a link."

"What is it?" Marie pressed. "What's wrong?"

"I'm not sure exactly." Hughie extended his hand. She threaded her fingers with his. The touch of her soft skin against his felt strangely familiar, yet it still sent a tingle down his spine.

He gave a polite nod to accompany Marie's goodbye wave to the host as a small bell above the glass front door rang at their exit.

Outside, Hughie walked with Marie down the dolled-up redbrick alley, strung with bare orange and black light bulbs, past the stationery shop with Halloween invites displayed in the window, the comics-and-games store, the antique jewelry shop, and the bakery displaying ghost cupcakes, werewolf brownies, and vampire cookies. Steps ahead, a thirty-something couple was indulging in pumpkin cake pops on a black wrought iron bench, and the *clang-bong-swoosh* sounds of the arcade echoed from a propped-open doorway.

Hughie handed Marie his phone so she could read Sam's messages, but he summed them up anyway, trying to make sense of what was happening. "Ximena's boyfriend showed up at her last shift at the pub. They got in an argument out front—Sam says they bicker all the time, and anyway, the boyfriend took off. Ximena started crying, but she pulled herself together, and then something scary happened . . . there's a video. Ximena recorded it late Wednesday night, but at first, she wasn't sure about going public, so she didn't post it until this afternoon." His eyes widened as he looked over Marie's shoulder. "It's trending locally."

"Trending in a good way?" Marie asked. Hughie shrugged, tapped the link, and they watched it, leaning against the alley wall, his upper arm pressed against hers.

Ximena looked exhausted but determined. "This video . . . uh, this video is for everyone out there who thinks the crossroads is a safe place to shop or get something to eat or go for drinks or play pool or watch a game or whatever."

Ximena had obviously recorded the video on her phone—the camera jerked slightly. "I used to work at the Grub Pub. Like, up until tonight—no way am I going back now. There's something . . . bad out there. This weirdo was following me behind the old chicken restaurant—the one they're using for that haunted house—to my car. I didn't get a good look at him. It was dark. But he was calling to me, trying to say . . . I'm not sure what. It sounded like *bless* or *less*. I know what you're thinking: that he was just an ordinary creeper. But that's not all."

Muted voices were audible in the background.

"This, this *devil dog* comes out of nowhere—barking, snarling. A wolf! I swear it was possessed. Like, supernaturally, by some evil spirit. I thought it was going to rip my throat out, but I got lucky. It lunged at the creeper instead, and so I ran. I'm a runner—cross-country team clear through high school. I ran all the way to old town, to my abuela's trailer.

"My boyfriend had to go get my car the next day, and he said that there were paw prints alongside the parking lot. Stay away—it's not safe! Stay the hell away from the crossroads!"

The video ended, and Marie gave Hughie his phone back. "Well," she said. "That's . . . a lot. I'm pretty sure, though, that there are no wolves in Kansas."

"It could've been a coyote," he theorized. "Aren't coyotes everywhere?"

"Also, you're touching me a lot," Marie added.

Hughie realized that as Ximena had been speaking, he'd all but rested his chin on Marie's shoulder. He stepped away, but she grabbed his forearm. "No, it's fine. Are you scared by the video or worried about the fact that today I apparently landed the job that Ximena quit because of . . . whatever happened to her?"

"That last thing, I suppose." Hughie tried not to sound alarmist or overprotective—he'd observed Louise bristling when her boyfriend acted old-school "manly"—but *something* had frightened Ximena, and Marie *did* work at the crossroads. Not only that, but Ximena was also a Mexican American of Indigenous ancestry, and Marie was Ojibwe. They were both brown girls. He hated to think that might be a factor, but he couldn't ignore the possibility, either.

Before Marie had arrived at his house to pick him up, Hughie's mom had been drafting speaker invitations for the KU Native American Law Students Association's symposium on the crisis of missing and murdered Indian women, girls, and two-spirit people—#MMIWG2S. Missing Indigenous relatives. He'd seen a mock-up of the poster for the conference—*No More Stolen Sisters*, it had read. Of course, Hughie's mind had gone straight to that. If there was someone targeting young brown women at the crossroads, that was something to take seriously.

Marie didn't look alarmed, though. As they started walking again, she said, "You should text Sam. Tell him that we hope Ximena is feeling better. Oh, and tell him to warn her not to read the comments."

Hughie raised an eyebrow. "Nobody told me Ojibwe women were this bossy."

"They should have told you Ojibwe women were strong leaders." Her lips pursed, the ends curling tight as she tucked in a grin. "Get used to it. But if it makes you feel better, I'll be extra careful leaving work at night."

"You're not worried?" he asked, keying the message into his phone.

"Yeah, no, not really. I'm not sure there's anything to be worried about." Marie led the way through the noisy arcade's front door and made a beeline for the air hockey table. "Or anything more than usual. I'm always on guard alone at night." She slid a striker across the surface toward him on the opposite side.

As Hughie slipped his phone into his pocket, Marie batted the puck with her own striker. "I have two theories," she said, raising her voice over the din of nearby machines.

"That's two more than I have," Hughie replied.

"One." Marie tapped the puck across the laminate, Hughie hit it back, and then she slammed it into one side of the table, so it ricocheted into the slot in front of him— point. Marie continued, "I know bad things happen all the time. But in this case . . . It's possible Ximena's boyfriend circled back after their fight to mess with her mind, like a trick—a mean trick."

"A mean trick coordinated with a possessed coyote?"

"That part could have been a coincidence. It could've been a coyote or coydog who happened to be foraging at the pub for scraps and wandered across the street to dig through the garbage can at the haunted house work site. What with the recent activity, especially the dog groomer, it could've been attracted by the new smells and decided to investigate. If Ximena perceived the stalker as a threat, it's not much of a stretch to guess that a coyote did, too."

"I can see that." Hughie served up the puck, and they batted it back and forth for a while over the playing surface. He caught on to the game fast and, with growing confidence, asked, "What's your second theory?"

"Ximena's video is a publicity stunt," Marie said matter-of-factly. "I'm sorry to say it, but . . . You saw all the shares, all the clicks. Like you said, it's trending locally. Did you notice so is Harvest House?"

Could the video have been an aspect of the Harvest House attraction, another layer added to the make-believe? It was the most obvious explanation. Hughie was embarrassed that he hadn't thought of that himself . . . but wouldn't Sam have known about the ruse? Would Ximena have wanted to worry her own family like that? Was Ximena that good of an actor?

Marie took advantage of his distraction to score another point.

Hughie protested, "Hey, I was thinking!"

"Hey, yourself!" Marie countered. "I'm not taking it easy on you anymore. This is technically a form of hockey, the unofficial state religion of Minnesota."

The rest of the date was likewise a success. Afterward, Marie dropped Hughie off at home. He finally complimented her sneakers, and they both said that they'd like to see each other again. Shortly after he got in, Hughie answered a video call from his sister. It was only fifteen minutes past the Wolfe family's traditional eleven o'clock curfew.

Leaning against the headboard of his bed with a dachshund curled up on either side, he said, "You couldn't wait until tomorrow?"

"Of course not," Louise replied from her dorm room. "I need to hear all about your date. Oh, but before we get to the juicy bit—did you hear? This girl Ximena Rodríguez posted a video—"

"You saw it?" he said. "Ximena is my friend Sam's sister."

"It's the talk of the dorm." Louise had a pen tucked behind her ear. "A couple of people on my floor swear they've heard stories like hers before. A lone girl at the crossroads at night, a threatening dude is following her, something bizarre happens."

"That's how urban legends work," Hughie said. "People claim they know somebody who knows somebody who—"

"Exactly. And the descriptions of the guy are super generic. He's young and white, but the body type and facial hair, they vary. And it's not only girls and women who've reported freaky experiences. One of the guys who commented on her video said that he'd mysteriously blacked out coming out of the Grub Pub—"

"It is a *pub*," Hughie pointed out. "He was probably drunk."

But Louise was on a roll. "There's a photo of this 1992 article from the *University Daily Kansan* circulating about a ghost at the crossroads. Apparently, people have been talking about an 'Indian maiden' haunting the crossroads for decades. Someone from Watkins Museum, a neuroscience prof, and a custodial supervisor were all interviewed. The historian says there's no known history of a woman dying there, but that doesn't mean it never happened. The neuroscientist chalks up ghosts to delusions or hallucinations. The custodian's quote is vague, but it leaves open interesting possibilities. Somebody should've written a follow-up. I did a web search, pulled up an obit, and turns out, the custodian was an enrolled Kickapoo member and worked for her tribal government after she worked for KU."

"Are you working on a story about the crossroads?" Hughie asked, skimming the article his sister had just texted him. Jenny Thomas, the custodian, had said, "People talking about the Crossroads Ghost, they should show her more respect." That could've meant a lot of things, Hughie thought, including that death wasn't something to make light of.

"I thought about it," Louise replied. "Obviously, I've done a little poking around. But there's not enough *there* there. If I was still at the *Hive* and not stressing over my first-semester college midterms . . . What's the name of that friend of yours, the new reporter?"

"Cricket? You're her idol. I can send you her contact info if you want."

"I want. Now, on to more pressing things—namely you and Marie." Louise, who was wearing sunflower-print pj's, moved to plop down onto her twin bed. "How did it go? No mushy details. I do not need that from my little brother. I'm thinking more of a power-ballad montage."

Hughie obliged, painting in broad strokes—the drives, the dinner, the way he bested Marie only once at air hockey though "victory was sweet."

Louise chuckled. "Speaking of sweet, was there any kissy-face action?"

"Kissy-face action? Is that the technical term for it? Is this an essay question?"

"I'm looking for a yes-or-no answer, and please do not mention tongues."

"No tongues to mention." Bilbo had awakened at the sound of Louise's voice. Hughie wasn't the only one missing her. "Marie walked me to our front door, but the porch light was on, and it was obvious that Mom and Dad could see us through the picture window, and who knows if Marie was even thinking about kissing—"

"You two will figure it out next time, assuming that's what you both want. Will there be a next time?"

"Lopice tos, heruse tos, heren vcafaste tomes."

"My Mvskoke is rusty," Louise replied. Because of the abusive US federal Indian boarding schools, it had been a few generations since the Wolfe family had a fluent speaker, but the siblings had been making an effort to learn. "She is kind. She is beautiful. She . . . ?"

"She treats me well."

34 DAYS UNTIL HALLOWEEN

On Sunday morning, the two-story building had already been refaced with a cutout creating the faux front of a historic farmhouse, with holes sawed for the windows.

Apparently, crew members had been hard at work since sunrise.

Hughie's parents dropped him off on their way home from church, and behind the building, Sam said "hello" by handing him a powered paint sprayer. Liking the feel of it in his hand, Hughie swept his gaze around the sea of wooden planks spread out on butcher paper on the ground. Nearby, fellow volunteers were busy sweeping, dusting, and scrubbing the windows—a condition of Mr. Boucher allowing them to use the property. "Let me guess: We're thinking gray?"

Sam laughed. "Darker than an elephant, lighter than the deepest, darkest black of night."

"Because why?" Hughie wanted to know. He'd imagined that the main challenge of staging the haunt would be finding old furniture and fixtures, working on special effects. "What exactly are we supposed to do with all this wood once it's painted?"

"You two are assigned to interiors," Ms. Fischer explained as she came down the stairs from the kitchen. "We're going to use all this to cover up the inside walls and create the maze. It'll give us a neutral background for staging each of the ghost stories. It's going to be quite the show, boys!" A couple of college guys on the other side of the workspace were attaching some of the already-painted boards to one another with hinges, securing weighted feet with noisy electric drills. Ms. Fischer added, "No holes in the walls. We leave the place better than we found it . . . though we may have to sand and restain the back stairs."

"I'm surprised the building hasn't already been torn down," Hughie said.

"What with the housing boom, Boucher has been talking about renting out the space for special events," Ms. Fischer said. "Weddings, anniversaries, reunions, that sort of thing."

"Is this everybody?" Sam asked, looking around at the on-site volunteers.

"Mostly, but I've got a couple of artistic types out searching for costumes at charity shops, a handful of people are just volunteering in costume on Halloween weekend, and . . . hey, come to think of it, how about you two playing Indians?"

"Come again?" Hughie asked. Had she really said what he'd thought she'd said?

"Indian ghosts, that is," Ms. Fischer added. "We're still working up ideas for the inside, but our grand finale is going to be a haunted Indian burial ground. *Lots* of ghosts, from back when Kansas was the Wild West. I'll be monitoring the bottom of the slide for any overly anxious souls to whisk out of the side gate and leave the savage specters to jump scare the rest." Undaunted by the boys' blank faces, she asked, "Haven't you heard the legend of the Crossroads Ghost? Boucher loves it. He's promoting it on his October menu! We've already found the perfect girl to play the part in the attic set. She'll be the star of the show."

Hughie didn't know what to say. He felt shocked and insulted on behalf of the Native people—the human beings, not "wild" or "savage" animals—who were Indigenous to what was currently called Kansas. But Ms. Fischer's plan to shine a spotlight on the Crossroads Ghost story was even worse. The deaths of Indigenous girls and women weren't anything to turn into a fun house. Hughie knew from his mom's #MMIWG2S advocacy that making light of those deaths both made more violence likely and made it easier for non-Indians to minimize those crimes.

With a brief grimace, Sam started painting, and the smell of it was thick in the air.

"Your hair isn't long enough for real Indians," Ms. Fischer went on, raising her voice. "But we should be able to find cheap black wigs. And you two have beautiful complexions! We don't want to paint people's skin; that would be disrespectful. Maybe we'll use ghostly white makeup instead. That might make more sense."

What had Hughie gotten himself into?

"Think about it!" Ms. Fischer said, then answered her phone as she went back inside.

Once she'd cleared hearing range, Sam stopped painting and slung an arm around Hughie's shoulders. "I know what you're thinking . . . and I know you're uptight about—"

"I am *not* uptight—"

"If a bunch of white boys dressed up in sombreros and charro suits were pretending to be ghosts, well, I'd think they looked like jackasses. But hear me out, Wolfe Man. It's just make-believe. It's not like any of the ghosts she's talking about were real people, Indian or otherwise."

Hughie didn't feel like debating the subject. Native people had lived in what was currently called Kansas for thousands of years. Hughie wasn't exactly sure which Nation had made its ancestral home at the crossroads— the Kickapoo, the Kanza, maybe the Osage or Očhéthi Šakówiŋ. It was possible some of those people, those real human beings, had died or been buried, that their remains might lay within the land. Not to mention the Crossroads Ghost, who might have been completely made up but also might have been based on a real woman. Hughie finally settled for the word that Ms. Fischer had used. "Don't you think it's . . . disrespectful?"

"She's a nice lady. She's friends with my mom. There's no way she means it like that."

And Hughie had given Ms. Fischer his word. They'd shook on it.

Promises meant something to Hughie. He still wasn't happy, but they were just getting started. Halloween was still more than a month away. Plans were fluid. During the previous year's theater controversy, Hughie had come to appreciate the power in taking his time, carefully considering his options, making a decision, choosing his moment and his strategy for change.

There was still time to persuade Ms. Fischer to reconsider her plan.

33 DAYS UNTIL HALLOWEEN

"Explain to me again what we're doing here," Hughie said, setting his backpack on the scuffed floorboard of the bus after school the next day. "You have a car."

Sam's slim chest puffed out. "I do. I really do."

Hughie nudged, "So why are we taking the bus?" Like all school buses, it smelled of sweat, old socks, and despair. Four rows up, a couple was smooching, the girl across the aisle was popping bubblegum, and most everybody else was jamming on their earbuds.

"Why are . . . we what?" Sam asked. Hughie followed his friend's gaze and identified the source of his smile: Cricket, the *Hive* reporter, was coming toward them down the aisle. Hughie asked, "Anybody ever tell you you're a sucker for a pretty girl?"

"For the record, I prefer the feisty over the pretty, and I'm a sucker for all genders." Sam tilted his head. "I mean, I'm discerning. I have standards. I'm attracted to energy, intensity. Competitive disc golfers, speed walkers, people who chew their hangnails. But I take an equal-opportunity approach to matters of the heart."

"Good to know," Hughie said. "My bad for making assumptions." It felt important to be reassuring, especially given that rainbow flags weren't flying all over town.

"I've been hoping to talk to you two all day," Cricket gushed, plopping onto the seat in front of them. "Hughie, thanks for the intro to your big sister." Cricket let her backpack fall to the side and dug her phone out of her purse. "By the time I'm a senior, I'm going to *be* her. And, Sam, that girl all over social media with the spooky story—she's your sister?"

"I am proud to say so," he answered, leaning forward to rest his forearms on the back of Cricket's seat. "Ximena had a bad scare and decided it was her duty to warn the masses."

"Are you interviewing him for the *Hive* or is this just a conversation?" Hughie wanted to know. Between his experience with last year's fall musical and his own journalist sister, Hughie knew the difference between being on and off the record, and Sam tended to ramble on.

"Interviewing, if that's okay with you, Sam?" Cricket replied, activating the video function on her camera app. "It's a fluffy human-interest story for Halloween."

"Not a problem," Sam replied, clearly delighted by the attention.

Cricket introduced herself into the camera as a *Hive* reporter, and they repeated their initial exchange, confirming that Ximena was Sam's older sister and the year she'd graduated from EHHS. "Sam, how does it feel to have a sibling go viral?" Cricket asked. "As of today's after-school bell, her video has received more than a thousand shares and more than fifteen thousand likes. Do you think she really saw a ghost?"

"It's a lot of attention, more than she expected," Sam replied. "But I talked to Ximena, and she's doing better now. I was worried when I first saw the video. I mean, she's my sister, and the whole experience obviously freaked her out. But for the record, Ximena never said she saw a ghost."

"But she did say the 'devil dog' was possessed. Can you confirm that Ximena's video wasn't a publicity stunt for the haunted house?"

Marie hadn't been the only one quick to explain away the video, Hughie realized. Obviously, publicity stunt was the preferred theory of local skeptics.

"Ximena was working at the Grub Pub," Sam said, "not at Harvest House, and she quit her job right after what happened. She wouldn't even go back to the cross-roads for her own car. Ximena made her boyfriend do it. *I'm* the only person in my family volunteering at Harvest House, and I haven't heard anything about a publicity stunt." Neither had Hughie, and if Sam believed that Ximena had been sincere, then Hughie did, too.

Cricket's expression lit up. "But if *you're* volunteering

for the haunted house, and Ximena is *your* sister, that connects *her* to Harvest House, doesn't it?"

Hughie blinked. Though the school newspaper had won state awards, he'd never considered it a bastion of hard-hitting journalism. "Anything you say could go viral, too," he warned Sam.

"Uh . . . Not really," Sam replied. "I mean, kind of . . ."

Cricket maintained her polished demeanor. "Setting aside the supernatural for a moment and assuming the incident occurred as Ximena described, Sam, does your sister have any idea who the man that she refers to as 'the creeper' could've been?" Animated, she continued, "According to the 'Legend of the Crossroads Ghost,' the vengeful spirit of a Native American woman is targeting young, dark-haired women. Ximena fits that general description. Could the ghost have contributed to what happened?"

Cricket could at least pick one question at a time, Hughie thought.

"Look," Sam said, "I don't know what the whole story is, but my sister is no liar. Something happened that night. Somebody should try to find out what."

Cricket shifted the phone. "And how about you, Hughie? What do you think of all this?"

"I'm with Sam," he declared. "We don't know what happened, but Ximena put herself out there to warn people. That took guts. Somebody should investigate. It's important that whatever happened to her doesn't happen to anyone else."

28 DAYS UNTIL HALLOWEEN

After almost a week to ponder the situation, Hughie still had mixed feelings about volunteering for Harvest House. The part of him that had fallen in love with theater felt drawn in by the idea of a community-created production, but he wished he had asked a *lot* more questions before committing to participate. Then again, the haunt was still very much a work in progress. *No big deal,* he told himself. But it wasn't something he'd talked to his family about—not even his sister or cousin Rain, at least not yet, and he hadn't mentioned it to Marie, either.

That breezy Saturday morning, Hughie and Sam approached the dozen or so people eating doughnuts and drinking coffee behind the building. Most of them were a few years older, drawn from surrounding local colleges. A few looked to be contemporaries of Ms. Fischer, men for whom a tool belt was a day-to-day accessory. Hughie and Sam made their way to the open boxes of doughnuts and discovered Jonas and Elias setting up a service station—thermoses and paper cups—for pub coffee and cocoa.

"Here you go, Sam," Elias said, holding out a steaming cup toward him.

But when Sam reached to accept it, Elias let the cup fall from his fingertips, causing it to hit the ground and splash the front of Sam's jeans. "Oops," Elias said, sarcastically. "My bad."

"Real mature," Hughie muttered with a side-eye at Jonas's petty grin.

Sam shrugged it off, in too good of a mood to let the Vogels get to him. "Yo, Oakley, Kelsey!" Waving, he and Hughie approached a duo putting out the last of a mismatched array of lawn chairs. "This is my friend Hughie Wolfe." To Hughie himself, Sam added, "Kelsey is the one with the hair." Both Oakley and Kelsey sported asymmetrical haircuts, but Hughie took "the hair" to be a reference to the fact that one 'do was dyed purple. With their visible tats and tie-dyed tees, the duo looked more Lawrence than the burbs or old town.

As they approached, Kelsey said, "Hey, Hughie, good to meet you. I'm in charge of the visual and audio effects."

"I'm in charge of costumes and sets," Oakley added.

"Everyone, take a seat!" Ms. Fischer called. "I have a few announcements."

Standing on the back step to the building, Ms. Fischer said, "Thanks again to each and all of you for volunteering for this project. You're probably going to get tired of hearing me say that, but too bad. Nothing's going to shut me up!"

"Thanks for the sugar high!" called out a volunteer in a Baker University tee.

Everyone laughed. "You're welcome," Ms. Fischer said. "You'll need the energy. With the initial goal of generating ticket sales, it made sense for us to focus first on getting the sign made and installed out front so—"

"Fear the reaper!" hollered a volunteer in all-black clothing and black makeup.

"Fear the reaper!" echoed about half the crowd.

Ms. Fischer grinned. "That's the spirit, so to speak! Our main goal for this weekend is to paint the front facade to make it look like a dilapidated farmhouse. From there, we'll zero in on the ghostly journey through the maze and the slides down and out to the burial ground."

It occurred to Hughie that few of those gathered appeared to be likely candidates for the ghostly Hollywood-style Indians Ms. Fischer had envisioned. Then he remembered that some volunteers would be working Halloween weekend only—maybe that would be a more diverse crowd.

As Ms. Fischer continued speaking, a debate rose up on the merits of using dry ice versus a fog machine. Hughie could well imagine that the dark of night, strategic lighting, and the power of suggestion would go a long way toward creating a compelling atmosphere, one well worth the ticket price to families and partiers seeking a Halloween activity.

"We have hit one PR wrinkle," Ms. Fischer announced. "There was a letter to the editor in the *Examiner*, and it

appears that uptight busybodies are cranky with us for . . .
I don't know . . . conjuring the devil or whatever. Our
official policy is to ignore the haters, but if a reporter or
anyone official asks you about it, refer them to me." She
adjusted her scarf. "And if you happen to spot anyone
lurking around or experience anything out of the ordinary,
raise a flag on that right away. We're here to honor the
spirits of the past, not stir them up." Ms. Fischer cupped
her hands around her mouth like a megaphone and raised
her voice. "You hear that, spirits? We're here to honor
you!" Amid the nervous laughter of his fellow volunteers,
Hughie wondered who she was trying to convince.

23 DAYS UNTIL HALLOWEEN

When it came to Halloween decorating, Hughie's father didn't go big, he went *huge*. Concept sketches were made in advance. Decisions included what to recycle or reimagine from previous years and what no longer made the cut. The early planning stages were as hidden from the Wolfe teens as those for Santa's visits had been when they were tots. Hughie had come to appreciate that his dad would take it to the max on every birthday, every holiday, making up for all those important family moments he'd missed while in the army.

Once spooky-season decorating began in earnest, the black cat was out of the bag, so to speak, and this year, without theater to occupy Hughie's spare time, he was eager to lend a hand. Waiting in the foyer of the house for his dad to reveal the decor plan, Hughie knocked on the inside of the front door and called, "How much longer?"

"One minute!" was the muffled reply from the front porch.

A spine-chilling, classic vinyl recording of groans,

cackling, creaking, banging shutters, rattling chains, howls, wind, thunder, screaming, and a ghastly sounding cat began playing from outside speakers.

The front door swung open, and Dad announced, "I've assembled the troops."

"Whoa." Hughie blinked at the enormous stacks of decorations. "How many skeletons did you order?" They were life-size, all of them.

"Many," his father said. "A whole clutter of skeletons."

"Fifteen, twenty?" Hughie asked, accepting a pair of box cutters. *"Thirty?"*

"Or thereabouts," his dad replied as they moved to the top of the driveway to free more bony figures from their packaging. "Your mother guilted me about buying all this plastic, so I had to promise to integrate them into all future displays."

Hughie examined the merchandise. The skeletons were sixty-inch-tall "decorative mannequins," with bendable joints and glowing red LED eyes. Lightweight. A long wire had been attached to each for easy hanging. Dad added, "You'll find a bunch of double-A batteries in a brown bag on my workbench in the garage. There's a switch on the back of each skull."

"How much did you pay for these anyway?"

"Hush, your mother's coming out any moment." With a glance toward the open garage, he lowered his voice. "If she asks, I picked them up last year on clearance."

Hughie was amused. "*Did* you pick them up last year on clearance?"

"My wife is a law student." His dad slung a newly liberated skeleton over one shoulder. "I plead the Fifth. It's our first year without both of you kids living here full-time. I got emotional."

"Retail therapy," Hughie said. "Let me guess: You're planning to lure Lou home with the Halloween display?"

Dad slung another skeleton over his other shoulder. "Let's just say . . ."

There was a tapping from the door that led from the garage into the kitchen. Hughie hurried to open it for his mom, who was carrying three mugs of hot apple cider. "Good news! Lou will be home tonight for dinner. I'm making my king ranch casserole."

"Tonight?" her husband echoed. "*Tonight!* This is Operation Scarification—go, go, go, go!" He waved away the cider. "If I need to pee, it'll slow me down!"

Moments later, Hughie and his mother were working side by side in the Adirondack chairs on the front porch. As they sipped cider and loaded batteries into skulls, Dad used painter's tape to indicate skeleton positioning on the house, trees, and shrubbery. "Honey!" he called. "What do you think?"

"I have full faith in your vision!" Mom sealed her approval by blowing him a quick kiss, and Dad carried on, moving the extension ladder around to the side of the house.

To Hughie, Mom said, "That video Sam's sister made is all over the neighborhood message board. Are you boys staying safe out there at the crossroads?"

"Supersafe, I promise." Reassuring parents was always important, but Hughie wanted her opinion on the situation, too. "Some people seem to think the video was a publicity stunt for Harvest House. Or that Ximena was on drugs, but Sam says she doesn't even drink. Oh, and some people figure it was her boyfriend trying to mess with her. Others think her imagination got wound up and, between the wind and a stray dog, she freaked herself out."

"And a few believe the crossroads is really haunted, and an actual ghost possessed a wild canine," Mom said, squinting at the plastic covering over the batteries. "I'm not convinced these things—the battery compartments—will hold up in the rain. We've got over a fifty percent chance of showers this week."

The packaging promised that the skeletons were weatherproof. Hughie peeked into a nearby brown paper bag of hardware supplies. "Waterproof duct tape."

The job took focus. The covers came off easily, but snapping them back on was tricky.

"It was your father's zest for life that first attracted me to him, so I'm in no position to complain about his big personality. We may very well put red caps and scarves on these fake bones and keep them up through New Year's Day."

"Like *The Nightmare Before Christmas*?" The old movie was a family favorite.

"Exactly, and speaking of which, 'tis the season for family movie night. Do you want to ask a certain Ms. Headbird to join us for a viewing party?"

Hughie had noticed that his sister had gotten a lot of mileage out of occasionally bringing her boyfriend to church and family dinners. Both his mom and dad liked and trusted Joey, which meant they were more flexible about Louise's curfew and even let her stay out all night for senior prom. "I'll ask Marie to join us," he said. "In a few weeks."

"Too soon?"

"*Way* too soon."

"Noted." Mom positioned another battery-loaded skeleton on the lawn, just beyond the miniature shire of hobbit homes along the front walk. "Your father sure does love a project."

For a moment, she watched Landon Fuller, whose family lived across the cul-de-sac, riding his bike in lazy figure eights. "It wasn't long ago that you were that age." Mom moved to open the next packaged skeleton. "What do *you* think happened—if anything—that night to Sam's sister at the crossroads?"

"I'm not sure," Hughie replied. He positioned the skeleton he'd just finished next to another. It was disturbing—eerie—to see them lying there on the grass, side by side. Mounted speakers were still playing the spooky soundtrack, and the dachshunds were howling inside the house. "How 'bout you?"

Mom got up and let the dogs out to run around in the fallen leaves. "Well, all we have is one eyewitness testimony, Ximena's, and eyewitness testimony isn't that reliable. No expert witnesses or electronic records, no photos or security video." Bilbo was barking frantically at the skeletons while Frodo seemed oblivious to them. "I've only had one crim law class, but . . ."

"You think Ximena should've gone to the cops?"

Mom frowned at the fake skeleton in her hands. "That's never my first call. But it does seem like more fact-finding would be necessary to determine what occurred."

Attracted by Bilbo's bark fest, Frodo rushed one of the prone skeletons, tore off its forearm, and pranced victoriously around the yard. Hughie didn't have the heart to take it away from him, at least not right away. "Me and Sam, we could talk to his sister in a more organized kind of way. We could look for clues." He remembered Cricket's questions from the bus. "Now that Ximena has had a chance to calm down, we could ask her for a better description of the guy and figure out possible suspects." Frodo's glee inspired Bilbo to give chase.

"Suspects?" Mom echoed. "Somebody's been watching one too many true-crime documentaries with his father. I don't want you getting mixed up in a scary mess with—"

"No scary mess," Hughie insisted. "Healthy curiosity. Besides, so long as I'm volunteering at Harvest House, it's probably best to find out if there's anything to be worried about." In response to Mom's raised eyebrows, Hughie added, "If someone's scaring girls and women, then who? If there's something dangerous or supernatural going on, then what?" Giving Mom a chance to think about it, he got up to intercept Frodo and, after a brief game of keep-away, grabbed the plastic forearm, its fingers dangling. By then, a dozen life-size skeletons covered the grass.

Dad came around from the side yard and surveyed the grisly scene, including the bony arm in his son's hand. He threw back his head, raised his arms, and shouted, "The dead shall rise!"

Mom chuckled. "All right, Hughie. Whoever scared Ximena, odds are they're long gone. You be careful, though—stick close to your friends, and keep me posted."

22 DAYS UNTIL HALLOWEEN

Getting into Sam's station wagon the next morning, Hughie asked, "You know how you told Cricket on the bus that somebody should investigate what happened to Ximena at the crossroads?"

"Hello to you, too." Sam yawned and turned down the radio. "Sure, what about it? It's not like the cops—"

"Not the cops," Hughie replied as his friend put the car in gear. "Us." Sam's eyes widened at that, and Hughie continued, "I mean, it's your sister who—"

"You don't have to sell me," Sam assured him, exiting the Wolfes' driveway. "I'm in. But how do we know it wasn't a one-off, a freak occurrence that'll never happen again?"

"How do we know it hasn't ever happened before?" Hughie countered. "What if the legend of the Crossroads Ghost isn't BS? What if there's something to it?"

Driving through the subdivision, Sam drummed his fingers on the wheel. "A real ghost?"

"Or at least a real threat? Maybe a real person inspired

the legend. Or was inspired by it." They drove past little kids trotting to the bus stop. Yard signs celebrating EHHS athletes. Trees turning gold and burnished orange. "How do we get started?"

"We're already started," Sam replied, grinning as he slowed at a stop sign.

"We are?" Hughie asked. "What's brewing in your devious brain?"

"Not devious. Obvious. Cricket has been working on a series of stories about the crossroads for the *Hive*. Cricket is good at asking questions, finding things out. Cricket—"

"*Cricket* just happens to be the person you're crushing on right now."

"Which in no way makes anything I said less true."

Now the only thing left to do was to loop in Cricket to their investigative effort. Hughie had trouble concentrating in class that day as he waited impatiently for the bell to ring so that they could get started. He met Sam after the final bell, and they staked out the after-school bus. When Cricket didn't appear, they tracked her down in the *Hive* newsroom.

It was empty except for Cricket, who was chewing a pen while typing. Looming behind her was a dry-erase board labeled NEWS, ARTS/ENTERTAINMENT, SPORTS, and FEATURES, with a list of stories and weekly web traffic totals next to each.

Cricket glanced up from her keyboard and spit out the pen. "Bus buddies! Are you lost?"

After much negotiation with Sam, it had been agreed that Hughie would do most of the talking so they could stay on track. "We're here to see you."

"Color me intrigued," Cricket said. "By the way, Sam, did you ever hear from Ximena about giving me a quote? My story about her viral video is already live, but I could still write a follow-up for my crossroads series."

Before Sam could reply, Hughie said, "Speaking of which, the two of us have decided to try to figure out what happened to Ximena that night—who the guy was, whether he's dangerous, if he's gone after anyone else—"

"Whether there's something legit paranormal going on," Sam added.

Hughie recalled that Louise had already talked to Cricket, so Cricket knew about the '92 article in the University of Kansas student newspaper and the local chatter about a bogeyman and other mysterious occurrences. "Sam and I are both volunteering at Harvest House, so we've got access. We've got connections, too—not only Ximena. Friends who work at the pub. But we're not sure what to do next. We could use your help."

Cricket glanced over her shoulder at the board, the tally of hits scrawled beside each story. "Graduate's Crossroads Video Trends Locally" was number one under NEWS. She pushed up her blue eyeglasses. "Tell me who you know at the pub."

17 DAYS UNTIL HALLOWEEN

On a dinner break from Harvest House, Hughie strolled into the pub, took off his jacket, and waved at Marie as she cleared a four-top on the other side of the dining room.

Taking note of a boozy dart game, he made a point to sit well out of range in Shelby's section. Through the rain-splattered windowpane, he could watch Harvest House volunteers unloading a front-end display of a bright red 1957 Chevy Bel Air.

Shelby greeted him with a glass of ice tea. "Wings or wings?"

"I'll have the wings," Hughie replied. "How's your shift?"

"Quiet. Boucher's gone fishing." She scribbled an order ticket. "Rumor has it that you've turned ghostbuster."

Hughie squeezed the lemon wedge garnish into his tea, shooting a stream into his right eye. "Ow!" He grabbed a napkin to cover it. "Ow, ow, ow. Is Marie looking this way?"

Shelby snatched up another napkin and dunked it in a glass of water. "Use this."

"Excuse me!" protested the forty-something bearded man who was reading the *Hannesburg Weekly Examiner*. "That's my napkin. And my water!"

"Hush up, Chuck!" Addressing Hughie, she added, "Splash it out in the restroom!"

"Shelby!" Chuck exclaimed. "I'm going to tell Mr. Boucher—"

"Go ahead," Shelby said. "You always order the ice water. You never drink the ice water. It's wasteful and makes more work for me, but if you must have another one, I'll get it."

Meanwhile, Hughie hurried to do as Shelby had suggested, leaving his backpack in the booth.

When Hughie returned, his eye was still bloodshot and teary, and Marie was seating an over-sixty ladies social club in the corner behind the foosball table. She'd apparently missed the entire incident. As Shelby delivered his chicken wings, she said, "You look terrible."

"Thanks for the help and for . . ." He glanced at Marie. "Covering for me."

"Oh, no, that was hilarious. I told Marie right off. She didn't laugh at you. She thought it was—and I quote—'cute' that you were stressed about what she'd think. I'm fond of you, Hughie, but I am not your confidant. I am a spy."

Swallowing spicy chicken, Hughie wasn't surprised. "For my mom or for my sister?"

119

"Both," Shelby replied. "In case there really is a creeper at the crossroads, my job is to keep you relatively safe and let them know if anything gets out of hand."

"The crossroads creeper, a very alliterative title," Marie said, coming over to wipe down what had been Chuck's table. "It's catching on. How is your eye?"

"Better," Hughie replied as Shelby made herself scarce.

"I figure you're doing this investigation or whatever it is partly for Sam," Marie said. "I understand that he wants to find out what happened to his sister. But you don't need to protect me, if that's still something you're worried about. The new pub rule is that nobody leaves by themselves after dark, and I don't think there's . . ." She did a double take at the window. "Isn't that Ximena? She looks like the girl in the video, but I thought she swore never to come back."

Hughie squinted, trying to confirm the identity of the young woman across the road. He recognized Sam jogging to meet her. From their body language, it looked like an animated discussion. Sliding out of the booth, he said, "Be back in a few."

"Sam, get in the car!" Ximena ordered. "It's not safe out here! This sham of a haunted house should be shut down for good."

Dark gray paint had dripped onto Sam's Honeybees T-shirt and forehead. "I'm being careful," he replied. "My good friend Hughie—look, here he is! Hughie is my backup. See how quickly he got here to protect me from you?"

Ximena wasn't convinced. "Oh please, I could take both of you."

"Hey!" Hughie protested. When she whirled on him, he added, "Fair enough."

Sam countered, "Ximena, think about all the blow-back you're getting online. Don't you want proof that you were right? Don't you want people to take your warning seriously?"

That stopped Ximena short. "I do. I would hate for—"

"Excuse me!" Ms. Fischer called, coming to join the conversation. "Excuse me, young lady! What is all this ruckus about?"

"That's Mom's friend from yoga," Sam told his sister in a low voice. "Nice lady, big talker, and she needs the money from this project. It's not like I can just up and quit on her."

Drawing closer, Ms. Fischer exclaimed, "I know you! You're the girl from the video!"

As one, Hughie and the Rodríguez siblings took a step back, but Ms. Fischer practically tackled Ximena in a hug. "Thank you, sweetie! I couldn't have asked for better pub-licity." She let go. "Tickets were overpriced—what can I say? I'm an optimist. But they're selling like hotcakes now."

"Please listen," Ximena began. "It's not safe here."

Hughie's phone pinged, alerting him to a text from Marie: *Shelby wants to know if U R coming back, or if she should box your wings for pickup later.*

Ms. Fischer crossed her arms over her chest. "Now, I'm sorry you got spooked—happens to us all—but you look fine to me." Strolling off, Ms. Fischer gestured for the boys to come along. "I hate to break up this family reunion, but our sets won't paint themselves."

Hughie reminded her he was taking a dinner break, but Sam said, "Yes, ma'am."

As he hurried off, Ximena exclaimed, "My own little brother. I can't believe it!"

Hughie said, "Sam wasn't kidding—I am here to look out for him." It occurred to Hughie that this was an opportunity to really have a conversation with Ximena about her experience. "Want to split lukewarm chicken wings with me across the street? Mr. Boucher's off on a fishing trip, and I'd like to hear your whole story—start to finish."

Hughie knew that Ximena probably didn't want to linger at the site of her scary experience. Still, she agreed to join him at the pub, even if she kept her thoughts to herself on the short walk over.

When they arrived at the hostess stand, Hughie made quick introductions. Marie glanced at him as if to confirm that his appearing with Ximena was about more than dinner.

"How about I take a quick break and join you two?" Marie suggested, gesturing to one of the waitresses to keep an eye on the door.

"Restroom," Ximena replied. "I'll be right back."

While she was gone, Hughie took a seat and Shelby

dropped off the chicken wings once more. They'd been warmed up in the kitchen. "I never thought I'd see Ximena here again."

Hughie said, "I think she's ready to tell her story—fill in the blanks of her video."

Marie grabbed the specials menus off the nearest four-top and crumpled them up. "When Mr. Boucher noticed that Shelby and I kept 'forgetting' to hand these out, he asked the other girls to leave them after they cleared and cleaned tables."

Hughie glanced at the word *Legend* on a menu mangled in Marie's fist. He told himself that he hadn't mentioned the Harvest House burial ground or attic set to her yet because he still hoped Ms. Fischer would agree to rework them both. Why upset Marie for nothing?

Meanwhile, Marie scooted to the middle of the leather booth, so that she, Hughie, and Ximena—upon Ximena's return—would be seated in a semicircle. "This is better than the two of us facing her," Marie said. "Less confrontational. Plus, since the creeper is a guy, my being here might make her feel safer."

"Mvto," Hughie replied. "By the way, this girl Cricket—she's a reporter on my school newspaper—is working with me and Sam to try to figure out what's going on at the crossroads, and she suggested we focus on 'who, what, when, where, how, and why.'"

Hughie would've been more prepared with questions,

but he hadn't been expecting to talk to Ximena right then. He'd assumed that Sam would be the one to lead this conversation.

When Ximena returned, she seemed calmer. "Marie, I don't want what happened to me to happen to you or anyone else. I appreciate that you're all taking me seriously and trying to do something about it. But you have to promise me that you'll be careful."

"We promise," Marie said, and that's when Hughie realized she'd opted onto the team.

Shelby returned with a tall cup of ice water for Ximena. "Hey, Ximena. Can I get you anything?"

"No, thanks. I'm good with water for now." As Shelby moved on, Ximena addressed Marie and Hughie. "What do you want to know?"

Marie asked, "Do you have any idea who the creeper could've been?"

"Sorry, I didn't recognize him or get a good look. At first, I thought he was young, but his voice sounded old—or tired—and he moved like his knees might go out at any minute."

"Could he have been drunk?" Hughie asked. "High?"

"Maybe. I was more worried about the devil dog."

"Did the dog bite the guy?" Marie asked. "Or claw his face?"

"No clue. I took off running." Ximena rubbed her temples. "I could hear barking, snarling, but then it went quiet as soon as I had a solid head start."

Hughie wasn't sure what to say next. "Feel free to have a chicken wing."

Ximena shook her head. Marie replied, "You go ahead."

So he did. For one, two, three wings, Hughie and the girls sat in companionable silence. As Hughie reached for his fourth, Marie said, "What else was going on that night? Was the pub busy? Did anything weird happen?"

"I was distracted," Ximena admitted. "My boyfriend—my ex-boyfriend as of last night—he was there. He's . . . he'd get so jealous. He'd accuse me of flirting for tips."

Hughie was tentative. "Do you think that he—"

"It *wasn't him*!" Ximena insisted. "Sam has asked me that a hundred times."

"Could it have been a friend of his?" Marie suggested. "Somebody he put up to it?"

Ximena blew her nose on a napkin, and that's when Hughie realized she was crying. "Doubt it. Has anyone else seen the devil dog? It came out of nowhere, like it had been watching and waiting. God help me, I felt watched the whole time I was outside that night."

Later that evening, as the boys were about to head out, Sam said, "I hate when Ximena is pissed at me."

"She's worried," Hughie replied, buckling his seat belt. "Your sister is positive that something freaky is going on around here, and she—"

Sam nodded from behind the wheel. "I'll promise to text her every time I get home from work. It's only for a couple of more weeks anyway."

"What did I miss?" Hughie asked, as they left.

"Minor drama. Ms. Fischer decided to scrap the Grim Reaper ghost story idea because it might be seen as religiously disrespectful. The angel Azrael and all that. She's trying, but nothing short of shutting us down will please the Bible thumpers. Then Kelsey pointed out that our car-accident set could upset people who'd lost someone that way, and Ms. Fischer seemed to take the thought to heart, but Oakley had a mini-meltdown about dealing with too many changes to costumes and sets that were already well underway. So only the Reaper got nixed."

Sam was driving toward old town rather than in the direction of home, and Hughie figured he needed to blow off steam. "What do you know about Ximena's boyfriend?"

"Justin? Boring, clichéd white dude. Skateboarder."

"Ximena remembers his car peeling out after their argument," Hughie said. "But what if Justin parked it alongside the road and ran back? It would've been easy to turn in to the plant nursery and hide his wheels behind the greenhouse."

"I thought of that, too," Sam said. "But Justin drove straight to Blue Heaven Trailer Park to wait for Ximena so he could apologize and my abuela invited him inside."

"Can your grandmother confirm what time he got there?" Hughie asked.

"Maybe—she has a better memory than I do." Sam turned down the radio. "I'll ask her and let you know if it doesn't sync up." They passed the plant nursery, swarming with pumpkin patch shoppers, and he turned onto a bumpy road, heading north.

"Where are we going?" As a nondriver, Hughie didn't know his way around beyond the destinations his family visited on a regular basis.

"Someplace I like to think," Sam replied. "Or not think, depending."

Not thinking sounded good. At a curve in the road, the headlights illuminated a small herd of cows and goats, then a field of pumpkins beyond the barbed-wire fence.

A couple of minutes later, Sam pulled over to the side of the road and got out of the car.

Following, Hughie used the flashlight app on his phone to look around. It felt liberating to be out on the land at night. Sam had driven them across a winding road to an old country bridge—Killer Crow Creek Bridge, according to the historic marker—built in 1911 out of cut stone with wooden railings. It was the crowning glory of Killer Crow Arch Park—a small structure over an overgrown creek that was flowing again because of the autumn rains.

Sam rested both hands on a wooden railing. "You know the haunting we're staging at the far end of the first floor, the ghost on the bridge? This place is its inspiration. It's a Lady in White story."

As the clouds drifted by, moonlight reflected off the water below. "What's a Lady in White story?"

"A ghost woman story," Sam replied over the fading chatter of katydids. "Long white dress. Tragic death. An accident, a murder, a love affair gone wrong, or a love that went to waste." Unrequited, he meant. "A Lady in White usually shows up alongside a country road." Sam sat on the edge of the bridge, his legs resting against the stonework, and Hughie joined him.

For a while, they listened to the wind snaking through the trees and the prairie grass.

Lightning flashed in the distance. Hughie glanced over. It wasn't like his friend to be so quiet. "Everything okay?"

Sam tilted his head far to one side and then the other, popping his neck bones. "When you were at the pub, Ms. Fischer made a crack about Kelsey and Oakley being queer. I know they're all friends, but I feel like I should've said something, and I didn't."

Hughie empathized. "You're allowed to pick your battles."

"You sound like my mom," Sam replied.

"Actually, I sound like mine." Hughie replied. A rustling noise arose from the bank of the creek, followed by faint splashing that startled the boys.

Sam managed to turn on his phone flashlight in time to glimpse a bushy tail vanish on the other side of the water. "Coyote?"

"Possibly *the* coyote. Can I ask you a question?"

Sam shrugged. "When it comes to my best friends, I'm an open book."

It was the first time either had acknowledged how close they'd become, and Hughie felt grateful and validated. "Do you *really* believe in ghosts? Like spirits of the dead. Separate from the whole thing with Ximena, the fact that it's almost Halloween—"

"For sure. Don't you?"

"After my aunt—Rain's mom—after she died, I could've sworn someone set a hand on my shoulder at the burial. When I turned to look, no one was there, but I remember this feeling filling me up. From then on, my cousins . . . We've all always been close, but it was like this bigger thing that folded in my auntie's memory, too." Hughie took a hitched breath. "We were in old town—Garden of Roses Cemetery, at the top of a hill. I'd swear that was my aunt's hand I felt. I know how that sounds—"

"It sounds nice," Sam replied. "Like, if that's how it works, death is somehow—"

"It was a hard day, and I'd had weird dreams the night before and—"

"Faith isn't a sign of weakness," Sam said.

"Now *you* sound like *my* mom," Hughie replied.

Sam echoed Hughie's earlier words. "Actually, I sound like mine."

16 DAYS UNTIL HALLOWEEN

With a little more than two weeks to go, the ongoing interior reinvention and logistical preparation of Harvest House was kicking into high gear, and Sam and Hughie were spending several afternoons a week at the site. As they pulled up after school on Thursday, they saw that chain-link fencing, covered by black privacy windscreens, had been installed, but since the rear exit was open wide, they walked in and greeted Ms. Fischer.

"The temporary fencing is partly for security," Ms. Fischer explained, "so nobody can sneak in for free, but it'll also help us control traffic flow." She gestured at the back double doors of the building and the attached loading ramp. "The slides are being installed later today. They'll go down the back stairs, through what used to be the restaurant kitchen, and plop guests onto hay-covered mattresses. The Indian ghost actors will do their jump scares out here in the burial ground, and visitors will leave out the gate. Merch will be for sale along the side of the road."

Every time Ms. Fischer said *Indian* or *burial ground*,

Hughie's jaw clenched. "What about parking?" he asked as a woman in a Sunflower Electric uniform passed by.

"Roadside," Ms. Fischer replied. "Plus, Boucher will be charging five bucks for a spot in the field behind the Grub Pub. He's donating that cash, too." As always, she sounded grateful and deeply moved by all the support.

A couple of college-age volunteers busied themselves installing outdoor lighting as Hughie's gaze swept what would become the outdoor haunt set. It extended beyond the bright yellow oak walnut trees into a grassy field dominated by a few evergreen junipers.

As he and Sam made their way through stacks of salvaged cardboard boxes, Hughie took note of the newly arrived supplies—utility knives, permanent markers, measuring tapes and masking tape, an unopened package of pencils, hot glue, and a pile of polystyrene foam skulls.

"Can we get your opinion?" Oakley asked from the top of a ladder that Kelsey was holding steady. "I think we need headstones for the Indian burial ground because otherwise how will people know it's supposed to be a *burial ground* and not just zombie Indians, but—"

"Indians probably didn't use headstones," Kelsey interrupted.

"Kelsey is a women, gender, and sexuality studies grad student, not an Indigenous studies grad student," Oakley countered.

Hughie's memory flashed again to his aunt's burial— Rain's mother's burial. He'd adored his auntie . . . the one who'd made the world's best green bean casserole and, for his eighth birthday, sent the FUTURE ASTRONAUT T-shirt that he'd worn until it fell apart. "Some Indians *use* head-stones," Hughie replied, emphasizing the present tense. This was getting ridiculous. He had to say something, before he cracked a tooth.

Sam peeled off to join the work crew, but Hughie kept moving. Inside the building, construction was underway—extenders for the slides—and Ms. Fischer's temporary office had been surrendered to the cause. After a few minutes, Hughie located her alone upstairs in the attic that was once used for private parties. It was a wide-open, empty space with a high ceiling and exposed rafters. Standing in such a big room, he felt small, and Ms. Fischer looked smaller, too.

Resolve had won the day. Hughie would be forthright in a way that left space for listening. "Ms. Fischer, I've been wanting to talk to you about something." He sneezed. "It's about the Indian ghosts, the Indian maiden, the burial ground."

"Bless you. We've been sweeping for days." Scribbling on her clipboard, Ms. Fischer frowned. Suddenly, she lit up, seemingly registering Hughie's words. "Yes! I'm hoping that you'll play an Indian ghost."

"No, it's not that. It's . . . my mom wouldn't approve."

"Why not? She does know you're volunteering at a haunted house?"

"She knows. It's not that. It's, we're Muscogee." At

her baffled expression, he added, "Indigenous." No reaction. "You know, Native American, American Indian?"

"Oh," she said, the pen still poised. "*Oh!* Wow, really? That's perfect!"

"No, it's . . . I don't think that we should . . ." He cast around for a way to say it, and inspiration struck. "I hear you cut the Grim Reaper display because Christians could find it offensive. We could also come up with something better than the burial ground and Indian ghosts. Since this is Harvest House, the ghosts of *farmers*—"

"Hughie, Halloween is just over two weeks away! We can't start changing things now." The floorboards creaked beneath Ms. Fischer's feet. "Oakley is a fireball of stress. It sounds like you're sensitive about these things, but you don't have to play an Indian ghost, if you don't want to. We can find something else for you to do."

Hughie suppressed a sigh. Time to shift gears. "I know what else I can do," Hughie told Ms. Fischer. "That's what I wanted to talk to you about. I could take over designing the attic set."

"You want to be assigned the Indian maiden ghost?" she asked, clearly confused.

"I want to come up with something you'll like even better." Sometimes you had to go for the win you could get, Hughie figured. If he could convince Ms. Fischer to change up the attic, maybe he could convince her to rethink the burial ground, too. "I'm a member of the Wolfe family, and our holiday decorating skills are legendary. Check this

133

out." Using his phone, Hughie showed off photos of the last few Halloween makeovers of his home. Granted, his dad had been the design director, but Hughie had learned a lot in the process.

Ms. Fischer nodded, and the air between them felt lighter. "I admit it, I'm impressed."

"I'd like to draw up a proposal for you by tomorrow," Hughie said. "I'm no artist, but I've got a good imagination." He figured that his dad would be tickled to help him brainstorm. "At least give me a chance. Listen to my pitch. You don't have to use it if you don't want to."

"Don't see how I can refuse an offer like that." Gesturing for Hughie to follow her downstairs, Ms. Fischer said, "By the way, I've noticed you're taking some long breaks at the pub. Don't get me wrong. I'm in no position to complain about free labor, but I'm curious . . ."

Using his index finger, Hughie traced a line in the dust down the carved wooden banister. "I'm a regular. My family goes to church in old town, so it's on the way home to stop for Sunday brunch. And my sister's best friend is a waitress there." He didn't mention Marie. The last thing he felt like dealing with was Ms. Fischer teasing him about his love life.

"You know Karl, the cook?" Ms. Fischer gave a dreamy sigh. "He was my high school sweetheart. We used to shoot hoops in my parents' driveway. It was so romantic."

Her and Karl? Hughie thought. Just then, Elias and Jonas Vogel walked through the front door, carrying takeout bags from the Grub Pub. Hughie, who had been doing a bang-up job of avoiding them at school, had hoped to slip off their radar.

Their reputation for fighting unnerved Hughie, but looking back, he realized the parking lot skirmish that got them suspended had happened only weeks after the Vogels' father's funeral. Hughie figured that timing was probably why they were only suspended instead of expelled.

Still, Hughie hated violence, and seeing the Vogels reminded him of having been bullied in middle school back in Texas. Hughie had thought he was long past all that. Since then, he'd literally moved across the country and made new friends and gained a lot more confidence. But the Vogels' animosity had brought back haunting memories. Part of him would always be that nervous seventh grader who got tripped in the school halls.

"Hughie, do you know Jonas and Elias? They're nephews of Karl's—speak of the devil. You all go to high school together, don't you?"

"I've seen them around, but we're in different grades."

Ignoring him, Elias announced, "Here's your pub order."

"Haul it out back to my crew," Ms. Fischer replied, pointing down the central hallway. "Straight on through— don't *mess* with anything, don't *touch* anything, absolutely *no photos*—then go under the arched bridge. You can leave the bags with the artsy kids in overalls. They'll take it from there." As the brothers sauntered off, Hughie heard one of them snicker.

Ms. Fischer tapped the wall, newly covered in long, netted black polyester.

Hughie touched the fabric. Taking over the attic design wasn't the only topic he'd hoped to address that day with Ms. Fischer. As a longtime resident of the area, she might be able to give background information that would help them figure out what was going on with the ghost, or the creeper, or both. "You dated Karl in high school, and you're still friends?"

"That Karl! He was a real hell-raiser back in the day. We both were. But that was a long time ago. He's a good old soul. Sad life—Karl's known more than his fair share of loss."

Taking reference photos of the stairwell with his phone, Hughie asked, "Loss?"

"Karl's younger brother Danny passed fairly recently. Second brother he's lost. Wicked sense of humor, that Danny, drove a sixteen-wheeler. Even when he was alive, most of the time, it seemed like he was gone. Danny was tough on his sons—too tough if you ask me—but it came from a place of love. Before that, there was Stefan, the baby of the family, the golden boy. I remember the funeral—people saying how he was too good for this world. They lost him in a car accident. Then there's this place." She held her arms to either side, palms up, as if gesturing to heaven. "The chicken restaurant. Opened and closed quick as a wink back in the eighties. Karl was still a young man back then, full of piss and vinegar. Leased the land dirt cheap from Mr. Boucher, spent everything he had, and went into debt."

"Why'd Karl shut it down?" Hughie asked as they crossed through the first-floor construction zone. The Killer Crow Creek Bridge at the far end of the space was shaping up to be a remarkable likeness of the historic stone bridge Hughie had visited with Sam.

"Most new restaurants fall straight into the crapper," Ms. Fischer said. "Ever since then, this building has been sliding into disrepair. Boucher has been renting space out front to food trucks and mobile outfits like that dog groomer.

"Between you and me, I think he let this place sit empty so long because watching another business go in would've been a punch to the gut for Karl, what with him working across the street. They're old friends. Everybody, even Boucher, knows that Boucher does a half-assed job of managing the pub. Karl's the one who's kept it above water all these years."

Ms. Fischer paused to take in the partly real, partly makeshift Bel Air sedan angled to one side, and Hughie wondered if it had put her in mind of Stefan's death. Someone had painted DEVIL OR ANGEL on the fake part of the car. She asked, "You got a girlfriend, Hughie?"

He hadn't wanted to go there, but he didn't know how he could avoid the question. "Sort of. Her name is Marie, and she works across the street. She's the new hostess."

Ms. Fischer chuckled. "Oh, so now the truth comes out! You scamp!"

Hughie took the teasing in stride. Artificial crows—with bendable talons, lifelike feathers, and light-up red eyes—had been mounted along the top of the bridge and hung with wires from the fourteen-foot ceiling. They'd been attached to black spray-painted mobiles, some of which were electronic and could spin on remote control, creating the illusion of flight.

"I bet your Marie knows Karl's nephews," Ms. Fischer went on. "They've been spending a lot of time at the pub lately. Karl's become like their father, now that Danny is gone."

As Ms. Fischer went on to tell Hughie about Danny's heart attack—she'd run into him at the grocery store only the day before—Hughie started to feel bad for the Vogel brothers, even though he recalled Sam saying that they had started becoming jerks well before their father had died. But the thought of losing a parent made him eager to get home to his own mom and dad.

Ms. Fischer concluded, "You'll be seeing more of them—Jonas and Elias—on this side of the road as we get closer to Halloween weekend." Ducking through the original restaurant kitchen, Ms. Fischer concluded with a hint of apology, "They're going to play, um . . ."

"Indian ghosts," Hughie finished. He'd see about that.

After a quick video call to his grandparents, Hughie and Dad embarked on the dachshunds' final walk of the day, grandly referred to as the Moonlight Puppy Promenade.

When the Wolfes had first moved to Emerald Hills, it had all looked boring to Hughie: arched streetlights, standardized mailboxes, manicured yards, and neutral paint schemes on four house designs that flowed architecturally from one to the other. But despite his father's ranting against the "control freaks of the homeowners' association," Hughie had come to appreciate how having a more uniform baseline made seasonal variations pop.

About a third of the households had decorated for Halloween, though none as enthusiastically as the Wolfes. As the holiday grew closer, more and more jack-o'-lanterns had begun to appear on porch steps. Families with elementary-aged kids skewed more to spooky-cute than scary—with yard signs that read TRICK OR TREAT in bright orange or BOO! in the shape of cartoonish ghosts. The Fullers had decided on colorful fake headstones that read HAPPY HAUNTING.

All that gave the dogs plenty to sniff and bark at, even as they searched for perfect piles of leaves to bound in, perfect sticks to gallop with, and perfect spots to "do their business," as Dad called it. Father and son carried biodegradable poop bags in their jacket pockets.

With the air of a connoisseur, Dad admired a massive fake spiderweb, featuring a massive black-and-purple spider, anchored to a lush front yard and two points of a two-story roof. "I admire their commitment to scale," he observed. "It would be better, though, if there were a hanging egg sac with a hole in it and a few baby-size spiders crawling away."

As the dachshunds barked back at a Chihuahua watching over her territory through a front window, Hughie could feel the evening slipping away. He had only so long to get his attic decor proposal together for Ms. Fischer and her assistants. But he was a slow-burn kind of planner, and he understood his father. Before bringing up the idea of brainstorming for Harvest House, he needed his dad to be fully submerged in Halloween-geek mode.

"When I was your age, from the beginning of the school year to the end of October, that felt like a solid hunk of time. Now, it's gone like that." Dad snapped his fingers. "Before long, you'll be off to college, too."

Three houses down, Bilbo stalked a squirrel across the street. Frodo tore apart grass with his teeth. Dad *tsk*ed at the sight of an LED ghost display in the trees. He could be a real snob when it came to holiday decor. Hughie asked, "How do you think time passes for ghosts?"

"Assuming there *are* ghosts? I'm not sure it does. Pass, that is." The rope lights were a spectral green. "Maybe it depends on the ghost. How they died, what's keeping them from moving on—unfinished business or a mystic force."

The labradoodle in the nearest backyard howled. "Mystic like what?"

The dachshunds howled back, and both father and son chuckled.

"Like Halloween! Lots of ghostly activity around this time a year, or so people say."

Hughie struck while the moment was ripe. "Speaking of which, I need your help with something. Today I talked to Ms. Fischer, the woman behind Harvest House, about letting me try to come up with a new staging idea for the attic." As a thunderstruck expression crossed over his father's face, Hughie added, "I'd appreciate it if you could help me—"

"*If I could?*" Dad pulled Hughie into a huge hug.

Crushed against his father's broad chest, Hughie continued in a somewhat muffled voice. "I'm supposed to get back to her tomorrow morning, so it's a tight deadline."

Still holding a leash, Hughie's father loosened his embrace, grabbed Hughie by the shoulders, and stepped back to bask in his son's grandeur. "Talk to me, O Child of My Demented Heart. Tell me everything! What are you thinking so far?"

Hughie laughed. "I want to go above and beyond and include the staircase from the foyer. It's underutilized real estate."

"I approve of your ambition! We can talk about transitions, but before we get into the nitty-gritty, tell me more about Harvest House." They began walking again, guiding the dogs farther to the side of the road as a new SUV passed by. Hughie explained that each set—or haunting—was supposed to pull from local history or lore. That was true of the Killer Crow Creek Bridge ghost and the Crossroads Ghost. "But the speakeasy flapper who danced to death, she's something Oakley and Kelsey came up with—and the 1950s car wreck with the teen couple, too."

Passing under an arched streetlight, Dad nodded. "There was a music trend—teenybopper songs about the tragic road deaths of young lovers. 'Teen Angel.' 'Last Kiss.' 'Leader of the Pack.' Dramatic, morbid—we're talking sappy on steroids."

"Your generation was not without its creepy side," Hughie said.

"I beg your pardon. That was long before my time." Father and son came upon a lawn filled with coffins made of spray-painted cardboard. "Oh, check it out! I gave them a hand constructing these. On Halloween, the tops will periodically swing open, and the vampires inside will sit up and scream."

"The vampires being the Kirshner-Robinson kids?" Hughie asked. The family had four daughters between the ages of six and twelve.

"They can hardly wait." As Bilbo began his pre-poop spin, Dad reached into his pocket for a bag. "Harvest House is planning on doing the 'Indian maiden' Crossroads Ghost, huh? And it's being marketed as family friendly? Did you mention that to your mother?"

"Not yet." Up until then, Hughie had been keeping the problem mostly to himself, trying to work out a solution, hoping to spare his loved ones any unnecessary grief. He wasn't fooled by how casually Dad had brought up the question. Hughie knew his father well enough to know he'd been thinking it over while they'd chatted. "The attic build-out is up next, so there's still time to make changes. I'm trying to come up with a concept that will wow Ms. Fischer, so she doesn't end up going there."

"Call it a plan," Dad said. "We're going come up with some *other* ghost. A fresh, showstopper kind of ghost that'll win over Ms. Fischer and the ticket holders, too. Let's think it through together. Can your ghost move things? Can they possess the living?"

"Moving things sounds good," Hughie said. "Possession, not so much. Too scary."

"Agreed." At the home to their left, the backlit profile of a Frankenstein's monster lurked in an upstairs window. It occurred to Hughie that his father, who had robustly defended seasonal and holiday decor at an HOA meeting, had won the war. One household after another had outdone itself with googly eyes in plant life, fake bats swaying from branches, witch and cat lawn ornaments, brooms propped beside doorways, and even an oversize cauldron.

"Come on, Frodo," Dad called. "Stop sniffing every blade of grass." To Hughie, he added, "We're expecting a S-T-O-R-M tonight, and I'd like to get the dogs home before it rolls in. You know how they get when something stirs the air."

Hughie did. He remembered how riled up the dachshunds had been on their visit to the mobile groomer at the crossroads. It was still unsettling, how close he'd come to losing his pups. Something else about that moment nagged at Hughie, too, but he couldn't quite remember what.

15 DAYS UNTIL HALLOWEEN

The fact that Ms. Fischer had decided to meet to discuss Hughie's proposal in the more fully realized so-called Indian burial ground was an unwelcome distraction for him.

Thankfully, Sam had volunteered to play the role of Hughie's assistant. Using a workbench as a tabletop, Sam held up Hughie's first presentation poster, face in.

It was labeled FOYER/STAIRCASE.

The setup reminded Hughie of auditions—the way Ms. Fischer sat with Oakley and Kelsey in a row in folding lawn chairs, drinking pub coffee from takeout cups. Cans of black-light paint had been stacked to the side. "Anytime you're ready!" Ms. Fischer called, taking a sip. "Fifteen days until Halloween, fourteen until opening night. Time's a-wasting!"

Ideally, Hughie would've rehearsed his presentation, but he knew what he wanted to say. *Focus on the message,* he thought. *Not on yourself.*

Sam flipped around the first poster board. It was a map

of the downstairs of the building with each of the major Harvest House sets labeled as such.

"Harvest House is a celebration of rural ghost stories with a historic flare," Hughie began, using an opening line suggested via late-night text from his sister. "Our goal is to be scary enough for the high school-slash-college crowd, but not too scary for families with kids. Each setting in the maze has its own vibe. The fifties roadside wreck, the Killer Crow Creek Bridge, the twenties speakeasy, the crossroads, and the, uh, burial ground." Hughie wasn't about to refer to it as an *Indian* burial ground. "It's kind of a mishmash. We need to create a flow by tying the whole thing together with a common, timeless element—birds."

Hughie hoped Ms. Fischer would consider what he was suggesting a solution, not a criticism. "We'll begin with that ever-popular Halloween staple, crows. When people first come in, the Harvest House foyer will be split up so that they don't see the staircase to the attic. Instead, they'll go straight ahead until they turn at the far end of the first floor. Along that first stretch of the maze, we'll add more and more crows until we reach a full flock or, uh, murder—that's what you call a bunch of crows—a murder of crows at Killer Crow Creek Bridge. Then, several more crows will fly toward the front staircase, slowly going down in number and starting to morph as the last few flap around, panicking, in circles up the stairs."

"Morph?" Kelsey echoed. "Morph into what?"

It was the cue Hughie had been waiting for. At his

nod, Sam advanced to the next poster, and Hughie recoiled from his audience, his fingers curled and raised as if in self-defense. His voice quavered, and his eyes flashed in fear. "Take thy beak out from my heart, and take thy form from off my door! Quoth the Raven, 'Nevermore.'"

Ms. Fischer and her assistants burst into applause. "I told you he was an actor," she said.

"'The Raven,' Edgar Allan Poe," Hughie continued. The shift in size from a crow to a raven was as dramatic as that from a pigeon to a red-tailed hawk, yet it was more subtle. Like a crow, a raven was a black bird, only larger, with a longer neck, bigger beak, and different tail. "In the attic, the backdrop will indicate that visitors are hiking through the countryside in the cold dead of night to the crossroads."

Sam continued to the next poster, and Hughie let it briefly speak for itself.

"You're thinking of a replica of the crossroads intersection?" Oakley asked, though that was apparent enough from the printed photographs mounted on the posterboard.

"Yes," Hughie said, his voice crisp. "We can use blown-up photos in sepia tone as a base to build on, adding lighting and a few three-dimensional accents mounted flush, and distorted mirrors for the windows. That imagery will linger in the guests' minds after they go down the slides and exit the burial ground to return to the real world. It'll make their entire night out at the crossroads feel like part of the Harvest House experience."

"Ooooh, 'Harvest House experience,'" Ms. Fischer echoed. "I like that."

"Very immersive," Oakley said. "Very meta."

"What about the Indian maiden?" Kelsey asked. "The legend of the Crossroads Ghost? She's the whole reason we're doing ghosts in the first place."

Sam advanced to the second to last poster, which looked exactly like the previous one, only it included increasingly monstrous birds, courtesy of a last-minute, late-night effort by Dmitri Headbird—the best visual artist Hughie knew. He'd had a long conversation with Dmitri and Marie the night before, breaking the news about the planned Indian maiden set and asking for Dmitri's help. Marie had been happy to hear that Hughie was fighting the system from the inside.

"I'm impressed," she'd said. "Shelby and I are doing our best to keep Mr. Boucher's October specials menu out of customers' hands. But it's like you're redesigning the pub kitchen itself." Hughie had taken Marie's enthusiasm and a dose of inspiration to heart.

It was time to flip the script. Hughie gestured to the visual aid. "As guests in the attic pass by the reproductions of the Christmas store and antique store to their north and the pub to their south, the ravens will gradually take on characteristics of . . . chickens. First, monstrous hybrids and then clearly chicken-like ghostly chickens—spectral, angry chickens, hungry for revenge." The raven-chickens and ghost-chickens Dmitri had drawn looked appalling, but in a cartoonish way that hopefully wouldn't give little kids nightmares. "Only one doorway is open for the guests to escape—K.V.'s Chicken Restaurant and Lounge!"

"We'll have to paint in the old restaurant," Sam said, breaking his vow to stay quiet. "Because we've already changed the look of the place to Harvest House, so it's too late for a photo shoot. But it's not like we don't know what it should look like, and—"

"Wait." With a confused grin, Ms. Fischer asked, "Who are the chickens targeting for revenge? And why?"

"Who else?" Hughie exclaimed as Sam held out the final storyboard, which featured a frantic, frightened figure bearing a strong resemblance to Karl Vogel from the Grub Pub. "The cook—and everyone else who's dared to down a drumstick."

Ms. Fischer burst out laughing. "Oh my!" she exclaimed. "What a tribute to Karl! People will be talking about it for years. Okay, so the first half of the attic will represent the crossroads, and then it'll transition into the chaos of a haunted restaurant. From there, our guests will slide down to the Indian burial ground, scream, scream, scream, and it's a wrap! Hughie, you're a genius!"

"What about vegetarians?" Kelsey groused. "The chickens have no reason to take revenge on us. Plus, what about the whole bait-and-switch problem? People are buying tickets to finally meet the Crossroads Ghost they've heard so much about."

"But this sends a pro-animal, anti-meat message,"

149

Oakley argued. "Mess with chickens, and they'll come back to haunt you!"

"Lighten up, Kelsey!" Ms. Fischer scolded. "It's all in fun. I swear, you kids today and your causes! It'd do you a world of good to go with the flow. Tell you what, I'll talk to Boucher about offering a Harvest House chicken special. *That'll* give everyone who ordered it an extra thrill." She laughed, gleeful. "We're cooking with gas now!"

"Just hear me out," Kelsey said, picking up a hot glue gun. "The Crossroads Ghost is the reason we decided to do ghosts instead of vampires. Everyone loves vampires."

Hughie was under the distinct impression that *Kelsey* loved vampires. As he collected his storyboards, he gratefully remembered how he'd spent some time with his mother the night before, talking through his reasons for axing the Crossroads Ghost from Harvest House. Hughie picked his words carefully. "If the Grim Reaper or Angel of Death or whatever is too disrespectful for some Christians, and if you wondered if the car-accident haunt might be too upsetting, then how can you play around with the idea of a girl freezing to death?" He took a deep breath. "This is a haunted fun house. There's nothing fun about that legend, especially not if you're Indigenous like me." Kelsey and Oakley exchanged a look of dawning mortification.

"Hughie is an Indian," Ms. Fischer said quietly, and then dodged his main point by adding, "Kids, this is brilliant! Ghost-chickens—I love it!"

CELESTE

How *dare* they scheme to mock me on my own grave! My kin, Hughie, raises his voice in my defense. He protects my memory the way I protect girls from The Bad Man.

Our enemies take our land and our lives, and then they take our life stories—what's left of us when we're gone—and corrupt them. Is there no limit to their greed or selfishness or lies?

Upon reflection, my outrage cools. I'm loath to admit it, but I'm partly at fault. A confession: my legend is mostly of my own making. Useful to deter skittish brown girls from crossing the country road alone after nightfall. A strategy to safeguard that sometimes slips into the temptation to play. In the early years, I'd wait until after sunset and then tap a shoulder, swipe a ball cap, knock on car windows. Once I fully manifested as a specter in the back seat of a Jeep Grand Cherokee and whispered, "Boo!"

10 DAYS UNTIL HALLOWEEN

Thwarted by Marie's work schedule and his own ongoing volunteering at Harvest House, Hughie had been eager for an opportunity to spend quality time with her. It had been more than three weeks since their date, and while they'd seen each other at the crossroads and at one of Dmitri's football games, they hadn't found a time to go out again— just the two of them. Still, when Sam texted their friends to suggest a pumpkin-carving party, and Marie responded with heart and jack-o'-lantern emojis, Hughie went with it, offering his own backyard deck for the occasion.

That evening, the Headbird twins and Rain drove in together from old town. After exclaiming over the Wolfes' outdoor decor, Dmitri and Rain briefly excused themselves to go upstairs and say hello to her auntie and uncle, who were "staying out of the way" with the dachshunds upstairs. "They're watching *The Nightmare Before Christmas*," Hughie said. "It's a family favorite."

"Rain told me," Marie replied, extracting a PEZ Jack Skellington and PEZ Sally from her purse. "I brought these to give to them."

"As if they don't already like you enough," Hughie said. With a glance toward the staircase in the foyer, he added. "Um, do you want to—"

"Later," Marie said. "If they come down to say hi to everybody."

"Oh, they'll come down to say hi to everybody," he assured her.

Beneath the crystal drum chandelier in the foyer, she shifted her weight in her ballet flats. He shifted his weight in his sneakers. Hughie thought about kissing Marie. He thought about whether she wanted to kiss him. He thought about how his cousin and Marie's brother could come back downstairs any moment, and how he could hear his dad laughing upstairs, and how that wasn't romantic.

While he was overthinking, Marie wandered past him into the kitchen.

It was strange. The two of them had been texting off and on regularly. They had no trouble picking up their conversation whenever he saw her at the pub. But being alone in person had a different, more charged vibe to it. Hughie struggled to make small talk.

"I should take this stuff outside," he said as he reached for the jug of apple cider and the paper cups. Marie followed with a platter of pumpkin-and-chocolate-chip cookies—courtesy of his mom's law-school stress baking.

"Yum, I can smell the cinnamon," she said. "I thought your dad was a no-refined-sugars kind of dentist."

"He is," Hughie said. "It pains me to admit that this

is usually a cookie-free household. Despite Dad's devotion to spooky decorations, he used to insist we give trick-or-treaters dental floss, sugar-free gum, and travel-size toothpaste. Thankfully, this year Mom overruled him."

"I adore your family," Marie said. From a shopping bag on the nearest chair, she grabbed paper towels and a fistful of carving knives. "Queen would have come, too, but she had plans tonight with her theater friends." Hughie had already seen pics of them at the vintage CDs and vinyl store. Queen had posted a selfie with a stocky, short boy, holding up a copy of the original Broadway cast's recording of *The Addams Family*. Marie added, "Sorry, I hope it wasn't bad to mention theater."

"Don't worry about it. I'm glad they're having fun." Hughie was still bummed about the fall play being canceled, but he could be happy for Queen. And he appreciated that at least the women in his day-to-day life—his mom, sister, Cousin Rain, and Aunt Georgia—had dropped the topic of him writing a script to submit for the spring production. Part of him longed to keep trying, but he was utterly lacking in inspiration.

Marie gently redirected the conversation. "My brother showed me the sketches he did for your Harvest House attic set proposal. I've never known him to work so fast."

"It was a short-notice ask," Hughie said, moving the cloth bag out of the way.

"That was probably for the best. Dmitri didn't have

time to spin in his own head, obsessing over making it perfect." Marie knelt to spread out pages from the *Lawrence Journal-World* so the deck floor wouldn't get sticky. "I appreciate your convincing Ms. Fischer to punt the Indian maiden ghost from Harvest House. I'm sure that took some doing. As you've probably noticed, Mr. Boucher's decision to put the legend on the October menus has turned it into a big topic of jokes and conversation at the pub. It's on my very last nerve."

Marie had had to deal with the Indian maiden stereotype throughout her life. The least Hughie could do is take it on at Harvest House. He doubled his resolve to address the so-called Indian burial ground next and offered a hand to help Marie up, which she accepted with a smile. He asked, "You still don't think there's anything spooky going on at the crossroads?"

Marie asked, "Are you asking about Ximena's creeper, the Indian maiden ghost, or both?" She tilted her head, considering his question. "At first, like I said, I assumed the whole thing was a hoax to drum up business," she replied. "Possibly not only for Harvest House. What with ghost tourism, everybody's all about the apparitions! Boosting a haunted rep for the intersection could bring more customers to the pub and to the antiques shop, too. I heard the year-round Christmas shop added a Halloween section."

Marie almost sounded like she was trying to convince herself.

"Now that I've met Ximena, I think she's telling the truth . . . or at least the truth as she knows it. But if anything is lurking out there in the dark, I doubt it's supernatural. Ximena was already upset by the argument with her boyfriend. The moonlight could've bounced off who knows what at a weird angle. A coyote in the parking lot could've been caught off guard and tried to defend itself." With her free hand, Marie tucked a strand of hair behind her ear. "How about you?"

What had he been thinking? Upon reflection, Hughie realized it had been a *horrible, frightening, dire* subject to try to pair with a potentially romantic moment, but he was too far in now. "Keeping an open mind," he said. "If I boil it down to ghosts, whether they're real . . . what happens when *we* tell ghost stories . . . The stories we Native people tell each other—not the stories told about us." Hughie was respectful of his culture and hers, and the fact that certain aspects of each were sacred and private. "Well, life is full of mystery, and death is, too."

"Poetic," Marie observed. "You've got layers, Hughie Wolfe."

"What about the local legend? Setting aside the Indian maiden cliché, do you think there's *anything* solid behind it? A kernel of truth?" Outside in the cool night air, Hughie felt fluttery. "I'll trade you a kiss for your honest opinion," he said, daring to flirt.

"The legend of the Crossroads Ghost?" Marie asked.

"Hughie, that's not local folklore. That's an episode of *Scooby-Doo*." She smiled again and moved closer to him. "Now, how about my kiss?"

"Holy Great Pumpkin!" an oblivious Sam exclaimed as he sauntered through the sliding glass doorway, startling both Hughie and Marie, who pivoted to a side-by-side pose to welcome him. Cricket followed Sam out. She said, "Hey, Hughie! About the skeletons out front? I have never seen *so many skeletons*!"

"I warned her, man," Sam said. "Oh! Guess what! I invited Cricket."

"Thank you, Captain Obvious." Cricket, who normally projected casual confidence, blushed to the roots of her auburn curls. "I hope you don't mind me crashing."

"Welcome to the Wolfe house!" Hughie was tempted to howl at the moon as a joke, but these were his friends, not his cousins.

Sam asked Marie, "How're you liking the job?"

"I was glad they let me take tonight off. It's going all right. From what I've gathered, Millie and Karl are the heart of the place. Mr. Boucher spends most of his time watching ESPN in his office. He bustles to the dining room to schmooze when somebody he considers important—the mayors and city council people, cops, his own buddies—shows up at the restaurant. We're on strict orders to let him know if any VIPs come through the door."

"How can you tell who's a VIP?" Hughie asked.

"Old town is tighter knit than the burbs. Most of them I can recognize. The rest usually announce their self-importance."

Just then, Rain and Dmitri joined the others outside. She wore her old-fashioned, beat-up Nikon on a strap over her shoulders, and he carried a stack of pumpkin stencils he'd created for the occasion. In no time, the group was stabbing, carving, and otherwise disemboweling a dozen orange gourds. Having seen pics of the house decorations texted by Hughie to Marie, Dmitri had brought several skeleton-themed stencils but also one of a space rocket for Hughie, one of BB-8 from *Star Wars* for Rain, a football for himself, and a wolf-head profile on a PEZ dispenser to lovingly tease his sister about both her PEZ collection and her budding romance with Hughie.

"Tell me about yourselves," Dmitri said to Sam and Cricket, "and I'll make you stencils, too." Hughie was grateful to Dmitri for the icebreaker.

It was a boisterous night of friendship, laughter, and picking pumpkin seeds out of the goo to be roasted later. Ms. and Dr. Wolfe showed up just long enough to *ooh* and *aah* over the freshly created jack-o'-lanterns, and Rain documented the festivities with her camera.

Later, in the great room, Hughie and Marie, Sam and Cricket, and Rain and Dmitri agreed to watch the original 1984 *Ghostbusters* and the 2016 *Ghostbusters: Answer the Call*.

But they had barely gotten into the 1984 film's opening scene at the New York City Public Library when Sam, kicked back on the cowhide sofa, received a text. "Attention, party people," he began. "Turns out the KU quarterback shared Ximena's video, and she says there have been a flurry of new comments—mostly from girls, plus a couple of guys who admit to being drunk at the time—reporting that something freaky happened to them at the crossroads, too."

"What do they say?" Cricket asked.

"Give me a minute. Let me go to my sister's account." After a moment, Sam read aloud, "This one says, 'Me too! For real. Same thing!'"

"That's it?" Dmitri asked.

"Could be a bid for attention," Marie said.

"Hang on," Sam replied, scrolling. "We've got ghost emojis, a few trolls . . . Here we go." He continued reading, "'Hugs! Been there—car wouldn't start at first. So scary!' And 'Your "creeper" came after me, too!' And 'Sorry this happened to you! Sounds like the same jerk from last winter. DM me if you want to talk.' A couple more mention the parking lot across the street from the pub."

"All roads lead to the old chicken restaurant," Hughie observed aloud as the "Ghostbusters" theme song pounded through the TV speakers. He paused the movie.

"We might as well call it Harvest House," Marie said, shifting on the cowhide cushion beside him. "The chicken restaurant closed before we were born." She tucked one foot beneath her and leaned forward so her forearm brushed against Hughie's.

"This could be the break we've been waiting for," Cricket said. "Can you ask Ximena to message the people who commented?"

"Sure," Sam said. "Ximena says that she wants everyone who claimed she was lying or being a drama queen to read these comments."

"Can I see?" Rain reached for Sam's phone. She began clicking through the network. A few minutes later, she said, "The girls who commented—I've been checking their accounts. They've also posted photos at Haskell and Native events at KU, the Indian Arts and Crafts Co-Op in Lawrence . . . These are Indigenous girls."

8 DAYS UNTIL HALLOWEEN

Ximena had referred Paige, one of the girls who'd commented on the video, to Sam, and Paige had agreed to meet up, though she'd asked for them to come to Lawrence. Gray clouds gathered in the sky, threatening thunderstorms. With Sam driving his station wagon, Cricket next to him, and Hughie in the back seat, they'd taken a brief detour to pick up Marie and Rain in old town. Hughie, in the middle, showed the girls Paige's social media profile on his phone. "She's a business administration major at Haskell and member of the Wichita and Affiliated Tribes from Anadarko, Oklahoma. She used to waitress at the pub. I'm worried . . ." The discussion that they'd started on movie night couldn't be avoided any longer. "We need to talk about this. Old town was founded by German immigrants, and it's mostly stayed white. The burbs are only slightly less blond. Paige and Ximena are not. Neither are the other girls who commented on Ximena's video."

"I've been thinking," Marie said. "The creeper could be racist, or working the system, picking victims who

don't usually get much support from cops or the media."
She exhaled. "Or maybe he's just into brunettes?" Thunder rumbled in the distance. As if trying too hard to lighten the mood, she added, "I'm into a certain dark-haired boy, but not in a stalker way."

"Glad to hear it," Hughie replied with a tight smile. It wasn't only the topic that was grim. He wasn't supposed to go as far as Lawrence with a relatively inexperienced driver. None of them were. Sam was taking back roads, avoiding highways.

"Could you slow down a little?" Rain asked, not for the first time.

"Why wouldn't Ximena and Paige get support?" Cricket asked from up front, as rain started to fall. "Ximena's video went viral. Everybody's talking about it."

"Yeah," Sam said, turning on the wipers. "But a lot of the comments were—"

"Everyone knows you're not supposed to read the comments," Cricket replied.

"Two, even three brown girls might be a coincidence," Marie said. "But what about the others who commented on Ximena's post? The ones who didn't want to talk to us."

"Or just didn't bother to reply," Sam countered.

"Not that we're rooting for there to be more." Rain was using two fingers to make Paige's profile pic bigger. "She doesn't look that much like Ximena."

"No," Hughie replied. "But if someone told you they

were sisters?" It went loudly unsaid that Marie also bore a resemblance to Ximena and Paige. No, they didn't look alike, but they were about the same age, build, and coloring. They all wore their dark hair past their shoulders.

Ximena was lighter skinned—her and Sam's mom, Mrs. Rodríguez, was white. "Nobody could tell the difference between the girls from a distance outside at night."

"*All* girls have to worry about . . ." Cricket trailed off. "Never mind. Erase that. I just heard what I was saying. If I went to the police . . ."

"They'd believe you," Rain said. "And if several white girls had been harassed at the crossroads, there would be an ongoing police presence and media coverage."

Cricket struggled to find the words. "I shouldn't have said—I'm sorry it's different—"

"It's different for me, too," Rain replied quietly. Her hair was the golden brown of wheat, and her eyes were that kind of hazel that seemed to shift color. Right then, they looked hazel gray. "Maybe facing off against a stranger at the crossroads at night, it wouldn't matter so much, but I've lived in old town my whole life. My granddad goes bowling and fishing with the good ole boys, the movers and shakers. My sister-in-law works for the local newspaper. That changes things for me, too."

"Could it be a copycat?" Cricket mused aloud. "Someone trying to make the legend come true? Someone identifying girls who could be stand-ins for the Indian maiden?"

Sam's navigation app directed him to turn onto Massachusetts Street in Lawrence. "Does anyone say *maiden* anymore? It sounds very Robin Hood."

The KU football team was playing Oklahoma State at home that weekend, and traffic was heavy. Hughie noticed that Rain was clutching the far side of the front seat. "Sam, slow down."

"I'm not speeding!" he exclaimed. "I have to keep up with traffic." Glancing at his passengers in the rearview mirror, he added, "Creeper or not, Ximena still swears something straight-up supernatural is going on. She's—"

"I'm way more bothered by the thought of a flesh-and-blood human predator," Marie countered as they passed local restaurants, shops, and music venues.

Hughie noticed that Rain seemed to relax as they entered stop-and-go traffic. He said, "Before we get too far ahead of ourselves, let's talk to Paige and find out exactly what happened to her." Hughie leaned forward to peer over the front seat at Cricket keying in notes on her phone. "Are you here as a friend or as a *Hive* reporter? Because if Paige wants to keep her name out of it—"

"Can't I be both?" Shifting to address everyone in the car, Cricket added, "Hughie, you and Sam came to me asking for help, remember? So trust me. I promise not to quote anybody without first making it clear that we're in interview mode." She showed them her phone screen. "This file is deep background, for my eyes only." Cricket turned her cell back around. "If we do find out there's a legit threat, we've got to get the word out . . . like Ximena was trying to. We've got to warn people."

According to the sign on the building, the Kansas Indian Arts and Crafts Cooperative was owned and operated by local Native artists and craftspeople. Paige had suggested meeting during the Friday night poetry reading, which the co-op hosted against the backdrop of its book nook. At first, Sam had been annoyed that she wanted them to drive all the way to Lawrence, but Rain had pointed out that if whatever happened to Paige the previous winter had been traumatic, she'd probably feel more comfortable talking about it in a safe community space.

Hughie had been to the co-op a few times with his mom, who considered it a go-to destination for gift shopping, but that night, the showroom was more crowded than he'd ever seen it. Most of the customers had formed a half circle around a performing poet while a few others moseyed through the store, checking out the handmade baskets or trying on beaded and silver jewelry at the display counter beside the register. Marie used a step stool positioned alongside a bookshelf to peer over the mostly intertribal audience. "That's her—Paige."

Cricket moved closer to Sam and slipped her hand into his.

Paige had pulled back her dark locks with a beaded barrette featuring a black-and-blue butterfly design. A maple-red strand of hair flowed from her temple halfway down her back. After the storekeeper introduced her, she raised her voice, almost in song.

> He calls me "less" . . .
> But I am shadow.
> He calls me "less" . . .
> But I am Moon's light.
> He calls me "less" . . .
> But we are Wind and wings.
> Spirit and vigilance.
> He calls me "less" . . .
> But he is not *us*.
> Together, we are more."

After three more poets performed—speaking of colonization and treaty rights and the hotly debated question of bologna versus Spam—the emcee announced a short intermission, and Paige made her way over. She said hello, adding, "Ximena mentioned that her brother's friends were Indian."

"Hughie Wolfe," he replied. "Muscogee. Or Creek."

"Me too," Rain said. "We're cousins. I'm Rain Berghoff."

"Marie Headbird," she added. "Ojibwe—my people are from Leech Lake. My mom is studying environmental science at Haskell. Do you know Claire Headbird?"

Paige visibly relaxed. "Loves Baby Yoda, carries peppermints in her purse?"

"That's the one!" Marie replied.

"Hi. I'm Cricket Stewart," Cricket said, "and I've literally never felt so white."

Marie lip-pointed at an Elder about to do a reading. "Isn't that . . . ?"

"Aunt Georgia!" Hughie finished. No sooner were the words out his mouth than he spotted Rain's grandfather and step-grandma in the audience on the other side of the room.

Aunt Georgia began with her head bent as if in prayer and, as she spoke, slowly lifted it.

> Our children, your textbooks.
> Lies of omission, lies of commission,
> Lies to soothe your conscience.
> Our children, your textbooks.
> Politics of delusion, politics of persecution.
> Politics as another name for power.
> Our children, your textbooks.
> Destiny mislabeled manifest.
> Our children, our stories.
> Native narratives for Native youth.
> All children, our stories.
> Native narratives to tell the truth.

Grampa Berghoff hooted and hollered, "Give 'em hell, Georgia!"

As the cheers abated, Cricket said to Paige, "I love your beaded earrings."

Marie peered at the woodlands floral design. "I made those earrings!"

This led to a lively discussion in which Marie explained that her father was a part-time trader on the powwow trail, and that her family was among the artists with a relationship to the co-op. Then the girls took off toward the glass display case so that Marie could show them more beaded jewelry she'd made. Cricket trailed awkwardly behind.

Sam said, "We came here to talk about the ghost or the creeper, not to shop."

"Relax," Hughie said. "Talking about beadwork is kind of a way of talking about, well, everything. Besides, we're not in a hurry, and we don't want to rush Paige."

Sam picked up a book about Water Protectors. "Do you think Cricket is okay?"

"Yeah," Hughie said. "She's just figuring out that she's white."

Once the crowd had thinned, the group made themselves comfortable in beanbag chairs toward the back of the store, surrounded by tall shelves of stacked, multicolored blankets, each with a tag verifying the respective artist and their tribal affiliation.

Paige chose an oversize pillow with a geometric design and welcomed the co-op's resident ragdoll cat into her lap. Cricket, sharing a chair with Marie, seemed to have relaxed. She was wearing a newly purchased beaded bracelet and holding a book entitled *Turtle Island 101: This Land Is Our Land.*

After they'd settled in, Hughie caught Sam checking the time on his phone. Hughie understood his friend's impatience. Sam had read the comments on Ximena's video, and people could be a lot meaner, cruder, more racist, and more dismissive online than they'd ever dare to be in real life. He was eager for answers.

Meanwhile, Cricket mentioned that she was a high school journalist and, after a moment's hesitation, agreed when Paige asked that what she was about to say be kept off the record. With that decided, Paige began again, "When I heard him . . . whoever it was . . . coming after me, I was so scared—like pee-your-pants scared." She was gently scratching the cat under its chin. "He kept saying 'less . . . less . . . less.' I keep thinking how I should've been carrying mace, or I should've taken a self-defense class, or—"

Cricket paused in taking notes on her phone. "It's not your fault."

"Right, right," Paige said, finding her center. "It was last winter, and I was so cold, but suddenly, the air got even colder. Like, my nose hairs iced over and my breath turned into a bright white cloud. For a second, I couldn't move. I've watched a few slasher movies and . . . my heart was banging into my rib cage. Then I realized, I wasn't the one out there alone. He was. I had someone on my side." She went quiet for a moment. "You're going to think I'm . . ."

"We'll believe you," Sam assured her. Hughie shot a sideways glance at Rain and Marie and didn't detect a hint of skepticism. Both girls were positioned toward Paige, their legs tucked to one side, their body language attentive without the confrontation of eye contact.

Not long before, the co-op had been abuzz with community chatter. Laughter, conversation, rising poetry, and applause. Now Hughie could hear the register cash drawer shut, footsteps on the floor tile, a clap of thunder outside.

Paige stroked the back of the co-op cat, who flinched at the sounds of the storm. "Birds. Out of nowhere, there were all these birds. Bigger than sparrows, smaller than crows. They swooped at him, screaming—not like an owl . . . I've heard owls before." Hughie put a reassuring hand on his cousin's shoulder as Paige continued, "They flew between us and at him. Time seemed to slow, and it was dark, but the snow and the wind . . . For an instant, it was almost like they formed the shape of a girl's face, a girl with flowing, long hair. Then the birds were everywhere. The noises they made—they sounded like a girl screaming, and she wasn't me."

Thunder boomed, lights flickered, the cat scurried off, and the group laughed nervously.

"It was a dark and stormy night," Sam intoned.

"*A Wrinkle in Time*?" Cricket asked.

"Snoopy," he replied.

Taking a breath, Hughie asked, "Any ideas who the guy was?"

"He didn't sound like Karl, the cook at the pub. I'd

worked there long enough to recognize his voice. Or Mr. Boucher, either. There were a few cars in the pub lot, I think. Food service at the bar stays open for a couple of hours after the dining room closes."

Voices and body language can be disguised, Hughie thought.

"You didn't call the police?" Cricket asked.

Paige shook her head.

"Wind and wings," Rain breathed. "The poem you read—it wasn't about you, was it?"

"No," Paige replied. "It was about her, the Crossroads Ghost."

Sheets of rain smacked Sam's windshield, rendering the wipers useless. Cricket had turned the radio to a station out of Topeka that was sharing regular updates on the weather.

"Sam, could you—"

"I swear, Rain! I'm barely going twenty miles an hour."

In the back seat, Marie said, "My family road-trips the powwow trail, coast to coast. I've been through worse than this." Comforting words, but then again, Marie's parents were much more experienced drivers. They probably wouldn't have turned onto this remote country road with zero visibility—like Sam had—just because GPS told them to.

Suddenly, the wheels hydroplaned, sliding at an angle, out of control for a breathless moment. Rain, Marie, and Hughie held on to one another in the back seat.

Cricket braced herself against the dashboard. *"Sam!"*

The rosary swung from the rearview mirror. Then, thankfully, the pavement gave way to a stretch of gravel that afforded traction. Sam slowed to a stop. "Take it easy." He was rigid, gripping the steering wheel. "Everything's under control."

As the radio DJ warned drivers against proceeding into rising water, Hughie's phone vibrated. "My mom. She wants to know if I'm out in this mess."

"I'm surprised she doesn't already know you're out in this mess," Rain said. "I'd expect Aunt Georgia to call and check on whether we got home safe."

Up front, Cricket cleaned her eyeglasses on her shirt-tail. "I told you to go back the way we came. Now we're lost."

"We are *not* lost," Sam said, straightening the car in his lane. "Yes, it's possible that we turned onto private property, but we're *somewhere* between Lawrence and old town."

"Pull over," Marie said. "You can't see anything."

Hughie checked the storm's trajectory on his screen. "No flash flood warnings. It should pass soon. We can wait it out. Make sure we're far enough off the road that nobody hits us."

Sam veered off and parked. He shut off the high beams and, after a moment searching, turned on his hazard lights. He gestured at the GPS. "We're on the edge of Killer Crow Arch Park. I know how to get to the crossroads from here."

The deep darkness of the remote field felt isolating, oppressive. Lightning illuminated falling water. Thunder boomed. "There's a ghost story about the bridge at this park," Hughie said, hoping they didn't end up stuck in the mud. "At Harvest House, we're re-creating—"

"Is this information we need right now?" Rain asked, and Hughie took the hint.

Sam put on a pop radio station. "As long as we're here, are we going to talk about what Paige told us? Where did all those birds come from? Why would they fly *in between* her and the creeper? What about the face of the ghost girl that appeared in the air?"

"Take a breath," Cricket said. "Birds . . . Birds are everywhere. It was dark, and the wind was blowing. Paige is a poet. She thinks in metaphors. Her imagination—"

"Power of suggestion," Marie added. "People routinely come in and out the pub's front door joking about the Crossroads Ghost legend. It was probably on her mind. But it's deeply disturbing to think a guy has been scaring girls for so long so close to where I work. What if he decides scaring isn't enough? What if he's already gotten more aggressive, and we just haven't found out about that yet?"

"Let's look at the pattern," Cricket said. "Break it down. If we assume Ximena and Paige had run-ins with the same guy—which seems fair given that their stories match up—then he's somebody who's been around the pub near closing time."

"Not just Ximena and Paige," Hughie added. "The girls who commented on the video and, well, who knows how many of the other stories flying around—"

"Did anyone hear that?" Sam asked, using his sleeve to clear the foggy windshield.

"It's the wind," Cricket whispered beside him.

Hughie's phone screen flashed a tornado watch alert. "What's the wind?"

"No," Sam replied. "There was a flapping noise."

"Like wings?" Cricket asked.

"Back to the creeper," said Marie, letting go of Hughie's arm. "He could be Mr. Boucher, Karl, or even the Vogel brothers. *Any* regular customer. A late-night barfly."

"Paige didn't think it was Karl or Boucher," Rain said.

"What about Ximena's ex-boyfriend, Justin?" Sam asked. "That night, he—"

"I know you're not his biggest fan," Hughie said, lightly bumping his shoulder against his cousin's. She was being quiet. "And I know he and Ximena were having their issues. Except, think about this: Why would Justin have gone after Paige so many months earlier—or anyone else for that matter?" After a pause, Hughie added, "I do hear flapping."

"Valid point," Sam put in. "But all along, he's—"

"It's not your sister's ex-boyfriend!" Hughie exclaimed.

"Fine!" Sam replied, withdrawing. It wasn't like Hughie to snap at him.

They were all tired, their nerves raw. Hughie wished they could continue the conversation the next day instead. Somehow the cheerful beat of the song on the radio was making it worse.

"What about the antiques store and Christmas store?" Cricket asked. "There's that garden center down the road. Do you think—"

"Eh," Marie said. "The shops are all run by middle-aged women, and they lock them up tight at six p.m. sharp. Plus, so far as we know, none of the incidents have happened during the day or even during the dinner rush. They're always late at night, when the parking lot across the street from the pub is nearly empty."

"I worked at the plant nursery this summer," Sam reported. "The owners are a husband-wife couple in their early sixties. Super nice. They're keeping the place open until ten o'clock for pumpkin sales to attract the pub's after-dinner—"

Thwap! Everyone screamed as something white, fleeting, and terrifying slid across the windshield. Cricket exclaimed, *"What was that?"*

Meanwhile, Sam fumbled to crank down his window for a glimpse at the would-be monster, caught on the brush alongside the road. "It's . . . it's a plastic bag."

"Not a ghost," Rain whispered. "Just the ongoing destruction of the planet." Which was in no way funny, but a huge tension release, and they all laughed.

"The storm is letting up," Marie observed out loud. Hughie pulled up the weather radar on his app. Rainfall had lightened from torrential to steady.

Sam shifted the car into drive. "Did you not hear Paige? I'm not saying that the legend isn't ridiculous or disrespectful." He slowed as they crossed Killer Crow Creek Bridge. "But what if Paige saw what she said she saw and there is a real ghost and it . . . did something to those animals? Like how Ximena said the coyote was possessed. The coyote scared her, but it went after the creeper. What if it was trying to help her like the birds helped Paige?"

Nobody answered. Despite himself, Hughie was scanning out the windows for any sign of a Lady in White. Sam was clearly frustrated. "If you think my sister and Paige made up—"

"Nobody is saying they're lying," Marie interrupted. "They were stressed. It was dark and windy. Your mind can play tricks on you. We all just screamed at a plastic bag."

7 DAYS UNTIL HALLOWEEN

"It's been pointed out that since I eliminated the Grim Reaper, the name *Harvest House* has lost some of its . . . harvest flavor." Ms. Fischer had settled for mounting a scythe horizontally above the entrance. On Saturday morning—exactly one week from Halloween—she gestured to the flatbed truck parked in front of the building. "Let's see what we can do about that. You boys haul these hay bales out front and build a couple of scarecrows. You'll find some old clothes in those paper bags. You can use that stack of newspapers to stuff them. Then when you're done, head up to the attic and help Kelsey set up and secure the crossroads photo-art installation."

Neither Hughie nor Sam was well muscled, and the hay bales weighed between fifty and a hundred pounds. "Whoa!" Sam exclaimed on the ramp attached to the truck bed. "Slow down!"

"I'm trying!" Hughie replied. "It's called *gravity*." Both were doing their best to ignore the fact that the Vogel brothers were making fun of them across the street in front of the pub.

"Stop, stop!" Ms. Fischer rushed over. "Put those down. I don't want you boys getting hurt." As they complied, she noticed Jonas and Elias being obnoxious. Ms. Fischer turned back to Hughie and Sam. "You two jump off and leave that there." Heading toward the road, she called to the Vogels, "Jonas, Elias! That's right, I'm talking to you. Haul your lazy butts over here and get these hay bales off the truck or I'm telling your uncle Karl what's what."

Hughie and Sam grinned at each other, hopped off the ramp, and waved.

"They'll probably kick our asses for this," Sam said.

"They're looking for an excuse to do that anyway," Hughie answered. "Life's short. Let's build scarecrows. It's not that hard. My dad has made them before."

Sam laughed. "Of course he has!"

Hughie keyed in a web search for how-to instructions. While the Vogels did the heavy lifting in front of Harvest House, Hughie and Sam gathered hammers, nails, and scissors from the back lot. Hughie was feeling pretty good about the day ahead until he read the names— HAROLD RUNNING NOSE, JIMMY DRINKS-A-LOT, CHIEF SPREAD EAGLE, among others—painted on the phony headstones in the Indian burial ground. He could've kicked himself for not seeing that coming. Still, why were so many people so determined to be asshats?

"Hey, Wolfe Man," Sam called, squinting up at the top of the building. "Hughie?"

"*What?*" Hughie replied.

Sam pointed up at the gutter. "Nests. See those gray birds?"

"They're called mourning doves," Hughie said. "Do they stay in Kansas all winter?"

Sam did a search on his phone. "Yeah! Or at least some of them do. That proves—"

"That proves there are birds on the property." Hughie made his way into the burial ground exhibit and bent to pick up a fake headstone. "Which fits Paige's story. Got it."

"What're you doing?" Sam asked, reaching for garden stakes and a ball of twine.

"Turning these around so that no one can read them."

"Wolfe Man, take it easy. They're trying to keep things light for the kids."

"*Whose* kids?" Hughie shot back. "If that's the way you feel, go on, and I'll catch up."

"Don't be like that." Sam dropped the supplies on a workbench. "You're not the only one who's got issues, you know. My dad is always complaining about all the people eager to make a buck off Día de los Muertos stuff in the stores, and . . . I'll help you."

By the time the boys circled around the building with their supplies, the hay bales were in position and the Vogel brothers had already left. Sam said, "I've been thinking about Jonas and Elias. They love messing with people, and they hang out at the pub a lot."

"Are you saying they're not only bullies—"

"I'm saying we should dig into it more," Sam replied in a quiet voice. "Especially since my big falling out with them was over Ximena, and she was one of the creeper's targets."

Ms. Fischer was checking the purple and green lighting in front to make sure it was well secured. "Getting chilly," she observed aloud. "I've been watching the long-range weather predictions for next weekend. Cold we can deal with, so long as there's not another big storm. You two know what you're doing, or should I text Oakley to come down?"

Hughie handed her his phone to read the instructions he'd pulled up. He needed to talk to her about what he'd just read on those headstones.

"Not bad," Ms. Fischer said. "But we're going to want jack-o'-lanterns for heads, not pillowcases. Pillowcases aren't scary, and we've got *plenty* of pumpkins to choose from." Ms. Fischer sipped her coffee. "You two are good kids, not like Karl's good-for-nothing nephews. Just let me know if they give you any more trouble."

"They're tight these days, huh?" Sam asked. "Karl and his nephews?"

"Oh yeah, he's been training those boys to fill in for him at the pub. Says he can't take so many hours on his feet. It's bothering his legs and his lower back." It didn't sound to Hughie like Karl was in good enough physical shape to chase young women in the dark of night, but then again, the creeper didn't chase. He creeped. Ms. Fischer added, "Restaurant work is tough. Long hours, a hot kitchen. Jonas and Elias, they don't have it in them, if you ask me. In my opinion, those boys are trouble waiting to happen."

With that, Hughie forced himself to swallow his frustration and disgust. Ms. Fischer already knew how he felt about the burial ground, and right then, if Hughie launched into a tirade, that would squash Sam's low-key questioning effort. Besides, changing Ms. Fischer's mind was starting to feel like a lost cause. Hughie might have to settle for nixing the Crossroads Ghost and turning the offensive headstones around. At least he had hopes that she'd see what he and Sam had done in the burial ground and take the hint.

It wasn't the first time Hughie had been faced with a tough choice. In that moment, the threat to girls like Ximena and Paige—especially Marie—mattered more. Setting his mind to stopping whoever was behind that threat, Hughie pulled a flannel shirt out of one bag. "Do you think the Vogels are really that bad?" He tossed another shirt to Sam. "I mean, they're obnoxious, but . . ."

"Mark my words: Jonas and Elias wouldn't be the first Vogel men with a short fuse, especially when it comes to women. But I'm no gossip, so that's all I'm going to say about that."

As far Hughie was concerned, Ms. Fischer was definitely a gossip, which, given the circumstances, was useful. However, he knew better than to push his luck and decided to try a different angle on the conversation. "Shelby—she's a waitress . . ."

"I know Shelby," Ms. Fischer replied. "She's a hoot."

As the boys buttoned the shirts, Hughie said, "Shelby said something about Karl taking care of his mom."

Ms. Fischer set down her coffee cup to help with the scarecrows. "Mrs. Henrietta Vogel. Goes to my church. Sweetest woman you'll ever meet. The fire went right out of her when she lost the first of her boys. Now she's got three urns on the mantel—two sons gone, and her husband, too. Karl's all she's got left."

"I knew Jonas and Elias's dad," Sam said. "Did you know the other brother?"

Hughie shot Sam a look that urged him to be more subtle.

Sam shrugged as if to say he was trying his best.

"Oh, gosh," Ms. Fischer threaded a six-foot garden stake through the sleeves of the shirt Sam was holding up, to act as a horizontal support. "That was a tragedy. Stefan was the only one to go to college—Kansas State. He wanted to be a veterinarian. Drove into an ice storm coming home for winter break and, well, let's just say it was a blue Christmas."

"That's sad," Hughie said, his anger abating. Louise's boyfriend Joey was a freshman at K-State, and they regularly drove back and forth to visit each other on weekends.

With Sam holding a stick in place vertically, Ms. Fischer

hammered in a second one to make a cross. "Poor Karl, he's a surefire magnet for tragedy. I've talked to God about it. I make sure to mention Karl and his mother in my prayers. She's always been such a sweetheart. I think Mrs. Vogel was more upset than I was when he dumped me."

"*Karl* broke up with *you*?" Sam exclaimed, sounding shocked.

Ms. Fischer's smile was bittersweet. "I appreciate your seeing it that way, but Karl is a shell of what he once was. That sexy, hot-tempered boy I fell in love with, it's like I lost him after the first time he lost a brother. Karl was never the same after that."

Hughie couldn't imagine losing a sibling. He didn't want to consider the possibility of life without Louise. He felt awful for Karl and for Karl's mother, too.

Once the scarecrows had been secured with twine and artfully posed with bendable wire and bendable wire mesh, Hughie and Sam excused themselves for a break at the pub.

At the busy hostess stand, Hughie thought Marie looked lovely in her white tee, black jeans, and beaded loop earrings. The streak of yellow mustard across her table-busing apron only added an extra dash of panache. She led the boys over to Grampa Berghoff, who was seated by himself at a two-top, reading the old-town newspaper. Blessedly, there was no sign of Jonas or Elias, who must've moved on for the time being. Marie asked Grampa, "I've got to go take care of that couple who just walked in. Could you tell Hughie and Sam what you told me?"

"Glad to," Grampa pushed aside a plate of fried cauliflower and ranch dipping sauce. "Marie was asking me about local history: the legend of the Crossroads Ghost."

From the way Sam straightened in his chair, Hughie could tell that his friend felt validated that it was Marie who'd raised the question. Up until now, the two had been leaning toward the opposite sides on whether the ghost might be real.

Grampa cleared his throat. "People have been telling ghost stories around these parts for a while, but now that I think on it, the stories sprang up after a young lady disappeared. Might be a coincidence. I might even be misremembering the timing—it's been so long. But as I recall, it wasn't *that* far back—the mid-eighties. Some people are stuck on the foolish notion that all the Indians died off before nineteen hundred, so they like to tell ghost stories set in the distant past, but don't you kids believe everything you hear. The story changes every time someone tells it." He caught Sam looking at what was left of the appetizer, and added, "You boys can finish that off for me. Anyway, I recall it was around Christmastime. A young American Indian woman went missing. A college student, might've still been a teenager. The way I heard tell it, she was bright, had a loving spirit. A promising future. Such a shame."

"So the Crossroads Ghost *is* real!" Sam exclaimed.

"A girl who went missing was—*is*—real," Hughie countered.

"I don't know how the crossroads got mixed up in the story." Scratching his bearded chin, Grampa added, "Or the talk about men wandering in the night and vengeful forces of nature. But the real-life girl was last seen fueling up a truck at that gas station by the mini-golf course in old town. Everyone talked like it had to be murder, but hand to God, nobody knows what happened for sure. The sheriff at the time seemed to think she'd run off with some boy, but her family and friends insisted that she never would've left them without a word. It just wasn't like her.

"The girl's people came up from Oklahoma. They tacked flyers to every bulletin board and telephone pole in the county. My church congregation was out looking. My late wife, bless her soul, helped organize and made sandwiches for the search parties."

Sam asked, "Do you remember the girl's name, or how old she was?"

"It's been a long time," Grampa Berghoff said. "I think maybe it was Estelle or Cecily. Sorry, kids. I can't say for sure."

Still, that was more information than the boys had had only moments earlier. After thanking Grampa, Hughie waved Marie over and asked if she had a minute to talk in private. Mr. Boucher was in the break room posting the shift schedule, so after she called to Shelby to watch the front door, Marie pulled Hughie into one of the two single-stall restrooms.

"A girl went missing in the eighties," he said. "A Native girl."

"I heard," Marie replied. "But Hughie, we can't get too carried away. We have nothing to prove she was connected to what happened to Ximena and Paige. That would be a *huge* stretch. The fact that her going missing might have turned into a cheesy ghost story doesn't mean she ever set foot at the crossroads."

Someone out in the hallway rattled the locked door-knob, and they ignored it. The restroom walls were decorated with framed vintage Coca-Cola ads that featured white women with hourglass bodies smiling while holding up bottles of soda. A small, boxy window was covered in white eyelet lace curtains, and the scent of lavender air freshener was palpable. "The suburbs are new," Hughie said, thinking aloud. "The Grub Pub—the businesses at the crossroads . . . back in the eighties, they were considered *way*, *way* out in the country."

"They're still out in the country now," Marie said. "There's just not as much of it."

He pulled out his phone and did a quick search. "In Kansas, 'the Hispanic population' has gone up almost sixty percent—wow, that's a lot—in the past twenty years. I don't know what it was in the eighties, but I'm guessing—"

Marie said, "Queen, Dmitri, and I stand out at school

in old town. So does your cousin, though not as much. Last week a teacher asked Rain if she was part Japanese."

"A teacher, really?" Were teachers even allowed to ask questions like that?

Hughie glanced at his vibrating phone. It was Sam, pointing out that Ms. Fischer was expecting them back on-site.

Someone knocked on the bathroom door. "Anytime now!"

Marie flushed the unused toilet and called, "Just a minute!" Moving to wash her hands in the sink, she added, "I hate to say it, but what if we assume the creeper is connected to the girl who went missing? That's a long time line. And what if he's stepped up his creeping over the years because now there are more girls around here who're his physical type?"

"Like you," Hughie mumbled.

"I know, I know," she replied, rinsing. "Look, I'm not loving this job. I get called 'honey' a lot—not sweet-Elder-grandma 'honey,' but drunk-leering, old-enough-to-be-my-dad-pervert 'honey.' Beats me how Shelby puts up with it. The only reason I'm still working here is because I want to help to stop this guy."

It was the fastest Hughie had ever heard her talk. "Okay."

The wall dispenser was out of paper towels, so Marie flapped her hands to air-dry them. "And I hope we're making some progress. You and Sam show up and voilà!

I serve up an order of information. But it's not easy. Jonas Vogel checks out my butt every time he breezes in, and the lady in charge of the historical society wants to know what flavor the hummus is—does hummus even have flavors?—and the two-top of sixty-somethings next to him is talking sexy to each other and I had to tell them to keep it down without ruining the mood because they really are kind of cute and we're talking murder, Hughie, *murder*—because *missing* isn't going to get you to *ghost* without *dead*. Not that I believe for sure that we're talking about a real ghost, but *what if*."

Marie was spiraling. He'd done that a time or two himself. "Do you need a hug?"

"Yes. No. I don't know."

Whoever was outside the door started pounding on it, and they yelled, "Shut up!"

Marie added, "On second thought, yes to the hug. A firm yes."

"Would it help if I kissed you?"

Marie frowned. "It might. Yes. Let's try—"

If Hughie had had the presence of mind to consider it, the pub restroom wasn't the most romantic backdrop. The pounding on the door wasn't the most romantic soundtrack. Worse, he and Marie had once again been discussing a *horrible, frightening, dire* subject. And the lavender air freshener was making him queasy.

Not that it mattered. His lips were soft, and so were hers. Hughie's fingers flowed into Marie's thick, soft hair.

She tasted like peachy mint, wry humor, and welcome . . . at least, until his pinkie got caught in her loop earring and broke it, sending seed beads tumbling to the tile floor and bouncing in all directions. "I'm sorry! I'm clumsy. Clumsy and cursed. I always spill those little beads!"

"Calm down. I can fix it." Marie wiped her moist hands on her pants and took off what was left of the earring. "That was a very good kiss. I feel much better now." She tilted her head. "Am I your first significant other, Hughie?"

"Uh, yeah." She was his *significant other* now? Spectacular!

After Marie's shift, she and Hughie caught a ride to old town with Kelsey, who dropped them off at the *Hannesburg Weekly Examiner* building. They'd texted Rain about the missing girl from the 1980s, and she'd suggested they come by to do some research. Sam had wanted to come along, but his mom had texted to remind him about his German test. "You'll let me know the minute, the microsecond you find anything out," he'd implored. "You promise. You swear."

They'd promised; they'd sworn.

Partly because Rain's sister-in-law was the news editor and partly because Rain was the second-best photographer in old town (after her grandfather), she interned for the newspaper during the summers and school breaks and on an occasional basis during the school year. Of late, the newsroom walls had been painted a buttery cream, and the industrial tile had been covered with high-traction, blue-gray carpeting, a fact that Hughie knew only because Rain had been complaining about liking it better the old way—grungy with wood paneling. She'd explained that the new owners cared more about appearances and profits than supporting editorial and photography staffers and leaned too heavily on wire service stories and community phone pics.

The small community paper was a shadow of its glory days. The advertising section was bigger than News. That, plus Sports and Announcements—births, engagements, weddings, and deaths—kept it in business, along with an aging readership that had an abundant interest in their neighbors and a dedication to griping about one another in letters to the editor.

The rest of the staff had left for the day. But Rain had a key to the building (and a key to the darkroom because she preferred shooting film to digital) and had propped it open for Hughie and Marie. "How's it going?" asked Marie.

Rain glanced up from a boxy desktop computer. "Not all the files survived various generations of tech updates. But if the *Examiner* covered the girl's disappearance—and we should've, since she was last seen here—there don't seem to be any follow-up stories from the past twenty years or so. We need to go back further."

Rain got up and crossed the room to a door labeled MORGUE.

Following with Marie, Hughie asked, "Is this where y'all keep the bodies?"

"Something like that," his cousin replied. She flipped on a wall light switch, and they continued downstairs to the basement. "It's an archive. Like I said, we don't have hard copies of every issue ever published. Things get lost. There was a fire in the nineteen fifties. What's the time line again?"

"Mid-eighties," Marie replied with a sneeze.

"Sorry about the dust." Rain said. She used a step ladder to scan the shelves and handed Hughie three stuffed manila folders labeled CRIME 1980–1989. "Here you go, cousin! Marie, could you check the Ms to see if there's a missing persons category?"

There wasn't. The trio divided up the folders of clippings, several of which were out of sequence or had jump lines with the continuation clip of the article missing.

About half an hour in, Hughie mused, "Lots of burglary."

"More disturbingly, lots of *gun* burglary," Marie said.

"Even more disturbingly," Rain added, "this gun burglary address is the same as this domestic-abuse call address."

"Hang on!" Marie exclaimed. "Here's a missing . . . goat. Never mind."

Using a couple of pushed-together wooden desks for a work surface, they skimmed column inch after column inch, page after page.

Hours went by. Marie yawned, which started everybody else yawning. Rain read aloud a couple of joking texts from Queen, who was worried that her performance in rehearsals was skewing more to Lily Munster than Morticia Addams. Hughie turned on an old radio on top of one of the shelves and turned up Kelsea Ballerini's "Miss Me More."

"Hey!" Marie said, perking up. "Celeste Highfield . . . this could be her!" Skimming the article, Marie added, "She worked at the pub, so there's a definite crossroads connection."

The cousins moved to stand behind Marie, peering over her shoulders at the bound copy of newspapers from 1985, from the week of December 22.

Missing KU Freshman Last Seen in Hannesburg
by *The Examiner* staff

Sheriff David Koch announced Saturday that Celeste Highfield, 18, of Oklahoma City, was last seen around 9:30 PM Dec. 20 at the Phillips 66 Car Wash in Hannesburg.

Margaret Burnham, who was working the cash register, said Highfield had come inside to pay for gas and bought two cups of coffee to go. "That night we had a real cold snap," Burnham said. "An ice storm was coming in, but it hadn't hit yet. I remember her being polite and bubbly. She had on a pretty, white sweaterdress under her coat, like she'd been to a holiday party. She was in a pickup truck, but I'm not sure if she was driving it or a passenger."

Highfield is a freshman at the University of Kansas and works part-time at the Grub Pub at the crossroads. Koch said that anyone with information about her whereabouts should contact his office immediately. High-field's family has offered a $2,000 reward.

Rain rubbed her forehead. "You know, Sheriff Koch retired ages ago, but he goes to First Baptist." Glancing at Hughie, she added, "Never misses a Sunday morning service."

Hughie felt the weight of Marie's shoulder against his. "We talk to him tomorrow?"

"He talks to *us* tomorrow," Hughie's cousin replied.

After the cousins walked Marie to her front door, they moseyed through the historic residential neighborhood to Rain's house. The homes varied in size from tiny cottages to regal two stories with wraparound porches, some of which had seen better days. The Halloween decorations skewed to handmade: construction-paper ghosts and black cats taped on the insides of antique glass windows, or a mix of colorful gourds arranged with jack-o'-lanterns.

As Hughie and Rain strolled down the uneven sidewalk, he could've sworn that one set of country curtains after another rustled as they passed by. Pausing at a stop sign, Hughie could hear a train whistle in the distance.

When they arrived at Rain's house, the living room sofa had been made up into a bed for Hughie. Someone had laid out an old T-shirt and shorts belonging to Rain's big brother. The clothes would hang off Hughie, but they'd be comfortable to sleep in. In their family, anybody's house was pretty much everybody's house. Anybody's stuff was pretty much everybody's stuff.

Hughie always felt at home at Rain's. If Harvest House was supposed to be a monster of the prairie, this was the place you ran for safety. An authentic farmhouse that old town had grown up around, it was decorated in family quilts and dark-wood furniture with deep cushions, brightened by antique-white walls topped by stenciled borders. There was a hint of pumpkin spice in the air that Hughie traced to a blown-out candle.

"Tired?" he asked, quietly so as not to wake his toddler cousin, Rain's niece.

"More like wired," Rain replied, setting her camera bag on the dining room table in the adjacent room. "I'll make us hot chocolate."

A couple of minutes later, when Rain found Hughie on the screened-in porch, he held out his phone to her. "Look what I found." Together, the two studied the website:

MISSING CELESTE HIGHFIELD. The photograph of Celeste online looked sharper than it had in the newspaper, and it was in color, too. Her dark hair fell well past her shoulders, and the sides had been curled out and back. She wore a royal-blue sweater with a lace collar. A heart-shaped silver charm on her necklace read BEST FRIEND.

If Hughie had to guess, he'd say it was Celeste's senior photo from high school. At the time she disappeared, she'd been five four and eighteen years old. She'd liked movies (especially *E.T. the Extra-Terrestrial*) and had been a competitive swimmer. She didn't wear prescription glasses or have any tattoos, but she was allergic to penicillin, and she had a scar through her left eyebrow from a sledding accident when she was six.

"She was loved," Rain whispered, settling beside her cousin on the porch swing.

"She is loved," Hughie said, reaching for hope.

He clicked to study additional photos of Celeste, fishing with a toothless bulldog (both of them in sunglasses), posed in front of a Christmas tree with two girls he assumed to be sisters or cousins (all in holiday pajamas), marching in a school flag team uniform, and waving with an Elder from a carnival Ferris wheel. Hughie and Rain watched videos of Celeste's teary friends and family—pleas for help bringing her home. Her best friend, Danielle, was wearing a heart-shaped BEST FRIEND necklace—exactly like Celeste's—and holding a plush toy E.T. doll. "I still talk to you, even though you're not here," Danielle said.

"Are you okay?" Hughie asked, taking back the phone. Rain had more and deeper experience with grief.

"I'm not *not* okay," she replied. "Who're you texting?"

"My mom. I'm reminding her to bring my church clothes when she and Dad drive in tomorrow, and I'm asking if she'll use her Indian Country contacts to find out whatever else there is to know about Celeste's case. You know, the kind of stuff people don't tell the media but they'll tell their cousins."

To lighten the mood, Hughie showed Rain a picture from his mom of Frodo and Bilbo sleeping on their backs, curled at odd angles, sprawled across the middle of his parents' queen-size bed. The text read *The hounds are taking over. Without you, we're evenly matched!*

Rain said, "Tell her hesci!" Rain's black Lab, Chewie, was curled up on the thick braided oval rug at their feet. It never ceased to amaze Hughie how dogs could be flailing, bouncy bundles of joy one moment and so comfortably unconscious the next.

"Sam is convinced that there's a ghost at the crossroads," Hughie said, hitting send. "Since we talked to Paige, I'm leaning more that way, too. What's your take? Do you think that someone could be . . . ?"

"Haunting the place?" Rain slurped a marshmallow. "Is this a religious question?"

"Only if you want it to be," Hughie said, giving her space. "It could also be a story question. Remember when we were talking about my theater script, which—don't ask—and you said, 'All stories somehow spring from stories that came before them'?"

"I said that?" Rain asked. "How smart of me! How do you even remember that?"

"I'm an actor." He appreciated that the cocoa was dark chocolate milk, not flavored water. His digestive system didn't love dairy, but his tastebuds sure did. "I pay attention to lines. Memorizing comes easy to me. I know you're a sci-fi geek, and ghosts are paranormal, but—"

"Hang on," Rain said. "There have been ghosts on *Star Trek*, and Force ghosts in *Star Wars*, and lots of ghosts in *The X-Files*. Let me think about it and get back to you."

6 DAYS UNTIL HALLOWEEN

"Are we seriously ambushing a sheriff at church?" Hughie whispered to Rain as they perched side by side in a wooden pew before the Sunday morning service.

"Absolutely," Rain said. "Except he's been retired since before we were born, and we're just going to ask him a few friendly questions." She tugged the sleeve of Hughie's dress shirt. "There he is now. Let's move."

They had only a few minutes before service would start. Louise hadn't made it that morning, and the rest of their family was too busy visiting to notice them slipping away.

The retired sheriff was a trim man in his early eighties with a neat gray mustache and a spry wife ten years his senior. They'd chosen a pew in front of the piano and next to one of the long, rectangular stained-glass windows.

"Let me handle this," Rain said. "He's on my grampa's bowling team." That was fine by Hughie. This was still his first year at First Baptist, whereas Rain had grown up in the church. She began, "Good morning, Mr. and Mrs. Koch. You remember my cousin, Hughie, from Texas."

After the appropriate nods and greetings, Rain added, "Sir, may I ask you a few questions about local history for a project I'm working on?"

Hughie forced a neutral expression. Rain hadn't lied about anything, but it would've been more than fair for the Kochs to assume she was talking about a school assignment. He remembered what Rain had said the other night about the benefits of being a light-brown girl from a family with long-standing ties to the community.

Meanwhile, Rain launched into an explanation about how she was tracing the roots of the legend of the Crossroads Ghost and said that her grandfather had connected it to a missing persons case from Mr. Koch's days as old town's sheriff. "Really, anything that you could tell me would help," Rain said, folding her hands in her lap. "It sounds like such a sad story."

Ex-sheriff Koch smoothed his mustache. "Yep, I saw a lot of tragedy over the years. As I recall it, the missing girl in question, Sally—"

"Celeste," Hughie put in, unwilling to stop himself. "Celeste Highfield."

"That's it," Mr. Koch agreed. "Thank you, son, my mind's not what it used to be."

"You can say that again," his wife added with a *humph*.

The piano started up, and Rain nudged, "The missing girl?"

"As I remember it, she was there one day, gone the

next. The trail went cold fast. I figure she might've run off with a boy or got mixed up with drugs. That's the way of the world. But be that as it may, she was over eighteen, a legal adult. We did all we could under the circumstances."

Hughie rested his forearm on the back of the pew in front of them. "What about the truck? Was it hers? Did you track it down?"

"Truck?" Mrs. Koch echoed. "What truck?"

"The pickup Celeste was last seen in at the gas station by the mini-golf course," Rain clarified. "It was mentioned in an article about Celeste in the *Examiner*."

"Oh, that's right, you take pictures for the paper," he replied, his gaze landing on the American flag up front, behind and to the left of the pulpit. "That was a right dandy one you took of me marching in the Fourth of July parade this past summer." Nodding toward his wife, he added, "This one's always had an eye for a man in uniform."

"Did the pickup truck turn up?" Hughie asked. Services would begin any minute.

"Like I say, it's been a while, but Celeste didn't own a truck. Who knows, maybe she stole it or borrowed it or was catching a ride that night."

"That poor little girl," his wife said. "Did you look into it, Davey? Did you try to find out whose truck it was?"

Mr. Koch's silence lingered for a moment, then another, until a piercing wail rose to the rafters. Hughie recognized it as the frustrated cry of his toddler cousin.

Hughie almost envied the tot, being able to fully express how she felt.

"If you'll excuse us," Rain said to the couple, "we should get back to the family."

After he returned to their pew, Hughie prayed for all the Celestes who, over so many years, had been failed by so many Sheriff Kochs.

That night, Mom peeked out through Hughie's window. "Bedtime."

Adjusting his binoculars, he replied, "Want to come out here?"

"On the roof?" she exclaimed. "You know I'm not thrilled about you going out there, let alone inclined to do it myself."

"But with all these skeletons crawling around, it's a party!" he teased. "Besides, tonight I scared the heck out of a neighbor just by waving at him." Hughie left out that he'd borrowed the bony hand of one of his father's decorations to do so.

Mom compromised by perching on the windowsill, keeping most of her body inside. "Are you cold out there? Do you need a sweater? Is your homework done?"

When people became parents, was a questions chip implanted in their brains? "No, my sweatshirt is fine." Hughie was leaning back, his legs spread in front of him. It looked like a skeleton with glowing red eyes was about to lunge over the gutter and grab his ankle. "And yes, French history—lots of guys named Louis, showy architecture, zesty about the guillotine."

"Zesty?" his mother repeated.

"That's what my teacher said."

"I wanted to let you know," Mom said in a gentle voice, "that Celeste's family suspects foul play. They're hoping that Koch was right and that she ran off, but so far as they knew, she was loving college and making friends." Hughie rubbed his eyes as Mom added, "The longer someone is gone, the less likely it is they're going to turn up again. There's been no paper trail, no electronic trail. I'm sorry, baby. I wish I had better news."

Hughie couldn't help thinking of his big sister at KU. She was a freshman, too.

"The family is Muscogee, and they're recent Choctaw descendants," his mother added.

It wasn't that surprising that Hughie and Celeste shared a tribal affiliation. The Muscogee were among the largest tribal Nations in the United States; Kansas and Oklahoma—where the Tribe was located—were border states, and Douglas County had an active Indigenous community. As he thought it over, Hughie had a sudden half memory of a Mvskoke voice on the wind that sunny September day when the dachshunds ran into oncoming traffic.

Mom reached out the window, and Hughie reached back for her. She gently squeezed his hand. "I'll be downstairs studying at the kitchen table if you need to talk."

Hughie spent another hour, maybe two, staring at the moon and stars. Then he crawled back through his bedroom window and went downstairs where Mom was waiting with a hug.

5 DAYS UNTIL HALLOWEEEN

On Monday after school, Hughie returned home to hear familiar voices coming from the laundry room. "You could've done your wash at my house," Shelby said.

"I can't pick up my sweaters at your house," Louise replied.

When he peeked in, the best friends were folding laundry. "Hesci!"

Louise squealed, dropping a handful of socks, and swept him into a huge hug. "Hughie! I miss you so much! You haven't texted me since—"

"Day before yesterday?" he managed to get out. Hughie had sent Louise pics of the scarecrows he and Sam had built for Harvest House. With the interior and exterior decorations finished, Hughie wasn't scheduled to work again until that Friday, opening night.

"I get to see him more than you do," Shelby teased, and Louise let go of her brother and turned back around, hands on her hips, in mock indignation. Shelby grinned and asked Hughie, "Speaking of which, any new leads on the crossroads mystery?"

Hughie started plucking Louise's stray socks off the floor. Given that Marie and Shelby worked together, it was fair to assume Shelby was in the loop on their progress. "We've been trying to patch together a time line. You've worked at the pub for three years?"

"Give or take." Shelby pushed up to sit on the chugging dryer. To Louise, she added, "Your brother is interviewing me. It's adorable."

"Agreed," Louise said, shaking out a long-sleeve Jayhawk T-shirt and laying it on the folding board. She carefully arranged the sleeves. *Click, click, click* sounded with each motion of the board, creating a perfect, stackable square.

Hughie tossed socks into the laundry basket. "You must know Mr. Boucher pretty well. Has he ever said or done anything that made you uncomfortable?"

"He likes to schedule me for both weekend nights," Shelby replied. "Like I don't have a life." She sighed. "Between school and work, I *don't* have a life."

Click, click. "You'll always have me," Louise quipped to her BFF.

"I mean, has he ever said or done anything that felt, uh, threatening or . . ." Hughie struggled to find the right word. "Icky?"

"Lecherous-icky?" Shelby shook her head. "Nah, he's all bluster with the customers and all business with the staff. He does talk down to us sometimes. It's a power trip for him, being the boss. But if he'd ever crossed that line, I would've been out of there ages ago."

Click, click. "We've talked to Ximena and Paige. Shelby, do you know of any other girls from the pub who've had a run-in with the creeper?"

"Hughie, are you being careful?" Louise pressed. "Shelby, are you and Marie being careful? The whole situation is—"

"Don't be a nag," Shelby said, using her fingernails to pick out a neon-green seed bead that had lodged behind one of the dryer's dials. *Click.* "We're leaving work in pairs now, walking each other to our cars at night." *Click, click, click.*

"What about other girls?" Hughie asked. "Has anyone else quit suddenly?"

Shelby set the green seed bead next to her on the dryer and used her fingernails to pick a turquoise seed bead out from a silver shelf bracket above her. "There's a *lot* of turnover in restaurant work, but we're a small staff . . . Why are there tiny beads all over the place?"

Hughie, who'd accidentally spilled his mother's beads the year before, exchanged a quick guilty look with Louise. "Bead fairy?" he joked.

Shelby picked yet another one—yellow—out of her hair. "The creeper targets brunettes, right? Other than Ximena and Paige . . . I'm blanking on whether we've had any other brunette waitresses or hostesses since I started working there. But I don't think so."

"Sorry, Junior Sherlock," Louise said. "I'm afraid you've struck—"

"No, wait!" Shelby exclaimed. "There was this one girl—Emma? Emily? Amelia? She went to Baker University. We overlapped by a few days, then she was gone."

Hughie made a note of that in his phone, and then pulled up the Missing Celeste Highfield website. "Shelby, do you know anything about this girl?"

She slid down, and Louise paused her folding to see what they were looking at.

"Celeste Highfield," Shelby said, reading. "Sorry, I don't remember hearing anything about her." Studying the siblings, Shelby added, "She looks enough like you to be your sister."

Louise took the phone, touched the screen as if she were smoothing Celeste's hair. "Do you think that whatever happened to her has to do with the Crossroads Ghost, the creeper, or both?"

Hughie replied, "That's what my friends and I are trying to find out."

At his bedroom desk, Hughie clicked a meeting link on his phone, and Rain let him in. She and Sam were already there. Marie joined a minute later, and Cricket popped in after that.

"Buckle up, kittens," Cricket said. "I've got news. Rain, can you give me permission to share my screen?" A moment later, a list of names appeared. Eleven, including *Paige* and *Ximena*, in one column. Six were asterisked.

"What are we looking at?" Marie asked.

"A list of all the sixteen- to twenty-five-year-olds I could find who appeared from photos to fit the physical profile targeted by the creeper and—this is key—had tagged themselves at the pub at night on social media. And by the way, people used to be a whole lot less careful about how much they shared about themselves on the web than they are now."

"Genius!" Sam exclaimed. "How long did this take?"

"Many hours, many networks."

"Very journalistic!" Rain said in an approving voice. "What do the asterisks—"

"Those are the ones I found a way to message, asking if they had any info about a series of harassment incidents at the crossroads."

"'Harassment incidents,'" Marie echoed. Hughie could hear Dmitri's worried voice in the background.

"Have you heard back from anyone?" Hughie wanted to know.

"Not yet," Cricket said. "I sent the last note right before we started this meeting."

"All right," Sam said, rubbing his hands together. "We're making progress with witnesses and the time line. Research on the crossroads is ongoing."

Cricket chimed in, "Property title, tax payment status, construction permits—that kind of thing. I'll check to see if the *Examiner* is available on microfiche. And I'm hoping to touch base with construction contractors, too. I want to get a full picture of how it's changed over the years."

"Super-exciting stuff," Sam said, trying—if only out of loyalty to Cricket—to sound convincing. "Now, what about the ghost angle?"

Hughie expected Sam's question to go nowhere, but Rain spoke up. "Not that I have high hopes this will work," she began, "but Cricket, you're a video reporter. Can you meet me at the crossroads later tonight to find out if—between your video app and my still camera—we can manage to capture an image of something supernatural?"

Cricket steepled her fingers. "Something supernatural that *may or may not* exist and, if it does, may or may not be the ghost of Celeste Highfield, who went missing in nineteen eighty-five?"

"Exactly," Rain said.

CELESTE

Not every night is about The Bad Man. He doesn't own the night.

Sometimes, like now, I'm watching out of caution, out of curiosity and loneliness. My visitors brought a beautiful black dog with them, and he's tracking their every move.

If these girls are friends, they're new ones. Their banter is marked by a forced cheer, their voices restrained. "Easy, Chewie," one of them says. "Good dog!"

These girls don't have dark hair that flows into the night. They won't attract The Bad Man, though he's not the only threat in these parts. I stretch what's left of my senses and detect no one else. They're safe, but the dog remains wary, his hackles raised. He's in guard mode.

He senses me, but he's no stranger to ghosts. Good dog indeed.

The girl who first drew my attention . . . her friend calls her *Rain* . . . She seems Indian to me. You can't always tell by looking, but there's something about the way she absently touches her beaded leather-tie necklace, the way she walks and holds herself, her expression, the rhythm of her speech, the smile of her eyes . . . It's all familiar, familial, soothing.

Moving her tripod, she says, "Cricket, I don't want to use a flash—it could attract attention—but I'm not going to get anything without one."

Rain and Cricket, that's who they are. I wonder what it would be like to spend time with them, how we'd all get along together. I long for my girls. I long for my life.

"I've been meaning to ask . . ." Facing the road, Cricket slowly begins turning all the way around again. She's making a movie! I didn't realize phones could do that. I wonder what else I've missed. Cricket says, "You're Hughie's cousin, and Louise is his sister. But when he talks about you two, it's like you're all three siblings."

"Uh-huh," Rain replies, distracted by her camera equipment.

"There was a question in there, but never mind."

"Celeste," Rain whispers. "If you're here, please know you're not forgotten. If you're here, please know we're looking for you."

Looking for *me*?

4 DAYS UNTIL HALLOWEEN

Thick, black plastic sheeting blocked the late afternoon sun. Two red safelights illuminated the darkroom. Hughie felt out of place in Rain's attic. He didn't know what to do with himself in the cozy space that she shared with Grampa Berghoff. So he rested on a wooden stool beside the enlarger to watch as she focused it to make a print. "This may sound weird."

"Go right ahead." Rain had pulled up her light brown hair in a ponytail, out of the way. "'Tis the season for weird." It was October 27. Harvest House would open in three days.

Hughie said, "The other night, when we were walking to your house from the newsroom, I could've sworn that we were being watched."

"That is probably because we were being watched. Everyone is always being watched. Don't get me wrong. This is my hometown, and I love it." The enlarger light clicked on, its clear beam illuminating shades of frosty gray on the glossy photo paper. "But we have our share of what Grampa calls Nosy Nellies. They mostly mean well. They're mostly harmless."

"Do you think they were worried that I—"

"They know we're related. We meet up at church and sit together with the family. You've met lots of our neighbors at our holiday get-togethers and Bierfest. If I was another old-town girl, they might be concerned about my being out so late. Because I'm a girl. Because I'm what they think of as a good girl. But because I'm *me*, they were more concerned about you."

"About *me*?"

"Yes," Rain replied. "Because the last time I was spotted out late at night, alone with a boy, he didn't come home alive." The enlarger clicked off, and it took a moment for Hughie's eyes to readjust to the red light.

That took a turn, Hughie thought. Of course, he'd heard the story before, bits and pieces of it anyway, through family and mutual friends. Hughie had heard about the accident, how a volunteer fire truck had struck and killed a teenage boy crossing the road on its way to put out a blaze caused by fireworks one New Year's Eve. He'd noticed that Rain tended to be skittish when riding in cars, always braced for what might go wrong. But she had never previously confided in Hughie about Galen Owen.

His cousin slipped the print into the tray of developer and carefully rocked it as an image slowly appeared. "Galen's death, it brought up a lot of feelings from when I lost my mom. When you're in mourning—once you're past the blur—the air around you, it gets still. You see things that you might've missed before." Rain took her time, moving the print to the stop bath, let it drip, and then placed it in the fixer and ended with the wash. Finally, she turned on the light, and suddenly, the darkroom was an everyday, old-house attic again.

Rain's smile was wistful. "Galen had this silver cat named Angel, a tabby, that still lives in the neighborhood. I notice her sometimes when I'm thinking of Galen. It's like Angel is watching over me for him. That sounds silly, I know."

It didn't sound silly to Hughie. It sounded comforting. Not for the first time, he considered telling Rain about the overwhelming sense of connection he'd felt to his aunt—to Rain's own mother—at the burial, but that felt wrong somehow. Like, when it came to *her* mother, Rain should've been the one who'd had the spiritual experience.

"I wish people would stop dying," Rain said. "Is that too much to ask?"

It wasn't the kind of question anyone could answer, but Hughie could be there for his cousin, a comforting presence. He could listen with love, and so he did.

Grief was tricky. It could mess with your mind. Last summer Queen had confided in him about how prickly and withdrawn Rain had become after losing Galen, how possessive Rain had seemed of his memory in a way that was so unlike her, how it had created a distance between the girls that persisted for months after he'd died.

Rain continued. "Has anyone ever mentioned that you and Lou lead a charmed life?" At Hughie's perplexed expression, she explained, "I'm not saying it's always easy. We've all got our stuff. But you both seem happy most of the time." With absolute sincerity, she added, "I love that. You're both such good people. You deserve it."

"So do you," Hughie said. "All this talk of ghosts . . ." He was only now realizing how much harder it must've been on Rain than the rest of them. "You can step back, if you want."

"Mvto, Cousin," Rain said. "You know, when I lost my mom and then Galen, I felt so powerless. Like simply surviving, day after day, was the best I could do. Now, what we've taken on together—trying to solve this mystery—it's a way for me to make a positive difference for other girls." Rain hung her latest print and squinted at it, searching the shadows for clues. "But my photos are a bust. I don't see anything spooky or even out of the ordinary."

Hughie was surprised by how much the sudden disappointment in her voice reflected his own. His phone pinged. With a sigh, he said, "Cricket says her video looks normal, too."

Later, they were eating cold leftover fried chicken in Rain's country kitchen while Hughie waited for her older brother to give him a ride home.

Rain asked, "You know how the aunties say you're like your dad?"

"The aunties say that?" Hughie took it as a compliment. "Everyone used to talk about me being 'shy and solid.' Once I overheard Louise tell our parents that I'd make a good accountant."

Rain said, "I think you'd be good at whatever you chose to do. And yes, the aunties say that you and your dad are both goofy and smart and good at taking care of people. But I think you're like your mom, too."

He wiped his mouth. "Are you saying I'm doomed to be a lawyer?"

"I'm saying you could be a lawyer or accountant or actor or astronaut or a scriptwriter, and you'll still make the world better. As far as I'm concerned, Hughie, you have more character than anyone you'll ever play onstage."

It wasn't like Rain to speak so openly from the heart, and it wasn't altogether comfortable for him to hear it. But he understood that she'd been thinking a lot about those she'd lost, and that it was important to tell the people who mattered most how much they meant to you while you still could.

He and Rain might've been young, but Galen had been even younger when he died. Celeste had been young, too, full of life, yet her loved ones had never seen her again.

3 DAYS UNTIL HALLOWEEN

The following morning, before the first bell, Cricket waved hello to Sam and Hughie on the crowded, enclosed bridge of EHHS that connected one section of the school to the other. She'd clearly been waiting for them. "I wanted to tell you in person. One of the women on my list of Grub Pub social media contacts messaged me back."

Seated on a long, sleek wooden bench, Cricket showed the boys a profile picture of a young, athletic-looking woman with a contagious smile, wearing a choker necklace. "Allie Deer—she's a member of the Iowa Tribe of Kansas and Nebraska."

Hughie unzipped his coat as he and Sam sank to either side of Cricket.

She added, "Allie looks enough like Paige and Ximena that—like Hughie was saying on our way to Lawrence—it would be easy to confuse them from a distance or in the dark. Allie was cruising through the crossroads *six years ago*. She stopped at the pub for a bite to eat. Afterward, in the parking lot across the street, she heard a man following her to her motorcycle, calling 'less, less, less.' Same ole, same ole, right? Except get this: once Allie reached the bike, she turned around, rushed the creeper, clocked him with her helmet, and rode off."

"That's assertive!" Sam exclaimed.

"Agreed," Cricket said. "But it's still—"

"Decades after what happened to Celeste," Hughie finished. Of course, it was necessary to put a stop to the creeper. But now that he knew about Celeste, that didn't seem like enough unless doing so would somehow help her, too. "Nothing eerie happened to Allie, nothing unusual beyond being followed by the creeper himself?"

Cricket shook her head, and Sam pointed out, "Ximena and Paige both seemed to have supernatural forces coming to their rescue. But Allie didn't need rescuing."

After school, it was Cricket and Sam who intercepted Hughie on the bridge.

"Hey, man," Sam said. "Read this."

"I found it in my locker," Cricket added.

Today after the final bell, meet me in the supply closet in the school basement. I am authorized to speak on behalf of a woman you messaged about a series of threatening and unexplained occurrences at the crossroads. However, the entire conversation must stay private. Come alone.

"What do you think?" Hughie asked.

"Of course it would be helpful to hear another story," Cricket replied. "But the note itself is pretty theatrical, and it's insensitive to ask a girl to come alone to a secluded area when she's clearly investigating 'threatening and unexplained occurrences' in a secluded area. Big no to that."

"We all go together?" Hughie asked.

"We all go together," Sam agreed.

When Cricket opened the door to the unmarked walk-in closet in the musty, dimly lit school basement, Brooke Johanson raised her gaze from the graphic novel she was reading and snapped the book shut. Brooke was a student library aide, known for her signature look—a blond bob and modest A-line dresses with jewel necklines. Rumor had it that she carried a skeleton key in her bra that could open every door in the school.

Her parents were among the proudest and loudest in the Parent Teacher Organization. Over the past couple of years, they'd advocated *for* banning library books and *against* color-conscious theater casting, and they'd tried to get the *Hive* adviser fired. Their latest target was a history teacher who'd supplemented the textbook with a title by a Black author. Hughie knew from his sister, though, that Brooke didn't share her parents' beliefs and even worked on the q.t. to undermine their efforts. He also knew she enjoyed cultivating an air of mystery.

Catching sight of Hughie and Sam, Brooke reached up

for a silver dangling chain and clicked off the bare single-bulb light. "Excuse me," she said, frowning. "I'll be leaving now."

"Wait," Sam replied, blocking her way. "Did you send Cricket this note?"

Cricket grabbed it out of his hands, tearing the corner. "I can speak for myself." She addressed Brooke. "Did you send me this note?"

"What's it to you?" Brooke hugged her book. "You were invited to a conversation, not . . ." She cast a disdainful look at Sam and Hughie. "A party."

Hughie put up his hands as if in surrender and took a step to the left so that they stood in a semicircle. "We're all here because girls are being threatened. We're all on the same side."

"Are you working with Cricket on the *Hive*?" Brooke asked.

Sam said, "Kind of. Not exactly. My big sister, Ximena, is one of the girls. Maybe you saw her viral video?"

Hughie added, "We're volunteering at that haunted house at the crossroads, and we have friends who work at the pub. We want to put a stop to the creeper."

Brooke pulled the light back on. "Close that door so no one can overhear. If you power down and give me your phones to hold, I'll dial back my cloak-and-dagger routine."

"Deal," Sam said, shutting the door. "Now, what's this all about?"

Hughie and Cricket exchanged a glance—she flashed

disappointment, and he suspected that her voice-recording app had been turned on—but they accommodated Brooke's request.

Brooke set her book and the phones on one of the industrial shelves of janitorial supplies and clasped her hands behind her back. "Cricket, how many people did you message about the crossroads? And did the messages all go out at once, or has this been an ongoing effort?"

"Six," Cricket answered. "All the same day. So far, I've heard from one, not counting whoever sent you. Details of her story overlap with the stories of other girls."

"Hang on." Brooke killed the light. "I hear voices."

As they waited quietly in the dark, Hughie could hear chatter coming from outside the closet, about a confetti cannon, girls' soccer, and the upcoming winter dance. Once the voices faded into the distance, he pulled the light back on. "We think the creeper is targeting brown girls with long dark hair." It bothered Hughie that there was no brown girl in the conversation, since they appeared to be the ones with the most at stake, but who was he to pull Sophie or her stepsister Buffy into all this? Plus, if they got involved, it might put them at risk.

Brooke strode over to the closet door, opened it, looked both ways, shut it again, and turned to face them. "Cricket, do you have those social media accounts bookmarked? Do you have screengrabs of the profiles? Did you save the pics tagged to the pub?"

"Yeah, so?"

"Who else has access to that?"

221

"These two, plus a couple of girls from old town—Hughie's girlfriend and his cousin."

Brooke appeared reassured. "Cricket, if you promise that you'll immediately delete the photos of a specific person you messaged—and that anything I say or she says stays completely, one-hundred-percent between us, no sharing, online or off, definitely not in the *Hive*—I'll arrange a face-to-face meeting."

"I'll have to talk to my editor be—"

"Cricket!" the boys exclaimed. In that moment of frustration, Sam's elbow knocked into the shelf behind him, causing a half dozen individually packaged paper towels to tumble down.

"All right, all right!" Cricket said, shaking her curls. "Take it easy. Agreed. We can discuss freedom of the press another day."

"Good." Brooke opened the door once again. "If my parents and their persnickety friends got ahold of the screenshots, this person could lose their job." She gestured for the boys to exit. "Hughie, Sam, I'm going to ask you to leave now. Cricket and I need to talk, woman to woman. Wait for her outside the pep club storage cage. She'll be there in a few minutes."

When Cricket finally rejoined Hughie and Sam in the school basement, she returned their phones—hers had already been powered back on. Then she held a finger to her lips and led them to the service elevator. "Can you get to school early tomorrow morning, an hour or so early?"

"Sure," Sam answered.

Hughie added, "Now that Sam has wheels, we usually ride together in the morning."

Upstairs, the trio exited the building to the parking lot and got into Sam's station wagon—the boys in the front seat, Cricket in the back. She said, "Brooke is connecting us to someone who was stalked by the creeper back in two thousand seven."

"That's between Celeste Highfield and Allie Deer on the time line," Sam said.

"If it's the same guy, he's been operating for a long time," Hughie added.

Cricket leaned forward. "We can go ahead and rule out Jonas and Elias Vogel—they're our age. Allie's story exes them out."

"But nineteen eighty-five is still more than twenty years before two thousand seven," Sam pointed out. "It doesn't confirm a potential tie to Celeste. It's still possible that her disappearance has nothing to do with . . . anything else."

"You couldn't have told us this *inside* the school?" Hughie asked Cricket.

"Possibly in the elevator," Cricket acknowledged. "Okay, definitely in the elevator, but I *promised* Brooke that I wouldn't say anything until we were out of the building and someplace where we couldn't be overheard." Cricket held up her phone, and the boys leaned in to study a photo of a girl with light brown skin, warm brown eyes, and heavy, long dark hair, toasting the camera lens with a mug of beer. "Say hello to Darla Cachikis."

"She looks familiar," Hughie said.

Sam blinked. "She looks . . . wasted."

Cricket scowled at him. "Say goodbye to Darla Cachikis." With that, she deleted the photo with flourish. "Schneider is her married name. You may know her as our very own EHHS nurse. We have an appointment to meet with her privately tomorrow before school starts."

That night, Hughie accepted a video call from Rain. She was squinting up at the phone camera, lying on the fringed rug in her bedroom, her head resting on Chewie's back. "I've been thinking about your question about ghost stories."

"Ready when you are." Some conversations were best had with a geeky cousin you'd grown up with watching spooky movies from behind sofa pillows.

"Are we dealing with a haunted place, a haunted person, or a haunted object?"

Standing on his back deck, Hughie was grateful for the distraction of the cold air. That night, the temperature had dipped into the upper thirties. Thinking over Rain's question, he watched the dachshunds sprint around the yard, a last chance to do their business before bedtime. Hughie had raked only the day before, and the lawn was already covered with autumn leaves again. "The crossroads is a place. We don't have any repeat victims, but based on the similarities in the girls' stories, we think the creeper is the same guy. As for objects—"

"Hang on," Rain said. "Could the creeper be more than one person? Slasher movies can be tricky that way. After you've ruled out a suspect, it turns out they've been working with someone else the whole time." She sat up to take a sip from a can of cherry Coke, and Hughie noticed the box of Cracker Jack and bottles of orange and black fingernail polish beside her.

"Karl and Mr. Boucher are in the right age range, and they've worked at the crossroads the whole time. I suppose they could be in cahoots."

"Cahoots," Rain echoed, sounding amused by the word.

"It's as good of a theory as any of the others we've got," Hughie said, hopeful that their spitballing would pay off.

"Granted," Rain replied, "ghosts are typically tethered to someone or something—that's what connects them to the mortal plane. Like I was saying, their options are to haunt a person, a place, or an object. In this particular case, the girls keep changing, so it's probably not a haunted person. That's the easiest one to rule out. So we're left with the possibility of a haunted place or a haunted object *at* the place—say, an object at the crossroads that has some significance to the deceased. Or maybe even a haunted object attached to a person who keeps bringing it back."

"There's an antique store located right there," Hughie said.

"That could work, but it doesn't have to scream 'haunted object.' It could be as basic as car keys or a necklace charm."

Hughie thought about it. "When Karl designed the interior of the chicken restaurant, he used old fireplaces and salvage from other buildings. But the original furnishings and kitchen appliances are gone."

"And the pub has been there the entire time," Rain reminded him.

Hughie pondered the possibilities. "What else have you got?"

"A ghost in the machine?" Rain suggested, reaching for a journal to check her notes. "Furnace, electric system? Any reports of blinking lights?" When Hughie shook his head, she added, "Renovations or remodels can supposedly stir up a ghost, too, but the building was pretty much in stasis until Harvest House started up."

"The timing of incidents is all over the place," Hughie said, then whistled to call in the dogs, who ignored him. "It's not like the spookiness happens one day a year or at a certain time of night or during a full moon or . . . If Celeste is the ghost, why would she be sticking around? Why not . . . go into the light or—"

"Become one with the Force? I don't know. It's possible the creeper has something to do with it. But I suspect she's the only one who could tell us for sure."

2 DAYS UNTIL HALLOWEEN

As Sam and Cricket strolled in front of him, swinging their joined hands, past the administrative offices, Hughie did a search of Mrs. Schneider's previous last name, *Cachikis*, and found out it was Greek. Hughie had never visited the nurse's office before, but last spring, Mrs. Schneider had spoken to his phys ed class for a series of sex ed presentations. She'd been frank and funny and fierce at silencing snickers.

Inside, Hughie was impressed by the double-sink cabinetry workstation and semiprivate patient cubicles. His school back in Texas had been built in the mid-1990s. EHHS was still fairly new, and the nurse's office looked like a real medical clinic. "Thank you for coming in early," Mrs. Schneider said with a warm smile. "And for indulging Brooke's covert tactics. She's been babysitting my kids for the last couple of years and knows every secret on the block and in this building. I'm sure to always tip like a Rockefeller. And thank you for agreeing not to share, uh, any photographic documentation of my misspent youth."

She laughed self-consciously, and Cricket rushed to assure her. "Already deleted."

Hughie glanced at the wall clock. The school would come alive soon. "We should get started," he nudged. Mrs. Schneider gestured for them to make themselves comfortable in the brightly lit reception nook, which included two love seats and an armchair with orange cushions around a bright white coffee table. Mrs. Schneider remained standing, pacing with nervous energy. "You know, kids, I wasn't much older than you at the time and . . . Well, you saw the photo—I was pretty sauced that night."

"Sauced?" Cricket echoed from the armchair.

Sam chimed in. "Drunk, intoxicated, tipsy, inebriated, sloshed—"

"I think they've got it," Mrs. Schneider said. "Yes, I was all of that. And again, I was very, *very* young, not to mention carrying a fake ID, and I feel obligated to say you shouldn't take that version of me as a role model. It was spring break at KU, and I couldn't afford to road-trip down to South Padre with my girlfriends. This guy I liked had invited me to listen to his band play at the pub."

Hughie was seated across from Sam on one of the love seats. "You were driving?"

"That was the plan—again, *not your role model*, but . . ." Mrs. Schneider paused in front of a graphic-art poster reminding students to stay hydrated, wash their hands, and sneeze into their elbows. "Let me start over. It was a foggy night, misty and chilly, and after I got across the road, I heard what sounded like a hissing."

"Could it have been the word *less*?" Cricket asked.

"It's hard to say for sure. I wasn't as alert as I should've been. I could still hear music coming from the pub. I turned to look, and there was a man coming toward me, acting like he was injured. To be honest, I didn't feel threatened. It was more like he was disjointed somehow . . . in physical or mental distress. There was this overwhelming sense of desperation about him. I heard what I thought was his voice, but then there was another sound, a wild, feral noise."

"What was it?" Hughie asked, leaning forward.

"A bobcat—a big one. It had to be a full-grown male. I have a twenty-pound house cat, a Maine coon, and it looked more like thirty. The bobcat growled and screamed—the noise was piercing, like a hawk, followed by a guttural, rumbling growl. The hiss may have come from the cat. The way it was acting, so aggressive—I worried it might have rabies."

"Coyote, birds, bobcat," Sam said. "What's next, attack of the squirrels?"

"Not now," Cricket scolded. Addressing Mrs. Schneider, she asked, "Did the man in the fog say or do anything else? Would you recognize a picture of him?"

"I didn't get a good look. I was more preoccupied with the wild animal in the parking lot. It scared me more than he did. I rushed around the empty building, back across the road to the pub, and yelled for help. A couple of men came outside to investigate. We caught a glimpse of departing taillights, but nobody managed to track down the bobcat."

That afternoon, instead of doing homework in her regular booth at the pub, Louise and Hughie sat at the bar, sharing a plate of fully loaded potato skins. According to the news on the TV mounted overhead, the blond, white woman from Pennsylvania was still missing.

The pub's bartender, Millie, said, "I appreciate the company, kids, but it's not like you to sit over here when you could be across the room visiting with Shelby and Marie."

The Wolfes had chosen the spot because Marie had texted saying that Mr. Boucher had decided to do the financial books at the bar on his old-school ledger, and Hughie wanted an opportunity to question him. Louise had been fully briefed on everything and had agreed to come along to help. Sure enough, Mr. Boucher was sitting at the bar frowning at the numbers, a steaming mug of coffee to one side.

"Hey, Millie," Louise began, fishing. "I bet you get a lot of customers who're more interesting than us. Lovelorn types, telling tales of woe?"

"I am a heart mender," Millie said, pouring Hughie

a fountain Dr Pepper. "A heartbreaker, too, make no mistake. But this isn't a barfly kind of place. Or a meat market. We've never even had what you'd call a proper bar fight. The old-timers tend to come and go, looking to shoot pool or shoot the shit. They mind their manners."

Louise's phone buzzed, and she angled the screen so Hughie could read the incoming text from Shelby in the breakroom. According to the message, Shelby had tried chatting up Karl about Celeste in the kitchen, and he'd claimed to barely remember her.

"How're you today, Mr. Boucher?" Louise called down the bar.

"Dandy, thanks!" he muttered. "Going broke as usual."

Louise forged ahead. "You know, Mr. Boucher, I just found out that many years ago, a girl—a waitress—went missing from the pub. Like, *missing person* missing."

Now she had his full attention. "Where'd you hear that?"

While Louise was doing a formidable job of projecting girl-next-door cluelessness, Hughie was making a show of staring at his phone in one hand and casually dipping a potato skin into ranch dressing with the other.

"Turns out my church in old town took part in the search." It was smart of Louise to remind Mr. Boucher that the Wolfes were a churchgoing family, if not for the sake of their shared love for Jesus, then at least for the positive word of mouth among the Sunday brunch crowd. The Wolfes were regular customers, and the family attended one of the more established churches in old town. It was in Mr. Boucher's best interests to indulge her questions.

"I recall the girl's folks coming up from Oklahoma," he said. "Her name was . . . Leslie?"

"Celeste," Louise replied.

"That's it. God-fearing people, Indian people, salt of the earth. I've always had a real respect for the plight of the American Indian. Back when I was a kid, I used to collect arrowheads."

Louise had learned a thing or two about interviewing people during her days as a high school journalist. She simply nodded, taking advantage of how much he enjoyed an audience.

Mr. Boucher added, "I sure felt awful for them, for her, the whole situation. Missed the excitement myself, though. Pops was still the boss back them. I gave him a hand when I could, but between the Army Reserve and long-haul trucking, I kept pretty damn busy back then."

"Thank you for your service," Louise said. "I'm sure your father was a good man."

"The best there ever was," Mr. Boucher agreed. "Maybe a little rough around the edges, but who am I to talk?"

"The missing girl must've weighed heavily on him. Did he ever say anything to you about it?"

"Once." Mr. Boucher's voice grew wistful. "Late one

night at that booth right over there"—he gestured across the dining room—"Pops and I broke out a bottle of scotch whiskey. He had nothing but good things to say about the girl. Pops felt kind of responsible for her disappearance, what with her being so young and his employee. He was real torn up about it. But these things happen. There was nothing he could do."

Hughie sighed and opened his notebook to his English assignment, "The Lady, or the Tiger?" Another dead end.

1 DAY UNTIL HALLOWEEN

Sophie Miller and Hughie didn't go to the movies or football games together. They didn't confide in each other or text memes back and forth. She had no idea how he felt about Marie. He had no idea what her deepest hopes and dreams might be. But Sophie and Hughie talked in the halls, in English class, and whenever they crossed paths at a school event. Chitchat mostly. Sophie and Hughie had high-fived when the *Hive* reported that the West Overland Braves had changed their mascot name to the West Overland Bison, and they had commiserated more than once about what a tough grader Mrs. Qualey was. But Sophie and Hughie weren't always simpatico.

On Friday, when he walked into English language arts and said "Hi," she kept her eyes focused on the marked-up essay on her desk. Hughie didn't think much of it at the time, but it wasn't like Sophie to go all the way through class without signaling that Hughie's presence was appreciated. It wasn't like her to ignore him when he asked what she was doing that Halloween weekend as they were getting up to leave.

Hughie jogged after her down the hall. "Sophie! Sophie, wait." If anything, she sped up. "Sophie!" He knew silence often meant no. No, she didn't want to talk. No, he shouldn't be chasing after her. Normally, he'd give her space. But it hadn't been that long ago that the Vogels had singled Sophie out for bullying, and he worried that she might need his help.

When Sophie turned abruptly and exited the crowded hallway for an interior courtyard, Hughie followed her outside and across several flagstones to a wood-plank bench with concrete legs. It was cloudy, cool. They were the only ones out there.

Turning to face him with one finger raised, Sophie said, "Not a word." She dropped her book bag on the bench. "Is it true that you're on"—she used air quotes—"'the design team' of that haunted house at the crossroads and that there's a racist Indian burial ground that's part of it?" After a moment, she added, "Well?"

"You said 'not a word.'" When that got him nowhere, Hughie added, "Who told you about the burial ground? It's supposed to be a secret until opening night."

"Samir Mitra said that Kelsey Carbunkle was talking it up to a friend of theirs who works the register at the new Hein's Market at the strip mall."

Kelsey, as in Oakley and Kelsey, Ms. Fischer's assistants. Hughie considered mentioning to Sophie that he hated the burial ground, too. That the haunted house was for a good cause. That his personal contribution to the Harvest House design had been the attic, and as a result, he'd managed to nix the inclusion of the legend of the Cross-roads Ghost, aka the stereotypical, tragic "Indian maiden." Hughie pondered explaining that being a volunteer at Harvest House was an excellent cover for low-key investigating the creeper. He thought that maybe he should tell Sophie about what had happened to Paige, Ximena, Allie, and Ms. Cachikis (without mentioning that she was now Mrs. Schneider) and warn Sophie herself to stay away from the crossroads. Instead, he said, "Yeah, I'm on the design team of that cheesy haunted house at the crossroads, and there's a racist Indian burial ground that's part of it."

Fists on her hips, Sophie tapped the toe of her right cowboy boot on a stepping-stone. "FYI, Uncle Tomahawk: it was only *after* Buffy told me about *you*, about how you took a stand on L. Frank Baum's racism last year in the-ater, that I thought *I* could make a place for myself at East Hannesburg High, too. You're a major reason I agreed to transfer here."

Guilt fell like rain. "Sophie, I know how it looks, but the situation is complicated."

"Making fun of dead Indians?" she exclaimed. "What's *complicated* about that?"

The sun would set on the crossroads in about an hour. A dozen grown-ups in Immanuel Baptist sweatshirts were protesting alongside the road, waving signs that read SAVE YOUR SOULS! and DEVIL'S PLAYGROUND! "This is social media gold," Sam said from the driver's seat as they pulled up. "People live to rant about stuff like this on the internet. Take a picture and share it with me. I'll post it later."

Hughie did as he was asked, thinking that—if anything—the protesters added to the ambience of the attraction. "What're they handing out?"

Sam slowed so that Hughie could accept a flyer through the car window. "God bless you," the middle-aged white woman said. "Fight Satan."

"Always do," Hughie replied as the car rolled forward. Scanning the flyer, he said, "There's a competing haunted house in the basement of their church. Instead of ghosts like Harvest House or zombies like that after-dark run in Lawrence, it's supposed to be scary because of . . . demons. Like *inner* demons—drug addiction, spousal abuse, infidelity, lust . . . Cautionary tales, amped to the max."

"For real?" Sam barked a laugh. "Are they *showing* lust and infidelity? Is this an *R-rated* Christian haunted house?" He parked on the far side of the closed shops with the rest of the volunteers, leaving plenty of open spaces for paying customers.

As the boys walked toward Harvest House, Sam blew a kiss to the protesters. Hughie ignored them until a sudden gust of wind sent stacks of flyers into the air. Hughie could've sworn he heard a faint hint of feminine laughter.

"That was weird."

As a sheriff's car pulled up, Hughie asked, "What's Cricket up to tonight?"

"She spent the afternoon going all Lois Lane, poring through building permits, restaurant inspections, boring stuff. Any document that could point us to a potential creeper or trigger a ghost. She's still at it." As if by unspoken agreement, he and Hughie paused in front of the antiques store until the deputy announced that the protesters were trespassing on private property and had to clear out immediately.

Seconds later, Hughie and Sam entered through the exit gate and Kelsey pointed them toward Oakley, who was handing out costumes and badges. As gofers, Sam and Hughie sported basic black T-shirts and jeans. Their job was to be flexible, responsive, and most of all, make sure the show went on. Kelsey said, "You're on ongoing cleanup duty and end-of-the-night cleanup duty. Candy wrappers, beer cans, cigarette butts, whatever—humans are filthy creatures. Plan to stay late to help Ms. Fischer shut down and secure the attraction. She's made a few last-minute tweaks. She may make more. If anything flops, we can change it on the fly. If anything fails to pop, make a mental note. We'll rethink it for tomorrow night."

Even though Hughie had known what to expect, the sight of the fully realized burial ground felt like a punch to the throat. Two dozen chalky-looking, bare-chested Hollywood "Indians" joked around, dancing wildly in cheap, white headdresses (the original multicolored feathers had been spray-painted), with streaks of red decorating their faces. They sported distressed jeans and cutoff sweatpants, dyed brown to mimic leather.

"We're going to freeze our nuts off," one of them griped, and in fact, the temperature that night was supposed to dip below forty. "What happened to the heat lamps?"

"Bad news, proud warriors!" Ms. Fischer replied. "The loaner lamps are a no-show. Keep moving, and you'll be fine." So much for any hope that they'd stay low-key in the mist.

"Hughie!" a voice called. "Hughie Wolfe!" It was Elias Vogel. "Woo, ooo, ooo, ooo, ooo, ooo!" he sang out, creating a staccato sound by tapping his open mouth with his palm.

"Woo, ooo, ooo, ooo, ooo, ooo!" Jonas joined in. "Woo, ooo, ooo, ooo, ooo, ooo!"

Within seconds the rest of the ghost Indians were in on the act. "Woo, ooo, ooo, ooo, ooo, ooo! Woo, ooo, ooo, ooo, ooo, ooo!"

Sam shot Hughie an apologetic look, and they turned their backs on the noise. *Sophie was right,* Hughie thought. He should've walked away from Harvest House. He hadn't made enough of a difference by trying to work with Ms. Fischer. Rain, Marie, and Cricket were investigating the mysteries of the crossroads without tangling themselves up in the horrific scene in the fake Indian burial ground. He should've found a way to do the same.

The boys went over to say hello to the other costumed actors—the 1950s car-crash ghosts (him in a black jeans jacket, white tee, and blue jeans; her in a poodle skirt and formfitting sweater), the 1920s flapper (in a sequined sheath dress, fascinator, and heels), and the Ghost of Killer Crow Creek Bridge (in a flowing white gown).

It was then that Hughie saw her, the *second* Lady in White. Her long, white dress was different—more rustic, made from dyed burlap. He watched as she put on a long, white, Plains-inspired headdress, which trailed all the way down her back to drag the ground. Oakley was helping her pin the headband in place.

"Ms. Fischer!" he called, louder than he'd intended.

"What is it, Hughie?" she replied, hurrying over.

"What's *that*?"

"Her name is Veronica, but tonight she's playing the Crossroads Ghost."

He was flabbergasted. "What about my chicken ghosts in the attic?"

"Wolfe Man!" For some reason, Sam was stepping into a head-to-toe chicken costume. "Oakley says they need us upstairs."

"Don't worry!" Ms. Fischer gave Hughie a pat on the shoulder. "We're still using those! We *love* what you've done. We reassigned you and Sam upstairs so that you'll be able to see for yourselves how much the guests enjoy it. But yes, it's true that we also reinstated the Crossroads Ghost. Putting her in the burial ground makes more sense.

240

You got want you wanted, and so will the crowd! It's a win-win-win for everybody."

Ms. Fischer's last words before the official opening of Harvest House were: "Remember, live audiences are unpredictable. If you must break character to take care of a guest or alert the leadership team, please do it. Be safe, be scary, be ready for anything. And no selfies while we're on the clock!" She concluded by explaining that to reduce the likelihood of drunken Halloween shenanigans, both Harvest House and the pub would close at midnight.

From the haunt's foyer to its attic, hidden speakers played sound effects to reinforce the ghostly settings. Music of the eras accompanied the 1920s flapper and 1950s teen lovers, a howling wind blended with *caw-caw-caw*ing crows at the arched bridge—their cries occasionally punctuated by coos, rattling, and clicks—and the attic soundtrack was an eerie mix of clucking and the oompah song of the "Chicken Dance."

Hughie's mood remained dour. Standing opposite Sam near the top of the side-by-side slides, Hughie could occasionally hear the ghost actors outside below whooping it up. "Woo, ooo, ooo, ooo, ooo, ooo! Woo, ooo, ooo, ooo, ooo, ooo!"

"Tell me again why I don't just quit now!" he said.

"We can't leave," Sam said, clasping his shoulders. "Ms. Fischer is my mom's friend. Plus, we promised. We worked hard on the attic. We've got a mystery to solve, potential victims of the creeper to protect, and it's *Halloween* weekend. Odds are either the ghost, the bad guy, or both will make their presence known."

"Fine," Hughie said. "But I may not be back tomorrow."

"Fine," Sam agreed. "We'll take it one night at a time." It was a very serious conversation for two friends wearing matching yellow chicken costumes.

The boys' new job was to help anyone who needed assistance into a seated position so they could slide from the attic down, down, down to the burial ground.

Meanwhile, the terrorized restaurant chef was played with comic enthusiasm by the former old-town mayor, who shrieked and bellowed at chicken specters flapping, clucking, and squawking on wires above him.

The early evening crowd had been heavy on tweens and family groups. As ten o'clock rolled around, the demographic shifted to high schoolers, college students, and other twenty-somethings. The guests also got rowdier, as zombie runners started showing up from Lawrence and more pub customers came through after a mug or three of beer.

According to Sam, who'd rushed across the street at about nine-thirty for a restroom break, Ms. Fischer was already almost sold out of I SURVIVED HARVEST HOUSE ball caps, bumper stickers, and T-shirts, and had called in an emergency overnight order for more.

"Brilliant!" a familiar voice exclaimed. "All these years, I *knew* my boy took after me, but he's surpassed even his old man. This blows away anything I've ever done."

"Yes, our child is very impressive," an equally familiar voice replied. "Very creative! But this haunted house is an ADA access nightmare—"

"Greetings, parents," Hughie said, his face framed by a giant beak.

"My son!" Dad exclaimed. "You're fowl!"

"We're wowed by you, baby," Mom added, tilting her head. "What's this?"

"Slides," Sam replied. "We're here in case you need help sitting down."

They didn't, but Hughie had a flash of panic about the scene his parents would find waiting outside. As they joined hands for the dark journey, he crouched as low as he could with fake claws protruding from his feet and clunky feathers attached to his booty. "Brace yourselves," Hughie said. "There's a bunch of actors . . . I'd say *in red-face* except they're painted white, pretending to be ghosts. They're dancing around, making goofy war whoops, chasing people." He winced. "There's a fake Indian burial ground down there."

Mom's grim smile would've warmed the hearts of her fiercest fellow Indigenous legal warriors. "I've faced down worse," she said.

After Hughie and Sam helped clean and lock up Harvest House for the night, a text from Cricket invited them to meet up in her finished basement. Cricket's mom let them in, and Hughie followed Sam down the carpeted stairs into

243

a seating area organized around a gas fireplace. No one was there. Then the boys drew back a hanging floor-to-ceiling, charcoal-gray room divider. "Is this a secret head-quarters?" Sam asked. "Like the Batcave or—"

"Looks like it," Hughie said. "A cross between the cave and the Gotham Clock Tower."

Though Hughie and Sam were still in chicken makeup, the girls spared them the obvious jokes. Cricket, Rain, and Marie were lined up in front of three laptops at a curved multiuser desk—the kind you would find in a business reception area or a doctor's office. They were doing simultaneous searches, using a list of questions about the crossroads, about half of which had been marked off.

A small mirror ball hanging from the ceiling gave the space an even more surreal quality, but Cricket was all business. "I've already messaged each of you links to start with."

"Before they dig in, let's take a break and catch everyone up," Marie said, and after a few more keystrokes, the three girls swiveled halfway around in their office chairs.

"Did anything paranormal or criminal happen today?" Rain wanted to know.

"Not today," Sam replied. "But tomorrow is Halloween."

"How about y'all?" Hughie asked. "Find anything interesting?"

"We spent the afternoon researching local sex offenders." Marie stood, wrapping her arms across her body. "Extremely disturbing, like never-leave-your-house-again disturbing."

"Assuming that your house is safe to start with," Rain added.

As the group moved to the seating area by the fireplace, Rain explained that they'd also been doing searches using online databases of newspapers from nearby towns like Lawrence, Baldwin City, and Eudora. Marie added, "Keywords include *crossroads*, *stalk*, *stalker*, *assault*, *ghost*, *paranormal*, *missing*, *murder*—"

Rain said, "The old-town newspaper didn't go online until the early two thousands."

"Too bad the creeper doesn't say something more unique than 'less,'" Hughie mused out loud, taking a seat on the beige love seat. "It's a lousy keyword."

Marie plopped on the couch next to him. "*Why* does he say *less* anyway?"

"'Less, less, less,'" Rain said in a soft voice. "He repeats it over and over again."

Sam shook his head. "Could be he thinks the girls are worth less than him."

"Or worthless—period." Cricket moved to warm her hands by the fire. "Could be he's angry that they're not interested in him. You know, how some guys are, if you're not into them. Just like that"—she snapped her fingers— "they decide you're a bitch."

Database searching was boring, tedious, and so far, yielding no helpful results. It was just after 4:00 a.m. when Sam finally exclaimed, "Found something!" He scrolled up.

"Tell me again: When was Celeste Highfield last seen?"

"December twentieth," Rain, Marie, and Hughie replied simultaneously.

Cricket added, "Why?"

"Because the parking lot of the chicken restaurant was poured on December twenty-third."

HALLOWEEN MORNING

On October 31, Hughie opened his eyes and reached for his phone on the nightstand. It was all lit up with text messages from Marie. *Where R U?* she'd asked five times. *U coming?* she'd asked twice. Hughie checked the time. 9:53 a.m.

As they'd been leaving Cricket's, it was decided that before the pub opened, Hughie and Marie would talk to Karl about the restaurant parking lot, since they were the ones who knew him already. As the young couple had left Cricket's at about a quarter till 5:00 a.m., they had planned to grab a few hours' sleep and then meet in front of the pub at 8:45 a.m. to discuss how to broach the subject and wait for the cook to arrive by nine o'clock for kitchen setup.

Hughie sent Marie a request for a video call, and she answered with, "Hughie!"

"I'm sorry!" He could tell from the background behind her that his girlfriend was leaving the hostess stand, heading for the front door for privacy. "I forgot to set my alarm."

Outside the restaurant, she replied, "We open in about five minutes. I can't talk long. The Halloween chicken promotion is of course today, and I'm working a double shift, and right now I'm looking across the street at the parking lot and wondering *what if* about Celeste and why you didn't *tell* me that Harvest House is still doing the Crossroads Ghost, especially after we found out about— hang on!" Marie smiled at approaching customers. "Good morning! Welcome to the Grub Pub. Please go on in and seat yourselves. I'll be there with your menus shortly." Focusing back on the phone screen, she lowered her voice. "Those awful costumes! Veronica—I know her from old town. She looks revolting! Plus, those half-naked white boys in feathers!"

As Marie ranted, Hughie was panicking because he'd messed up and he felt like he was letting down Celeste, and because Marie was—for the very first time—mad at him.

When he didn't reply, Marie nudged, "Hughie?"

"I'm sorry," he said again, racking his brain for how to somehow fix the situation. "You saw Veronica in her costume?"

"All over social media," Marie said. "I've seen images. I've seen video. I thought you'd decided to stick with volunteering at the haunted house because you were able *to get rid of—*"

"*So did I!*" Hughie ran a hand through his hair. It

would've helped if he'd told her about the Indian burial ground when he'd reached out to Dmitri about making artwork for the attic proposal or even when he'd reconciled himself to tolerating the outdoor set if it meant maintaining a better cover during their investigation at the crossroads. "Except then Ms. Fischer moved Veronica out back. I didn't find out until yesterday, and I thought about quitting, but Sam talked me out of it."

"Are you blaming Sam? Never mind. I have to go to work—now." Marie ended the call.

Hughie ached to rush over to the pub to talk to Marie, but he knew she was busy and thought maybe it was a good idea to give her a chance to cool off a little. Meanwhile, his mind was cycling on the Harvest House parking lot and what—or who—might be under it. With the Halloween chicken special in full swing, though, it wasn't a good time to interrupt Karl in the kitchen to ask about that. So in a way, Hughie was relieved when his parents declared that he needed to go visit Aunt Georgia to "help her out around the house," and he suspected that they had an ulterior reason for doing so.

Aunt Georgia had been the first Elder that Hughie had really connected with after moving to Kansas. They shared a fascination with science and—between her founding the Native youth summer camp and his role in diversifying student theater—they both had a tendency to shake things up.

Hughie wandered into her backyard and settled on the small concrete bench alongside her vegetable garden. He'd offered to help Auntie in the yard, but she'd shooed him off after lunch so that he could work on revising an essay for English language arts. To think, Hughie had entertained the thought of writing a whole playscript. That never seemed so laughable.

Hughie tapped his pen on the notepad. The statue facing him was inscribed SAINT FIACRE, PATRON SAINT OF TAXI DRIVERS AND GARDENERS. "You just couldn't be the patron saint of writers?"

"Going that well, is it?" Aunt Georgia asked, coming through the chain-link fence gate with her parrot, Dolly, on her shoulder. "Leave that be, Hughie, my boy, and come dig in the dirt with me." She bustled to the patio table to pick up a basket of gardening tools and carried it into the backyard. "Let's clean up and tuck in my veggie bed for winter."

Hughie joined her on the soft grass. "Mom told you about Harvest House, didn't she?"

"She didn't have to. That place is the talk of the town. Your mama is more concerned about you and your friends looking into this real-life scary business at the crossroads. If you don't mind me saying so, she's not the only one on edge. Your shoulders are bunched up. I haven't seen you crack a grin since you got here, and you turned down a slice of my pecan pie."

Hughie surveyed the remains of Aunt Georgia's fall

root vegetables—radishes, carrots, beets, turnips, and potatoes. Aunt Georgia herself was wearing a Jayhawks basketball sweatshirt, faded blue jeans, and gardening gloves, and she looked ready to get to work.

As they started weeding, Hughie told her about the strides he and his friends had (and hadn't) made in tracing the creeper to 2007 and the ghost legend to the mid-1980s. He talked about his decision to volunteer at Harvest House with Sam. He shared his thoughts behind designing the attic space, about Celeste, and how Native people were being disrespected. "Plus, Marie is upset with me. This morning she told me off, and yesterday, Sophie told me off—"

"Sophie?" Aunt Georgia was confused. "Who's Sophie?"

"Sophie Miller," he said. "She's Potawatomi, a new kid at school. She's . . . I don't know . . . disappointed in me because I'm volunteering. Like I'm a sellout or an apple."

"Now, don't be using that word about yourself. You know who you are." The crisp air caught a chillier undercurrent. A cold front was beginning to move through. Aunt Georgia started a pile of rotten veggies and dead plant material to toss and a pile of healthy vegetation to add to her compost.

As Hughie followed her example, it struck him as bittersweet that the garden had to die out for fresh life to spring up. But there was something respectful and comforting about tending to it. Aunt Georgia added, "I hear what you're saying. The problems are knotted up together, but you've given it thought. You made your choice for good reasons. You gave your word to Terri Fischer and decided that you've got bigger fish to fry."

Hughie was listening, but he was also enjoying the feel of sticky leaves and stems against his hands and the grit of soil beneath his fingernails. Aunt Georgia continued, "About this Sophie girl—y'all don't have to agree on every blessed Indian thing that comes up. You know how often I speak of the wisdom of my dear sister, Debra?"

Hughie did his best to recall Debra, keeping in mind that somebody called "sister" might well be a cousin. "I, uh, don't remember your mentioning—"

"Right. I love her, I do. But Debra is a thoroughly unpleasant stick-in-the-mud, and most of what falls out of her mouth doesn't make a lick of sense. You can like someone, even love someone to your very last breath, and still disagree."

Later, Mom dropped Hughie off at the pub. He planned on having dinner there—and groveling to Marie—before Harvest House prep began in earnest for Halloween night.

Waving goodbye to his mother, Hughie noticed Ms. Fischer participating in a TV interview in front of the haunted house and jogged in that direction instead. He'd given it a lot of thought on the ride over. Aunt Georgia's words had offered him permission to disagree with Marie and Sophie, to do whatever felt true to himself. Last year, Hughie had walked away from the role of the Tin Man in the school musical because of L. Frank Baum's racism. After having given his word to volunteer, Hughie had made a good faith effort to work with Ms. Fischer, to try to make Harvest House less bad. Had she deliberately double-crossed him by relocating the Indian maiden to the burial ground, or was Ms. Fischer genuinely that clueless about what she was doing?

Hughie decided to try talking to her one more time before making a final decision.

The reporter said, "Locals are buzzing about the family-friendly ghost theme of Harvest House. Do you plan to open again next year?"

Ms. Fischer sported a glittery white poncho decorated with a ghost face that read BOO! over black leggings and black athletic shoes. "Originally, Harvest House was meant to be a one-time thing, a fundraiser, but if the property owner lets me do it again next year, who knows? I haven't had this much fun in ages, and people have been so generous donating their time and supplies. I'm not the only person in these parts who's ever struggled to pay medical bills."

"It sounds like the crossroads will be haunted for a long time to come," the reporter replied. Turning to face the videographer, he added, "This is Aiden Hunter for KTCS-TV Topeka, here with Terri Fischer of Harvest House, wishing you a safe and happy Halloween."

As the news team packed up, Ms. Fischer exclaimed, "Hughie! You're here early!"

Hughie fought to keep his cool. "I'm getting food at the pub first."

"Did you hear that interview? People are clamoring for more! Your chicken ghosts nearly stole the show! The burial ground—it gives them that thrill they're hoping for, but everybody's talking about the replica of"—she gestured broadly to the crossroads—"all this and the way you tied in the history of the chicken restaurant. It's very—"

"Glad to hear it." How could Ms. Fischer not understand how what she was doing was hurtful and insulting? "But if you do open again next year or every year, I'd appreciate it if you punted the Indian burial ground and Crossroads Ghost. How about zombies? Everyone loves zombies. A bunch of people who came last night were dressed as zombies."

"That's the problem," Ms. Fischer said as the news crew loaded their equipment in their van. "Zombies are overdone. I considered vampires—Kelsey wanted vampires—but you know, they skew sexier than the family demographic we're aiming for."

As if suddenly realizing that there was a news crew within earshot, Ms. Fischer slung an arm around Hughie and began walking him toward the pub. "I understand that you're not loving the Indian burial ground. I hear you. I respect your feelings. You are a valued member of this team. But Hughie, it's *make-believe*, and you've got to admit that you kids today are so damn sensitive. People want to be able to cut loose and have fun."

"What people?" he asked. "My mom and dad were here last night. My big sister and her boyfriend have tickets for tonight. My girlfriend—"

"I appreciate your family's support." Before Hughie could say they were supporting *him*, Ms. Fischer added, "I bet there are a lot of Indians who might get a kick out of this place."

He technically couldn't argue with that, but it didn't change anything. *So Native people don't have a hive mind,* Hughie thought. *So what?*

"Enough already!" He made a decision. "I can't be part of what you're doing," Hughie said. "I gave you the benefit of the doubt—figuring you didn't know any better—but now I think you just flat-out don't care about the people you're disrespecting. I'm leaving. I quit!"

"What?" Ms. Fischer exclaimed. "B-but you worked so hard on the attic!"

"You're welcome," Hughie replied, storming away. At least he'd *tried* to make a difference. Not that he owed it to the world, not that he'd always have the energy for conversations like that. But having made the effort offered him some comfort.

Then again, this was the second time—the first being *The Wizard of Oz* musical—that he'd walked away from something he'd originally wanted to do because of anti-Indigenous bigotry.

Hughie resented the nagging feeling that he was becoming a quitter, that he was the one letting other people down, when he never should've had to deal with any of that crap. It wasn't right. It wasn't fair. If he'd known Harvest House would feature the Crossroads Ghost and Indian burial ground, he never would've volunteered in the first place.

HALLOWEEN MOONRISE

More than anything, Hughie wanted to patch things up with Marie. Unfortunately, that would have to wait. The pub was nearly a full house. "Monster Mash" was playing on the overhead speakers, and a family dressed as the Incredibles and a trio dressed as the witches from *Hocus Pocus* were standing in line ahead of him. All the employees and most of the guests were decked out in costume, too.

The TV above the bar informed Hughie that the remains of the blond, white woman from Pennsylvania had been found and that a college classmate of hers had been arrested. Critics were demanding to know what had taken so long.

Hughie's heart went out to the victim and her loved ones. He was glad that there had been a resolution to the case. But he thought about Celeste and all those missing people whose stories never made it to the news. What Cricket was doing, reporting on the crossroads creeper, was important. Hughie reflected on how Louise planned to become a professional journalist. He'd never seen an Indigenous journalist on the TV news.

"Hughie!" It was Ms. Fischer, pushing her way through the line behind him. "Excuse me, excuse me. Hughie! I need to talk to you."

Hughie thought it took a lot of gall for her to chase him across the street. Sure, he'd promised to volunteer, and yes, his word meant something, but ridiculing Indigenous lives and cultures was not what he'd signed up for. His decision was made.

Arms crossed against his chest, he turned to face her. There was a tone in his voice that had never before been unleashed on a grown-up. *"What?"*

Ms. Fischer looked windblown and frantic. "I'm sorry, Hughie. Really, I am. I never intended to hurt anyone, especially an upstanding kid like you who's helping *me* out. Next year, we'll change things up, I promise. No more Crossroads Ghost. Maybe we can go with farmer ghosts in the graveyard instead of Indians—or whatever you think is best. For now, we can turn the headstones back around, like you and Sam did, and spray paint different names on them—"

"Hang on," Hughie said. "Are you serious? What about the burial ground?"

"I'll tell all the Indian ghosts to tone it down. No hollering or chasing people around."

Ms. Fischer was scrambling to fix the situation. It

might be a fumbling last-minute effort, but Hughie believed she was sincere. He believed that if he stayed involved, next year's Harvest House would be better. Besides, he loved seeing people's reactions to what he'd done with the attic. But he drew one more line. "That tacky headdress comes off Veronica," he insisted. "No more feathers on any of the fake Indians, and she stands in the graveyard with all the rest of them without drawing any extra attention to herself."

"Deal," Ms. Fischer said, extending her hand.

Was he completely satisfied? No, but it was progress.

Hughie took the win.

Once Hughie reached the hostess stand, he drank in the sight of Marie wearing an antique bridal gown and standing next to Rain, who was sporting her second-favorite Leia Organa cosplay outfit. "Nice dresses!" He rocked back on his heels, tentative. He'd planned out what to say to Marie on his way across the street to the pub. Then he'd mentally revised that after receiving the amazing news from Ms. Fischer about Harvest House. Neither of those plans had factored in the possibility of his cousin being involved in the conversation.

"Found mine in the giveaway bin at a secondhand shop," Marie said with a smile that suggested maybe, hopefully, she wasn't still angry with him. "Some of the buttons were missing, but I sewed on new ones and rehemmed the torn skirt."

Had his cousin somehow diffused Marie's anger? "What brings you here?" he asked Rain.

"It's an excuse to wear this," she said, gesturing to her earth-tone outfit, worn with a long dark wig, partly woven into the shape of a headband and falling in a single braid to one side. "The inspiration scene raises the question of who the Ewoks got the dress from and whether they routinely roasted and ate humanoids on the Forest Moon of Endor."

Rain's costume looked terrific, and Hughie brushed aside the fact that in the wig, in the dark of night, she fit the creeper's victim profile, too. It was Halloween. They all deserved to have a little fun. He didn't want to taint the moment with a warning.

Marie smiled at Rain. "Mr. Boucher is crowing that this might be the pub's all-time-record sales day. Hughie, please take her away so I can do my job."

"I'm watching over her," Rain protested. "What if the creeper comes out tonight? It's only natural that I try to protect my friend."

"And it's only natural that I try to protect both of you." Anticipating their eye rolls, he added, "In the face of danger, you're both as capable as I am—hey, more so— but I'm a guy, and the creeper goes after girls. Not guys."

A circus clown, who was waiting behind Hughie, sounded his brass horn. *Honk!* "Anytime now!" he said. "Funny men are hungry men." *Honk!*

Marie grinned at him over Hughie's shoulder. "Happy

Halloween, and welcome to the Grub Pub. Do that again, funny man, and I will confiscate the instrument."

The crowd was exuberant—Hughie had never seen the place so packed. Seasonal coloring place mats—ghosts, jack-o'-lanterns, black cats—had been distributed to placate sugar-fueled little kids. Hughie could only imagine how backed up Karl must be in the kitchen.

Marie led them to a recently vacated two-top, and Rain took a seat.

Hughie began, "Marie—"

"It was the whole situation I was upset about," she said. "Those cringy costumes!"

Hughie tried, again, "Marie—"

"I mean, I work here, and the pub is handing out copies of the 'Legend of the Crossroads Ghost' on the back of menus. Who am I to talk?"

"I should've told you what was going on. I tried to quit, but Ms. Fischer talked me into coming back. She promised to make some changes for tonight and rethink the whole thing in the future. I do think she gets it now and next year will be different. Better. I'll make sure of it."

"For real?" Marie exclaimed. "Oh, wow. Wow! I should've had more faith in you."

"The whole thing was pretty touch and go." Hughie promised to fill her in on all the details later when she didn't have a line of ravenous costumed customers to deal with, and they agreed to talk to Karl after Harvest House and the pub closed for the night.

HALLOWEEN NIGHT

So far, Halloween at Harvest House had been glitchier and, for Hughie, busier and more stressful than the previous night. Yes, the volunteers knew what they were doing. Mechanical and sound bugs had been fixed. The Indian ghosts were much more subdued after Ms. Fischer had given them a talking-to, so at least there wasn't any whooping. But one of the actors tripped over a headstone and sprained his ankle. A fake crow fell from the ceiling, striking a customer in the face and scratching her eye. A group of frat boys on the stairs decided to moon the people in line behind them in the foyer below. One of the 1950s costumed teens—the boy—showed up drunk and threw up on set, which a half dozen fourteen-year-old girls proclaimed a "fantastic" and "disgusting" special effect. Then one of them caught a whiff and threw up, too.

Oakley pulled Sam off attic-slides duty with Hughie because it was faster and easier to scrub Sam's face and get him out of the chicken suit and into a leather jacket and white tee (he already was wearing jeans) than to scrub ghostly white full-body makeup off any of the guys outside. And even though it wasn't what you'd call a high-profile acting job, Hughie was miffed that Oakley had drafted Sam into a leading-man role apparently without even considering Hughie, who had stage experience.

"Hey, baby brother!" Louise exclaimed, entering the attic and gesturing to the set. "You did all this? Dad wasn't kidding. It's spectacular."

As Hughie soaked up her praise, Louise's boyfriend positioned himself in front of a slide. "Nice beak, Hughie! You've never looked so *cock*-a-doodle-doo."

"Bite me, Joey," Hughie replied. Strictly speaking, it wasn't the kind of language he typically used in front of his big sister, who insisted on viewing him as an angelic gift from the Creator. But Hughie had endured enough *cock* jokes at his expense from previous guests, and he wasn't about to take them from anyone he knew personally.

"Hughie!" Louise exclaimed with a laugh. "What's gotten into you?"

"All I said was 'bite me'!" Hughie replied. As the couple *whooshed* down the slides, Hughie yelled after them. "It is a chicken *restaurant*, after all. And I'm supposed to be *a chicken*." *Too bad Sam wasn't here to hear that,* Hughie thought.

After midnight, after the last guests exited from the haunted cemetery, Hughie turned in his costume and helped clean up. Though nobody was supposed to bring in food or drink, he found a half-eaten granola bar, an empty margarita can, and a package of suspicious-looking gummy mummies, as well as an orange-and-black hair scrunchie, a KU student ID card, an open package of pirate-flag-print facial tissues, and an unopened condom wrapper labeled GLOW IN THE DARK. A more extensive breakdown of the sets was planned for the following afternoon after everyone got a good night's sleep.

Sam, still dressed for the 1950s, came in through the front doorway as Hughie descended the stairs to the foyer. Before Hughie could say anything, Sam raised his index finger to his lips to say "hush." Supposedly, the sound effects had been turned off, both upstairs and down, but Hughie could faintly hear 1920s music and tipsy voices.

"The Vogels?" Hughie mouthed, in no mood to deal with them. They sounded drunk or high or both. Hughie grabbed Sam's arm and dragged him onto the staircase, well out of sight of the first-floor maze. "Where's your coat and stuff?"

Hughie had stashed his own in the fake oven in the attic.

"Kitchen cabinets," Sam whispered back. At Hughie's glance up the staircase, Sam clarified, "The *real* kitchen cabinets." He gestured at the first-floor maze with his thumb. "Back there." *Beyond* the Vogels, Hughie realized. In other words, if they went to fetch it, then it would just be the four boys—Jonas, Elias, Sam, and Hughie—no teacher in the hall, no restaurant full of people, no Ms.

Fischer to keep the brothers in line. All things being equal, it was usually best to avoid trouble if you could.

"Who's there?" Elias called. More quietly, he said to Jonas, "Did you hear something?"

"Could be Sam skulking around," Jonas replied. "That you, Sam?"

Sam took a step down toward the foyer, but Hughie pulled him in the opposite direction. "The girls are waiting for us," he said. "We can leave our stuff for now. It's not that cold out." It was that cold out.

"Let's find him!" Elias yelled. The sound of bottles clanking in a toast echoed through the building.

"We're coming for you!" Jonas warned.

Hughie and Sam had a head start and sober reflexes. They rushed up the stairs, through the attic maze, and down the slides to the cemetery where Ms. Fischer was reviewing yet another list on her clipboard. "Did you two see the Vogels?" she asked. "They're supposed to be cleaning up."

"Inside," Sam replied as Ms. Fischer retrieved a beer bottle from behind a foam-and-cardboard headstone.

"They're drinking again, aren't they?" she exclaimed, marching off to confront them. "That's it! Heaven help me, I'm telling Karl!"

"Busted," Sam whispered, following Hughie out the exit gate. "How was your night?"

"More of the same." Hughie shrugged. "Nothing freaky. No creeper. All the ghosts were make-believe. I was the brunt of every clucking fowl joke you can think of, except this time there weren't two of us to deflect them."

"Sorry to bail," Sam said. "But it turns out the gods of doomed romance were looking out for me. My summer fling—the guy who ghosted me—and his new boyfriend saw me in all my ghostly James Dean glory. Of course, I wish them the best, but—"

"You were loving it," Hughie said as they came around the front of the building. Sam's "tough summer" hadn't only been about the falling out with the Vogel brothers, Hughie realized.

"Could've been worse," Sam admitted, falling in stride. "But I'm over him. Cricket's playing my heartstrings like a fiddle. You got any exes I should know about?"

Hughie glanced at the sign. HARVEST HOUSE: FEAR THE REAPER! "No exes—period."

"Marie is your first love? That's so sweet."

"Hey, I have vicarious experience. I've watched many rom-coms with my sister."

As they crossed the road, Sam said, "Cricket is my first capital R relationship, and my ex in question was my first kiss. So we are equally clueless." By the light of the full moon, he gestured to the neon-green bicycle chained to the take-your-belongings sign pole outside the pub. "Speaking of . . . that's Cricket's bike. Have you seen her tonight?"

Hughie shook his head. "I hope she didn't decide to confront Karl by herself."

The boys hurried inside, nearly colliding with Millie,

the bartender. She was dressed as Medusa—her crowning glory a headband of layered and dangling rubber snakes. "Whoa, Nelly! Where's the fire? I was just about to lock up the front."

"Sorry!" Hughie exclaimed as Sam helped steady Millie. "Are you okay?"

The Grub Pub dining room had emptied. The tables and booths had been wiped down, the darts cabinet shut, the foosball and pool tables reset, and the floor cleared of crumpled napkins, broken crayons, and crumbs. "Dead Man's Party" was playing on overhead speakers.

"I'm just fine, but you two sure gave me a start. I'm surprised to see you boys here tonight. Marie and Princess Leia took off across the road to find you a few minutes ago."

Hughie realized the girls must've entered Harvest House through the front door as they'd come around from the back of the building. "Let's find Cricket and go back over to meet them at Harvest House."

"Did you see a cute redhead come in?" Sam asked Millie, gesturing alongside his shoulder. "About this high, talks a lot?"

"Sure did. Said she was from the suburban school paper, doing a story on the haunted house. Brash, pushy—I liked her. Didn't have my back turned for a minute when the little scamp snuck off to the kitchen to bother Karl." Millie yawned. "This was the busiest night we've had since I don't know when. I'm out of here! You boys turn off the music, and I'll lock you in behind me. You can leave through the back exit."

Hughie and Sam thanked Millie and wished her a good night. Hughie's nerves were on edge. The sooner he and Sam reunited with all three girls, the better he'd feel.

Sam slipped behind the bar. He flicked off the sound system, and Oingo Boingo fell silent in the middle of a chorus. Sam was muttering something about hating that song when they heard Karl shouting and Cricket's voice, more faintly, in reply.

Hughie experienced a surge of adrenaline, fearing for Cricket's safety. The boys barreled through the swinging door to the steamy, cramped kitchen. Behind the food counter, Karl was sweaty and irate. "Back off, Nancy Drew!"

"Why don't you answer my questions?" Cricket was standing in front of the dishwasher, holding up her phone, and the audio waveform on her voice-recording app spiked on the screen. "Doesn't she deserve that much?" Cricket and Karl ignored Hughie and Sam, who, as if by mutual agreement, positioned themselves to either side of her— not that she seemed to need the backup. Stumbling to the center of the room, Karl looked frankly terrified.

"You already know, don't you?" The big man crumbled, an only half-controlled collapse onto the freshly mopped floor. "You just want me to admit it." Cricket didn't seem surprised. Sam shot Hughie a wary look, and Hughie felt his fingers curl into fists.

"It happened so long ago, before you were born," Karl said, wiping watery eyes and splotchy cheeks. "My brother . . . My little brother killed his girl—murdered her—but he's gone, too. Gone, gone, gone. There's no justice to be had. He froze to death that same night." Karl gazed at them, as if begging for forgiveness. "I'm the only one left to punish."

"What did you do?" Cricket pressed, crouching to look him in the eye. "Tell us."

Karl swallowed hard. "I found them. I found them together, dead in the lot across the street. Cold as ice. I buried them. If my mother had found out—she's always been fragile. After Pops passed away, I became the man of the family. It fell on me to take care of them all."

"What did you do?" Cricket repeated. Hughie spared a moment to wonder why Rain and Marie hadn't returned looking for them. He hadn't meant to stay so long at the pub once he'd found out they weren't there. But it's not like he could leave now.

Karl said, "I told everybody that Stefan died on the interstate, near Alma, and that I'd had him cremated there. I bought an urn. Filled out a form and took out an obituary in the *Examiner*. Must've driven back and forth ten times before it occurred to me to check Boucher Barn and found Stefan's truck there. Long story short, I unloaded it cheap up in Des Moines. Nobody checked. Nobody asked any questions. Why would they?"

It was Hughie who spoke the words out loud. "You

buried your brother Stefan and the girl he murdered—Celeste Highfield, the girl who inspired the legend of Crossroads Ghost."

"I did," Karl replied, his bloodshot eyes shiny in the fluorescent light. His next words more of a confirmation than a revelation: "They're under the parking lot across the street." Karl sobbed, accompanied by the chugging of the dishwasher.

After a long moment, Cricket stood. "I guess that's everything."

Hughie drew his friends aside.

"I can't believe he just came out with it," Sam said, speaking low in the doorway.

While texting Marie and Rain, Hughie whispered, "I can. Think about it. This has been weighing on him for years. He works all the time, he's exhausted, it's hot in here, and all anyone can talk about is the haunted house, the ghost across the street. It didn't take much to break him."

"Thanks a lot," Cricket said with a smirk. "Never mind, I know what you mean." She moved to kneel next to Karl, and Hughie grabbed Sam's shoulder to stop him from going after her. In a soft voice, Cricket asked, "If you found them dead, how do you know he killed her?"

"Her head, her skull . . ." Karl gulped a breath. "He bashed it in. His hands were brown with her dried blood." Karl shuddered. "You're going to think I'm the devil, but I'm not. I'm a good man, a Christian man. Or at least I was."

"Nobody thinks you're the devil." Cricket held up her phone, so Karl could watch her close the app and power it down. "Listen to me," she said. "Whatever happened between Celeste and Stefan, that was a long time ago. We can't change it now. But to this day, someone at the cross-roads is frightening girls who look like her. This person came after Ximena, and she wasn't the only one. Is it *you*? Are you trying to continue what your brother started?"

"I . . . I don't know what you're talking about," Karl said, fighting for composure. "I don't understand what's been happening. None of it makes sense."

Hughie's phone vibrated: a thumbs-up from Rain. Tension seeped out of his shoulders. She and Marie were safe. Sam moved to sit cross-legged in front of Karl, and this time Hughie didn't stop him. Sam said, "Karl, I know we just met, but I believe in ghosts. Whatever you tell us, I'll keep an open mind."

Karl gripped Sam's forearm, as if to anchor himself. "You're a kid, but we were all kids back then, not much older than you." He began rocking in place. "That god-damned chicken restaurant! People say I lost my nerve, that I didn't have the courage to go after my dream. They think I backed down when the going got tough. But that's not what scared me off, the business part. That's not why I shut the place down."

For a moment, he seemed to lose the ability to speak.

"Take your time," Hughie said, standing apart from the others. "Breathe."

271

Karl began again, "My mom was so proud. She'd tell anybody who'd listen how proud she was. It was a few weeks after we opened. Late. A Thursday night. I was the last one out the door, and when I walked into the moonlight . . . Stefan. My dead brother, the one I'd buried . . . It was like I shared his mind, his memory. I could remember carrying Celeste's body through the cold of night . . . like I was the one who'd killed her. I could remember her blood, sticky, on my—his—palms and fingers. I could remember the wind and what it was like when I—he—got so cold that he couldn't feel the chill anymore.

"I closed the place down two weeks later, and I haven't set foot across the road since." Karl let go of Sam. "I should've known better than to let Terri talk Boucher into letting her use the building, but God help me, I've loved her since I was fifteen years old, and she damn well uses it."

"Terri?" Cricket asked.

"Ms. Fischer," Sam said.

Karl got up and washed his face in the sink. "That bite in the air you sometimes feel here at the pub, all over the crossroads, that's Stefan. Sometimes I can even smell his Drakkar Noir aftershave."

While Karl sipped a glass of ice water in the kitchen, Hughie joined Sam and Cricket in the hallway. "Karl is a mess," Cricket said. "I'll keep an eye on him. You two go on."

"I don't think so," Sam replied. "I can stay with him."

Cricket adjusted her eyeglasses. "I'm the one who pushed Karl to the breaking point. I feel responsible for his mental health, and right now he's alone in a room full of knives."

"I'm more worried about *you* being alone with him in a room full of knives!" Sam countered. "Did you think about that, huh?"

Leaning against a cardboard skeleton, Hughie said, "I could go find Marie and—"

"No!" Cricket and Sam said. She added, "The crowds are gone. All the ghost and creeper sightings have taken place close to Harvest House."

Sam added, "Wolfe Man, have you never seen a horror movie? No solo excursions!"

"How about this?" Cricket said. "I'll wait with Karl in the dining room while you two fetch Rain and Marie. If you're gone too long, I'll come meet you and bring him with me."

"Uncle Karl?" Elias called, coming in through the back exit with Jonas behind him. They had their coats on, but they hadn't changed clothes or washed off their ghostly makeup yet. "What're you losers doing here?"

Jonas lightly punched Elias in the arm. "Oh, hi, Cricket."

"Oh, hi, Cricket," she mimicked. "Do you think I don't know what you're like? You strut around all puffed up as if that makes you important. Well, believe me, you two are the least important things happening right now."

"Hey." It was the first word Hughie had spoken to the Vogels directly. He wasn't nervous around them, not now.

Not when there was so much else happening. "Your uncle isn't feeling well. Can you help Cricket take care of him in the dining room until he's doing better and then drive him home?"

The crisis seemed to take Jonas and Elias off guard. It hadn't been that long ago that they'd lost their father—the second of Karl's brothers to die. "Did you call nine-one-one?" Jonas asked.

"It's not that kind of emergency," Cricket said. "At least I hope not." She waved at Sam and Hughie to get going. "It's a family matter. He may want to tell you himself."

HAUNTED HALLOWEEN

Crossing the road beneath the lone streetlight, Sam wanted to know, "Are we going to talk about the fact that Karl was freaking *possessed* by his dead brother Stefan?"

"Or," Hughie replied, "he was traumatized by finding his brother's and Celeste's bodies and imagined the whole thing. Or he's just full of it." Hughie felt frustration well up inside. "Sam, who cares? What difference does it make? Karl Vogel isn't the one—"

"Can you imagine carrying all that for so long? He's been really suffering—"

"*Shut up*, Sam!" Hughie was fuming. Sure, he understood that Karl had been mourning his brother, and grief could wreak havoc on the mind, body, and soul. But *Celeste* had died, too. *Celeste* had been the one who was murdered. Her family and friends had traveled to this place, looking for her. If they'd covered every inch of land near old town, he was sure they'd searched the crossroads, too.

All these years later, they were still searching, still hoping, and the whole time, Karl knew he had buried her without consideration of their wishes or their traditions, without respect for her life and their loss. It had been more important to Karl to protect his deceased brother's reputation than to offer Celeste's loved ones the truth.

"Locked." Hughie rattled the front doorknob of Harvest House. "It's going on one o'clock. Ms. Fischer may have already taken off for the night."

"Fear not, cranky Wolfe Man." Sam wrenched open a first-floor window. "I hung the gray cloth over the inside of this wall myself. The lock has been missing for years."

"Impressive, but . . . why would Ms. Fischer leave with Rain and Marie inside? I'm sure she did a final walk-through before locking up."

"Valid point," Sam said. "I'll go around to check around back."

As he jogged off, Hughie heard his cousin's voice coming from inside, calling to Marie, and took advantage of the open window to climb in. "Hey!" he called "Down here!"

"Hughie?" Rain rushed down the stairs. "Where's Marie?"

"I thought she was with you," he said.

"She was. We went to the attic, and when I turned around, Marie was gone."

"She must've taken a slide to the haunted cemetery. Sam is on his way there now." Hughie quickly filled Rain in on what Karl had told them and Cricket in the Grub Pub kitchen.

"Murdered," Rain whispered, rubbing her eyes. "That poor girl."

"It also sounds like Karl was possessed by the ghost of his brother Stefan."

"Possessed as in . . ." At his nod, Rain added, "Could *Stefan* be the Crossroads Ghost? Maybe it's not Celeste at all?"

"Karl is an emotional guy, full of regrets. He was mourning his brother." Hughie whispered, "What if Karl somehow subconsciously invited in the ghost of Stefan? What if the ghost of Stefan Vogel *is here with us right now*?"

It was then that they felt the cool draft and heard the voice. "Em vnicvs."

"That was Mvskoke!" Rain exclaimed. "Sounded like it was coming from upstairs."

"That's not Stefan Vogel," Hughie said.

"Celeste?" they said at the same time. Fluent Mvskoke speakers of Celeste's generation were rare, but she could've picked up a few words and phrases from a grandparent or great-grandparent.

Wind battered the building. "Ivpecicv!" the voice urged.

"Cousin," Hughie breathed, "this haunted house is . . . *actually haunted*!"

"Come on!" Rain said, hurrying up the stairs.

On the second-floor landing, they heard a scream from outside. Rain yelled, "Marie!"

"Letkv!" the voice commanded.

If only Hughie and Rain had a straight path across the attic! Side by side, they hurried through the twisty attic maze, rushed through the open doorway in the painting of K.V.'s Chicken Restaurant and Lounge, and darted across the floorboards to the slides. Hughie threw his body into the opening for maximum velocity, while Rain trailed slightly after him. The foam mattresses at the bottom had already been packed up, and Hughie landed with a thud onto the ground outside. At first, he was confused. Marie, dressed as a bride, was struggling against Sam, still in his 1950s teen biker ensemble.

"Let me go!" Marie cried.

In a scratchy, hollow voice, Sam replied, "Less, less, less."

They weren't playing. This was deathly serious.

"Sam, *stop it*!" Hughie shouted, leaping to his feet as Rain landed at the bottom of the slide with a soft "Ow" beside him. Hughie yelled, "What the hell is wrong with you?"

"It's *not Sam*," replied Marie. "He's stronger than Sam."

Hughie tried to free his girlfriend from the grip of his best friend. "Sam, stop!"

"Less . . . less . . ." Sam's eyes were filled with blood and stars.

"Holy shit!" Hughie exclaimed, tripping over a headstone. Stefan was possessing Sam. Stefan was possessing Sam the same way he'd possessed Karl that night long ago at the chicken restaurant, the same way Stefan must have possessed countless more teenage boys and young men over the decades. He was threatening Marie the same way he'd threatened Mrs. Schneider and Allie and Paige and Ximena and who knew how many other girls and women.

Hughie heard Rain on the phone, yelling at Cricket to bring Karl, saying that they needed his help. Meanwhile, Stefan-Sam picked up Marie, oblivious to her kicking and pummeling him. "Less."

Marie managed to connect a solid punch, striking Stefan-Sam's nose. Blood gushed over his mouth and jaw and onto his white T-shirt. "Less, Celess, Celeste," Stefan intoned, and this time, there was no trace of Sam's voice. "Must save Celeste."

Now Rain was talking to Karl, explaining what was happening.

"Stefan!" Hughie called. "Bring Mar—Celeste to me."

"Celeste. Less. less." It had been worth a try, but Stefan-Sam didn't even acknowledge Hughie. "Less, less, less," he said, his voice raspier. Like a vinyl record, skipping, repeating, circling in a moment in time.

"Hughie, Rain!" Marie yelled as Rain ended the call. "Help!"

"Less . . . less . . . less . . . less . . . less."

"I'm trying," Hughie replied. "I think he's in pain."

"I don't care about his pain!" Marie shouted, squirming as Stefan-Sam arms clamped her shins and forearms in place.

"Less . . . less . . . less . . . less . . . less."

Hughie remembered his theories only moments earlier in the foyer, about how Karl longed for his brother. Hughie thought about how the volunteer work crew had boldly created a haunted house, how generations of pubgoers had swapped stories of the Crossroads Ghost, eager for a little spookiness in their lives, too. Had that made them more vulnerable somehow?

"Less . . . less . . . less . . . less . . . less."

Right then, all the pieces clicked into place for Hughie. Influenced by the local legend, he'd been musing on the possibility of an Indigenous ghost, and the Mvskoke voice he'd heard on the wind when the dachshunds ran into the middle of the road had only strengthened that subconscious expectation. After hearing Karl's story, though, Hughie had begun to wonder if he'd been mistaken—if Stefan had been the Crossroads Ghost all along—but that didn't align with the disembodied voice speaking Hughie's tribal language.

There was only one explanation: There were *two* ghosts at the crossroads, and they'd been at odds for a very long time.

One ghost—Stefan—had possessed others to stalk his victims.

The other ghost—Celeste—had protected them.

Hughie wondered if Celeste had willingly chosen her in-between existence. She'd been defending girls and women for so long, but she couldn't always go it alone.

She'd called on assistance from the living, the forces of nature, again and again.

This time, she might well need his—Hughie's—help to put an end to it for good.

"Less . . . less . . . less . . . less . . . less."

Hughie thought about how Rain mourned her mother and her friend Galen, how Marie ached for her extended family and life on the rez, Sam's mixed memories of Jonas and Elias, and how the Vogel brothers reminded Hughie himself of the bullied kid he'd once been. Hughie thought of Cricket's low-key awkwardness at the co-op poetry readings, how she was learning about the legacy of colonialism while working to prove herself an ally and friend.

Maybe everyone is a little bit haunted, he thought. *Maybe, dead or alive, that's part of what being human is all about. Maybe the Crossroads Ghosts are haunted, too.*

Hughie let his head fall back on his shoulders and opened his arms to the heavens. "Hesci, Celeste Highfield. My name is Hughie Wolfe. That's Marie Headbird and Sam Rodríguez. The ghost controlling Sam is Stefan Vogel. Celeste, to save my friends, I invite you in."

CELESTE

"Hughie, *no!*" Marie shouts. Her Elders have no doubt taught her that opening oneself to the dead is a terrible idea. Her Elders are right.

Yet what Hughie just said, could it be? Could I have been mistaking Stefan for The Bad Man? Was that Stefan calling for me all this time? "Less . . . less . . . less . . . less . . . less."

I cannot ignore the damage he's doing to Sam and to Marie, still trapped in his arms.

I cannot ignore the desperation of Hughie and Marie. Their bond reminds me of the one Stefan and I once shared. Still share?

I've never done this before, never merged with a human being. Hughie isn't an animal, isn't a breeze or misty fog, he's flesh and bone and blood. Human.

"Celeste, please," Hughie implores. He's separate from the others, wrenching himself open to me, willing to risk everything for those he loves. He and Stefan are so much alike.

If I could breathe deeply, that's what I'd be doing. If I could breathe deeply, my breath would be mingled with Hughie's . . . *now*. "Stefan," I begin, my voice scratchy, foreign, catching. "She isn't Celeste. I am. Release the girl. I am Celeste. She is Marie. Set Marie down."

"Less . . . less . . . less . . . less . . . less." He doesn't recognize me in Hughie's body, in the same way that I failed to recognize him in so many others' before Sam's. All this time, we could've been together—could've traveled on together—and instead, we've crossed purposes in our ignorance and pain. "Marie! Tell Stefan your name. Talk to him as if speaking to a child."

Marie stops struggling, shocked perhaps. Rain is teary, but she runs up and kicks Stefan—still in Sam's body—hard, behind his right knee, and he folds to the ground as though Sam's bones are nothing.

"Oof." Marie lands hard on her back. "I am not Celeste Highfield!" she shouts. "I am Marie Headbird! I am Marie. I am Marie, Marie, Marie!"

"*I* am Celeste," I say, and the voice sounds more me, less Hughie. Yet I hear his voice, too, deep in my mind, whispering what he knows. "Celeste," I insist aloud. "*Celeste.*"

Stefan lets go of Marie, gaping at me. Do Hughie's eyes look like Sam's, like shining, bloody heaven? I feel Hughie's heart beating, his lungs filling, his *mind*. Marie rolls free, springs into Rain's waiting embrace.

A big man, breathing hard, rushes through the open

fence gate, leading Cricket and two of the boys in ghostly face paint.

The big man grabs Sam's forearms, shakes Stefan. He says, "Brother, it's me, Karl. I failed you. I failed our family. I'm so sorry that you died."

"I'm dead?" Stefan asks, gazing at me over Karl's shoulder. *"Celeste?"* The blood and stars fade, revealing Stefan's blue eyes as if superimposed on Sam's brown. Another breath and Stefan's face hovers in front of Sam's in the moonlight. His smile is hopeless.

"Why did you do it?" Karl asks Stefan. "Why did you kill the girl?"

Kill me? I take a moment to unravel Karl's words. I remember him better now, the older brother. *He* was the one with the temper. I recall the way he and Terri would fight, the way I once saw him raise his hand to her. But my Stefan was never like Karl.

Stefan was gentle. Stefan was joy and passion and hugs that felt like coming home.

"He *didn't* kill me," I reply. "He'd *never* hurt me. It was an accident. The ice. I slipped. I fell. I hit my head." It all comes flooding back to me—the way I floated up from my body, the hunk of roadside concrete that had dented my skull, the nothingness that followed, until a voice called "Less, less, less, less" at the crossroads, at the intersection of Four Directions, at the border between an old community and a new one.

I interpreted the call as a threat to a girl who reminded me of myself.

I held on to protect her, to protect them all. It came as no surprise that girls like us would be targeted. It happens more often than most people want to admit, even to themselves.

The predators, they count on that and use it against us.

Not every man I battled was Stefan in his confused, desperate state. Not all of them called in love and desperation for "less." Not every man I frightened away was innocent.

Karl lets go and falls to his knees, praying.

I am not impressed. Let him boil in his regret, for all I care. He should never have underestimated Stefan. He should never have kept us secret or blanketed us with concrete and asphalt. Too many white men hunt brown girls on stolen land. If Karl believed that's what happened, he did everything in his power to cover it up, to cover our bones with lies.

"I saved you?" Stefan asks, more of a plea. He knows better—we both do.

I reply, "You tried."

The two white boys cower behind the three girls.

Marie reaches to grasp Rain's hand. Rain reaches to grasp Cricket's.

The "Legend of the Crossroads Ghost," it makes my death romantic, tragic entertainment—crocodile tears for an Indian maiden. *Tell them what happened,* I silently implore Hughie. *Tell my family, tell everyone I loved. Tell the world, everyone who'll listen. Rewrite my story, my legacy. Tell it with respect, tell it true.* Hughie promises to do that and more. He promises to ensure my bones find their way home. He says his mama will help us.

Stefan runs to me, folds me—and Hughie, too—in Sam's embrace. "Let's go, Celeste," he says. "Let's run away. We can still dance, make love, steal a future . . . We can finally celebrate Christmas!"

"No, Stefan. This isn't the way. Release the boy. Release Sam Rodríguez so he can live his life, so they can all live their lives. Ours are over. We have to get out of their way."

"No, no, *no*!" Stefan exclaims. "We don't have to—"

"You're talking about invasion," I say. "Appropriation, colonization. Taking is wrong. Stefan, I know your heart. You were never greedy. You always released those whose bodies you'd claimed."

"You're being generous," he says with a reluctant nod.

Stefan has been trapped in torment. He didn't possess the clarity to know what he was doing was a violation. He does now. Small comfort, I'm sure, for those whose skin he wore, mistaking it for his own. I can only hope they blamed it on drunken hazes, cases of overactive imaginations. I hope they let it go.

Stefan closes his eyes, and Sam falls to the ground, sweating, shaking, though the glowing specter of Stefan remains standing tall.

I close my eyes, and Hughie falls away with a sigh of relief and gratitude.

We remain, me and Stefan. Visible but incorporeal.

I consider Karl, the brother, the cost of his lies and lack of faith.

The eighteen-year-old girl I once was still resents him. The specter I've become rejects that, so it doesn't weigh her down for eternity.

Stefan glances at Marie. "I'm sorry," he tells her. "I thought you were someone else."

Though the gaze of the dead is directed at her, Marie doesn't flinch.

Three girls, stronger together. The moment is in balance. I am their fourth.

I hope that I'll always be watching over them, but it's long past time to leave.

Stefan is still a teenage boy—spirit and soul. I am still a teenage girl, forever eighteen, though I've had too many years to reflect on what that means.

My death was sudden. Gone in an instant, a promise on my finger, a hopeful heart.

I can only imagine Stefan's demise—prolonged, excruciating. How he must have carried me, burning body heat. How his fear built as I felt heavier with every step. The sweat beneath his clothes, how he hurried when he should have paced himself.

It would've been faster to leave me, run for help. But he didn't, couldn't.

My sweet Stefan hadn't been ready to accept that he couldn't save me. He hadn't been ready to accept that the future we'd planned would never come to pass.

"So, this is it," he says. "Until . . . unless?"

"Until . . . unless?" We have our beliefs, but soon we'll find out what an afterlife is truly supposed to be. For now, we kiss and bid the crossroads goodbye.

THE SPRING PLAY

The student actor playing Stefan-Sam echoed, "I'm dead?"

His castmate, Celeste-Hughie, performed by Hughie, fell to the stage.

The East Hannesburg High auditorium briefly went dark, as new actors took their marks to assume their roles as Stefan and Celeste. Meanwhile, the crew quickly changed the backdrop from present day to the mid-1980s, and the contemporary characters disappeared behind the curtain, except for co-playwright Hughie Wolfe.

Music arose from a string quartet. A spotlight fell onto Hughie, standing stage left. "This story is told with the express permission of the Highfield family and the Vogel family."

"The year is nineteen eighty-five. Celeste Highfield— a Muscogee girl, one with Choctaw heritage—and Stefan Vogel—a white boy—are college students in love at Christmastime."

A second spotlight, this one sepia, shined on Queen

Washington of Hannesburg High playing Celeste High-field in a snow-white sweaterdress with a lace collar, and on Brent Baker from EHHS in the role of Stefan Vogel in a black suit with a red tie.

It was the first joint production of the two high schools.

Their actions mirrored Hughie's words, bringing history alive. "After attending a Christmas concert at Hoch Auditorium on the University of Kansas campus, Stefan and Celeste climb into his pickup truck, stop for gas in old town, and then drive out to the country, to Boucher Barn. It had been the site of their first date, a fraternity dance in September.

"Snow begins to fall. Stefan offers Celeste a promise ring with a floral design. Tiny ruby petals around a tiny diamond center in ten-karat yellow gold. She accepts.

"They linger longer than expected in the barn doing what young people in love do, not realizing that, outside, a winter storm is building in intensity."

As the actors playing Stefan and Celeste kissed, the barn backdrop unfolded and a screen behind it rose to unveil the crossroads where a sign outside K.V.'s Chicken Restaurant and Lounge read OPENING SOON!

Given the conversation around color-conscious casting the previous year, it had caused quite the kerfuffle when Hughie had insisted that Indigenous actors play certain parts.

He'd countered that sometimes it didn't matter who took on a role, so it should be open to everyone, but sometimes it really did. Hughie and Queen had offered the new recruits—including Sophie, Rain, and Marie—extra support during rehearsals, and that opening night, Sophie's stepsister Buffy had shined bright, playing multiple roles.

"Later, Stefan's pickup truck sputters, but it won't start. The Boucher farmhouse is dark. No one answers the pounding at the door. So Celeste and Stefan begin hiking to the nearest establishment—the Grub Pub at the crossroads, where his brother Karl works."

A third spotlight fell on Marie, illuminating her on stage right while the actors between her and Hughie walked against the backdrop of a rural winter road. Marie was the one who'd joined Hughie in crafting the script. True to their word, they rewrote the school nurse as a cafeteria worker from a different school. "It's colder now, freezing, and they don't have gloves. They didn't pack a blanket or flashlight. In the dark, Celeste slips on ice. Falls. Her head injury is fatal."

In the spotlight, Queen took a tumble. It was an impressive piece of physical acting.

Hughie picked up the thread, sharing insights from Sam. "Stefan refuses to accept that she's gone. Panicking, he tries to stop the bleeding. He picks up and carries Celeste.

"Snow and sleet reduce visibility. If he stays along the road, perhaps a car will come along. She's not heavy, not at first, but it's more than two miles, closer to three, and he's so, so cold.

"Stefan sees the one streetlight in the distance and makes the mistake of treating it like a beacon. He perseveres. He prays. He crosses the road to reach it.

"Hypothermia takes his life at the edge of a dirt parking lot across the street from the pub—he was so close! His spirit cannot accept that he didn't save her life."

Marie said, "Stefan's older brother Karl finds the young lovers' bodies the next morning. Karl—horrified by Celeste's bloody injury and the dried blood on his brother's hands—assumes the worst. Karl blames Stefan for what he believes to be Celeste's murder.

"To protect his family name, his brother's memory, Karl buries the young couple's bodies and keeps that a secret. He lies, saying Stefan died in a tragic car accident. He leaves Celeste's family and friends in anguish without answers. For decades, he denies them the truth."

Karl had not only given them express permission to use his name, to tell the whole story; he'd insisted on it. He'd called it "making amends."

"You may be wondering why it matters that Celeste was Indigenous." Marie unleashed the grief and anger in her voice. "Year after year, decade after decade, local law enforcement fails to find her body or even to question Karl, despite the fact that Celeste and his brother Stefan had been dating since the first week of that school year, despite the fact that her friends saw them together that night at the Christmas concert, despite the fact that Karl paved over the land where she was buried only a few days later. Year after year, decade after decade, the local news media failed to prioritize or follow up on her story. For too long, the police and journalists and society itself have failed Indigenous crime victims, failed our sisters. We demand change now."

At that point, the narrative moved into the realm of artistic license.

The ghost of Celeste, played by Queen, reached out, and all the other Indigenous girls involved with the production returned to the stage to hold hands in a show of strength, solidarity, unity, and hope.

Hughie and Marie had anticipated mixed reactions from the audience, and that's what they got. In the front row, Sam and Cricket were first on their feet, and the Wolfes, Headbirds, and Berghoffs were among those cheering loudest. Aunt Georgia whistled her approval. But the crowd was about fifty-fifty in its standing ovation. From the time the production was first announced, grown-ups—especially Parents Against Revisionist Theater—had chimed in with their opinions. Critics had bristled at the focus being so firmly Indigenous and at the idea of questioning law enforcement. They'd complained that people should let go of the past, supposedly so the dead could rest in peace.

The co-playwrights were expecting that. They didn't write the show to please everyone. They wrote it to fulfill Hughie's promise to Celeste. They wrote it to make people think.

The playbill featured information about the crisis of murdered and missing Indigenous girls, women, enby, and two-spirit people from tribal communities. It also included the newly published obituaries of the deceased (Stefan's was labeled CORRECTED), used with permission from the *Hannesburg Weekly Examiner*.

Hughie concluded the performance with a poem, written by Paige.

White like Snow, swirling in Wind,
Brown like Earth, fiery heart.
Respect the true Harvest, the Green Corn.
Today's truth becomes tomorrow's herstory.
We dedicate this performance to a protector.
And to so many like her
For whom we ache, advocate, pray, mourn.

AUTHOR'S NOTE

Are you fascinated by the spooky in-between spaces where ghosts are believed to dance and sing? I am. I've written both realistic Native-focused fiction and fantastical gothic fiction, and this novel takes place at an intersection—or crossroads—of my mind.

One of my favorite teen memories is visiting a commercial haunted house in Kansas City with a cousin and our moms. I remember our clinging to one another in the dark, enjoying a safe scare, complete with decorated sets and costumed actors.

I've long considered writing a novel about a pretend haunted house that turned out to be really haunted, but it wasn't until the Grub Pub appeared in one of my previous novels, *Hearts Unbroken*, that the story began to take shape in my mind. I didn't want to write about a corporate haunt but rather one that was more of a community project, so that Hughie and Sam could play a major role in its conception and production.

My stories often engage with other literary works and

oral stories. *Harvest House* speaks to the legends created by non-Native people about Native people. For example, the Indian burial ground trope is a longtime Hollywood staple—appearing in movies and on TV—that is thankfully falling out of favor. I most recently encountered the trope while on a ghost tour of Chicago and, later, while streaming the TV show *Supernatural*. Indian burial ground storylines usually feature a construction or renovation project that disturbs vengeful "spirits." As shown with the "ghost Indians" of Harvest House, the trope draws on offensive stereotypes of Indigenous people while promoting the harmful myth that Native people are extinct. As for the Indian maiden ghost trope, in this novel, the legend Mr. Boucher writes up for his October specials menu is representative, and Louise does a fine job of deconstructing that.

Meanwhile, the land currently called *North America* is the real-life setting of a real-life human-rights crisis characterized by missing and murdered Indigenous women, girls, and two-spirit people. It has prompted the use of the activist hashtag #MMIWG2S.

Because of this crisis, you may be wondering why, in *Harvest House*, Celeste dies of an accident rather than foul play. Simply put, Native girls and women are by no means wholly defined by harm done to us, and there aren't nearly enough books that show joy and love in our lives. Of course, any fatal accident is tragic, but it's not against the natural order. I decided to highlight the *missing* aspect of the crisis—zeroing in on the roles and responsibilities of law enforcement and especially the news media—and to leave the *murdered* part to other Native-authored novels. While Stefan isn't guilty in this story, the harsh reality of those cases can't be denied. As Celeste says, "Not every man I battled was Stefan . . ."

Although Stefan is innocent, Karl most certainly is not, and I wanted to underscore the pressing need to return Celeste's body to her family and community. Native remains and cultural items should always be returned to lineal descendants, culturally affiliated Indigenous organizations, or relevant tribal communities.

Mvto for reading *Harvest House*. I do believe in ghosts. I also believe everyone, in some way or another, is haunted by some aspect of the past. Whether you're Native or non-Native, if you have ever experienced violence or lost a loved one to it or if you are searching for a missing relative, my solidarity, heart, and prayers go out to you.

INDIGENOUS LANGUAGES

The Native languages referenced in *Harvest House* are living languages.

My sources were the Muscogee Nation (MN) website, the College of the Muscogee Nation (CMN) website, the Mvskoke Nation Language App (MNLA), and the Ojibwe People's Dictionary (OPD) website.

MVSKOKE–ENGLISH GLOSSARY

em vnicvkvs: help them (MNLA/Words)
em vnicvs: help her/help him (MNLA/Words)
Heren vcafaste tomes: She treats me well (MNLA/
     Describing People)
hesci: hello (CMN)
Heruse tos: She is beautiful (MNLA/Describing People)
Hvtvm cehecares: I will see you again (MNLA/Words)
ivpecicv: hurry up (to one person) (MNLA/Commands)
letkv: run (MNLA/Commands)
Lopice tos: She is kind (MNLA/Describing People)
mvto: thank you (MN)

OJIBWE–ENGLISH GLOSSARY

miigwetch: thank you (OPD)
nookomis: my grandmother (OPD)

MVTO

Candlewick editor Andrea Tompa was a guiding light in solving the mystery of how to best tell this story for young adult readers. I'm grateful for her precise logic, respectful questions, generous suggestions, enthusiasm, and graciousness throughout the editing process. Thanks also to my previous Candlewick editor, Hilary Van Dusen, who acquired the manuscript. Her editorial efforts on the companion book, *Hearts Unbroken*, certainly influenced this one, too.

Likewise, I'm deeply appreciative of art director Pam Consolazio, copyeditors Shasta Clinch and Julia Gaviria, and cover artist Britt Newton. The loving care they poured into this book has made it so much stronger. Britt's eerie cover art beckons, and I'm especially delighted that the novel features the evocative, storytelling art of a fellow Muscogee citizen. From there, the thoughtful interior design lures readers deeper and deeper into the ghostly mystery.

Moreover, I'm a tremendous fan of Candlewick in the whole. Executive editorial director Liz Bicknell was one of the first editors to encourage my writing, back in the day, and she continues to shine as a leader in the field. Meanwhile, I've been blessed by working with marketing pros Jamie Tan, Stephanie Pando, and Sawako Shirota, all of whom are consummate professionals.

Speaking of blessings, my deepest thanks go to my career-long literary agent, Ginger Knowlton, her colleagues James T. Farrell and Holly Frederick, and everyone at Curtis Brown. My career now stretches more than twenty years, and Ginger and her colleagues have steadfastly supported me throughout.

My writing life is far from a solitary one. Love goes to my dear friends in Native Kidlit, the Vermont College of Fine Arts community, and Austin SCBWI. I'd also like to thank my wonderful assistant, Gayleen Rabakukk, and our Cynsations team as well as my events agent (and organizational wizard) Carmen Oliver of the Booking Biz.

As for me, this novel was more daunting because it touches on personal themes and because it was completed during the busiest professional year of my life.

Thank you to Christopher T. Assaf for his assistance brainstorming the plot, sharing his photography expertise, and reading an entire draft aloud to me. Thank you to Dr. Edgar Alexander Hallock for answering medical questions; to Schuyler Bowen for filling me in on what happens behind the scenes at commercial haunted houses; and to my devoted Chihuahuas, Gnocchi and Orzo, for cuddles.

All stories exist in conversation with each other to varying degrees. In addition to *Hearts Unbroken*, the following literary titles either were referenced in or some-how influenced *Harvest House*: *The Amityville Horror* by Jay Anson; *Elatsoe* by Darcie Little Badger; *The Wonderful Wizard of Oz* by L. Frank Baum; *The Hunger Games* by Suzanne Collins; *Custer Died for Your Sins: An Indian Manifesto* by Vine Deloria Jr.; *Apple: (Skin to the Core)* by Eric Gansworth; "Young Goodman Brown" by Nathaniel Hawthorne; *Leviathan* by Thomas Hobbes; *The Haunting of Hill House* by Shirley Jackson; *A Wrinkle in Time* by Madeleine L'Engle; *We Are Water Protectors* written by Carole Lindstrom and illustrated by Michaela Goade; *Symposiacs* by Plutarch; "The Raven" by Edgar Allan Poe; *The Catcher in the Rye* by J. D. Salinger; *Frankenstein* by Mary Shelley; *Rain Is Not My Indian Name* by Cynthia Leitich Smith; *The Strange Case of Dr. Jekyll and Mr. Hyde* by Robert Louis Stevenson; "The Lady, or the Tiger?" by Frank R. Stockton; *The Lord of the Rings* by J. R. R. Tolkien; as well as authors Louise Erdrich, Simon J. Ortiz, George Orwell, and William Shakespeare more generally. That said, *Turtle Island 101: This Land Is Our Land* doesn't exist. I made it up, but there are similar non-fiction books by Native authors, and I encourage you to seek them out.

From the world of TV and film, I'd like to nod to *The Incredibles*, written and directed by Brad Bird; *Ghost-busters: Answer the Call*, directed by Paul Feig, written by Paul Feig and Katie Dippold; *Supernatural*, created by Eric Kripke; *Star Wars*, created by George Lucas; *Hocus Pocus*, directed by Kenny Ortega, written by Neil Cuthbert and Mick Garris; *Ghostbusters*, directed by Ivan Reitman, written by Dan Aykroyd, Harold Ramis, and Rick Moranis; *Scooby-Doo, Where Are You!* created by Joe Ruby and Ken Spears; *It's the Great Pumpkin, Charlie Brown*, created by Charles M. Schulz, directed by Bill Melendez (especially Snoopy); *The Nightmare Before Christmas*, directed by Henry Selick, written by Tim Burton, Michael McDowell, and Caroline Thompson; and *E.T. the Extra-Terrestrial*, directed by Steven Spielberg, written by Melissa Mathison.

Fiction references and influences also included characters such as Batman, the character created by Bob Kane and Bill Finger; BB-8, created by Lawrence Kasdan, Michael Arndt, Neal Scanlan, and J. J. Abrams; the Care Bears, created by Those Characters from Cleveland; Casper the Friendly Ghost, created by Seymour Reit, Joe Oriolo, and Vincent E. Valentine; the Flash, created by writer Gardener Fox and illustrator Harry Lampert; Kermit the Frog, created by Jim Henson; Lois Lane, created by Jerry Siegel and Joe Shuster; Nancy Drew, created by Edward Stratemeyer; and the Teenage Mutant Ninja Turtles, created by Kevin Eastman and Peter Laird.

From the stage, I'll add *The Wolves* by Sarah DeLappe; *Mamma Mia!* by Catherine Johnson, based on the songs of ABBA (composed by Benny Andersson and Björn Ulvaeus); and *Little Shop of Horrors*, music by Alan Menken, lyrics by Howard Ashman. These are such a nifty segue to more tunes—"Miss Me More" by Kelsea Ballerini; "More Than a Memory" by Lee Brice, Billy Montana, and Kyle Jacobs, recorded by Garth Brooks; "Last Kiss" by Wayne Cochran, recorded by J. Frank Wilson and the Cavaliers; "Teen Angel" by Jean Dinning, recorded by Mark Dinning; "Dead Man's Party" by Danny Elfman; "Through the Eyes of Love," by Marvin Hamlisch and Carole Bayer Sager; "Monster Mash" by Bobby "Boris" Picket and Leonard Capizzi, recorded with the Crypt-Kickers; and "Leader of the Pack" by George "Shadow" Morton, Jeff Barry, and Ellie Greenwich, recorded by the Shangri-Las.